Aladinma

Eighties to Nineties: A Reconnect

PETER OBIDIKE

ALADINMA
EIGHTIES TO NINETIES: A RECONNECT

iUniverse books may be ordered through booksellers or by contacting:

iUniverse
1663 Liberty Drive
Bloomington, IN 47403
www.iuniverse.com
1-800-Authors (1-800-288-4677)

ISBN: 978-1-5320-8819-3 (sc)
ISBN: 978-1-5320-8820-9 (e)

Library of Congress Control Number: 2020912254

Print information available on the last page.

iUniverse rev. date: 07/23/2020

CONTENTS

ACKNOWLEDGEMENTS

Freezing the experiences of the eighties to nineties could not have been possible without the gift of a sound mind from God and inspiration from my dad, Engr P.N. Obidike. His writings published in the PUNCH triggered some irreversible *busy body* writing in me that diversified into this work.

God made things fall in place for me; giving me my oga at the top and *ntuch*a (gossip) partner. One of my bosses understood the implication of *ntucha* by couples that he would always place a disclaimer to my wife. Anytime something came up in the office that entailed long hours; he was sure to exonerate himself whenever he met my wife. That was to make sure he was not the subject of our *ntucha!* My wife was the first person to read eighties to nineties, made the first set of corrections and got the work ready for the subsequent reviews.

My next acknowledgement goes to *nwa* Iheakaram, chidozie Iheakaram, *nwa* professor Iheakaram. He was the second person that reviewed this work. I chose Dozy as he is fondly called because I knew him to be a master of English right from University days. It was no surprise he knew English given that his dad is a professor in the subject. He did not disappoint me and delivered the review even in the midst of his tight schedule at work. He was the first to point out to me that I was mixing first person and third person points of view in the whole writing!

Chinedu Nzekwe came to my rescue to help me understand what Dozy was referring to. As if both of them had *tuchaalad* me at some point, he went ahead to practically describe to me how I was switching that first person and third person views. He said it was like shooting a movie where the camera is following the character as the story is told; and suddenly the character turned and faced the camera. That was an awesome analogy that helped my understanding of the concept in my "irresponsible" conflicting use of "he" and "I" in telling my story. Chinedu is the producer of "Anchor Baby", an international award-winning film with the lead character Omoni Oboli.

Not forgetting all fans of www.peterobidike.com, my various yahoo groups and Facebook friends who have critiqued my essays all these years.

To you all I am deeply grateful

INTRODUCTION

This story reflects the life of a public servant's kid in Aladinma, a quiet neighbourhood in the Imo State capital city of Owerri in Nigeria. As expected from a religious and hardworking family, the kid imbibed the family values and grew with the resilience needed to navigate the changing times from an analog to a digital age. In all his learnings, though, nothing prepared him for the fight brewing inside a Dallas courtroom during a US federal criminal trial against a copyright thief where his character and resilience would be tested to the limit.

With the new media in vogue, Ginika was chatting with his wife, and suddenly an idea came to his mind. "Honey, I intend to write an online real-time script for my Facebook fans using a pen name." Ginika had earlier been successful at writing short essays and commentaries on topical issues and getting accolades from his numerous fans on the various social media channels. He planned to publish the script weekly over a one-year period, which would then culminate in the publication of the story in book form. This, he hoped, would surprise his readers, who would have read the whole book without knowing it. Ginika was somewhat surprised, and his wife was even more surprised, to learn of a movie preview making waves. They both were even more surprised when they learned it had been written by Uchewuba, the brother of a close friend of the couple. Being enthusiasts of newly published works, Ginika and his wife immediately looked forward to the preview. Behold—it was a full, undistorted reproduction of what Ginika had been writing for his numerous fans on Facebook for the past fifty-two weeks!

This started a full-blown copyright fight to prove who owned the copyright of Uchewuba's soon-to-be-released movie, *The Converted*. What was expected to be a local fight between childhood friends soon turned into a local court case and subsequently took on an international dimension as the owner of Facebook became involved in an international lawsuit in Dallas in a bid to determine the actual content owner of the script.

The uproar that greeted the legal battle between the childhood friends, along with the international dimension to the story, soon made the script an instant success story, and the rights for its publication were sought by big publishing companies and motion film directors around the world, pending the determination of the rightful owner of the intellectual content.

The court eventually ruled in favour of Ginika after two years of bitter legal battle. The movie premiered a year later, six months after the release of the book. On the day of the premiere of the movie, and as the world feasted on the success of the story, Nkiru, Ginika's wife, had one thought in her mind: how on earth had Ginika pulled this off without her knowledge? This apparently referred to the revelation that Ginika knew Uchewuba was collating his online posts with the intent of publishing the same story in the United States, but he decided not to interfere, knowing the tussle he hoped would result from the act and the publicity of the work that the court fight would make the story so popular. But some other consequences were not what he had bargained for.

The voice of the judge kept ringing in Ginika's ears as he saw Uchewuba, in handcuffs, being led away from the courtroom: "Stealing became your nature and was enshrined in your DNA so that any area of life you found yourself in, you did nothing else but steal, be it money or intellectual property. This serves as a warning to the youth of today—stealing does not pay. The long arm of the

United States law will find and bring you to justice. It is better to channel your energy into more productive things. Mr Uchewuba had the opportunity and capacity to do that but chose the wrong actions."

CHAPTER 1

Ogadimma Gets Transferred

Onye tiri nwa na ebe akwa,
Egbe tiri nwa na ebe akwa,
Wete uzuzu, wete ose,
Ka umu nnunu racha ya ohoho ohoho.

And so the singing to calm little Ginika down continued on that sunny Saturday afternoon until his aunt Ekemma, who was carrying him, noticed the suspicious movement of a white Volkswagen Beetle, which passed several times in front of their government-reserve-area residence in Onitsha, Anambra State, Nigeria. Ekemma signalled, *"Ndi ntori mmadu!"* (Kidnappers!) to Emeka, the eldest son of Ogadimma, who was washing his school uniform in front of the house, and everyone quickly ran into the house. The news in Onitsha at that time was saturated with stories of the disappearance of little kids, and every family had issued strict warnings to their children not to venture outside once they noticed any strange activities.

Ogadimma had instructed his children to stay indoors until later in the evening when their parents came back from a visit to one of their fellow parishioners in Christ the King Catholic Church. Emeka was the first to break the news to his dad, Engineer Ogadimma of the Federal Ministry of Works, who listened with some element of fright in his eyes. He thanked God that the suspected kidnappers had not intruded into their home and taken away Ginika as if his small self could not have been a victim as well. The residents of Onitsha had lived and worked in fear of the tales of kidnappers using children for rituals in the tail end of the River Niger, which separated the city from the neighbouring Asaba town. The cities were connected by the popular Niger Bridge. At first, rumour had it that the rich and powerful in society were behind these kidnappings. No one, however, had substantiated those claims, and the stories died a natural death as the bustling city moved on with its huge trade and commerce business among the Igbos of South East Nigeria.

The next day, the Ogadimmas attended the seven o'clock morning mass at the CKC Church before going on another social visit. Their second outing was to see the monsignor in charge of a newly opened seminary at Nkpor, a suburb of Onitsha. Monsignor Chigbu was a childhood friend of Ogadimma, and they both hailed from the same village. While Ogadimma had been busy selling palm kernels to augment his primary school fees and support his poor farmer parents, Chigbu had been busy attending to church matters and following the parish priest to houses in the village for prayers. He later received a scholarship from the bishop at Awka, the Anambra state capital. Chigbu attended the seminary and eventually became a priest. The monsignor was always, to Ogadimma, a typical case of *ukwa na adara ndi na amaghi api* (the breadfruit always falls for those that don't know how to process it) since he felt that Chigbu's joining the priesthood was a waste of the talent the village would have gained if he had ended up as an engineer like himself or a doctor.

The family had lunch with Monsignor Chigbu and came back home for their routine Sunday afternoon nap. Later that Sunday evening, Ngozi, Ogadimma's wife, took Ekemma, Ginika, and Emeka to see her mother, who lived in Odakpu, an obscure neighbourhood in the town, for a taste of her mum's Sunday *ofe akwu* delicacy (a local stew made from fresh-pressed oil from the palm fruit). It was always fun for Emeka and his siblings when they visited Granny since each visit guaranteed them some chops, biscuits, eggs, and malt drink to wash things down. And they could never get enough of the rich aroma of Granny's ofe akwu. There was something about this ofe akwu that the kids had not been able to figure out, but it sure tasted different— and so nice that they looked forward to winning the week's lottery to be the one to accompany their mother to Granny's place.

When Ngozi returned from Granny's place that evening, Ogadimma informed her and his children of his transfer to Owerri. The first thing Emeka, who was ten years of age, asked was, "Is Granny coming to Owerri too?" When he was told that Granny lived her own life and would not be going to Owerri, the poor boy broke down in tears and wondered how they would get their Sunday share of Granny's rice and ofe akwu. Not even the promise that Granny would always visit Owerri and could bring some of her specialty for them would pacify the little boy and his siblings, who had joined in the crying even though they didn't understand what a transfer to Owerri meant. The option of going on holiday to stay with their Granny did not pacify them. The crying continued until the kids were tired and eventually went to bed that night.

This was not the first transfer for Ogadimma, who had spent a lot of years in the service of the federal government of Nigeria. Being on the staff of the Federal Ministry of Works meant constant transfers across the various states of the federation. His last transfer had been from Mubi, a city in the north-eastern part of the country to Onitsha in the South East. He was to take up the role of a principal resident engineer in the ministry's regional office. That last transfer from the north to the east had been a blessing indeed because, in addition to the elevation in rank that came with it, the transfer was an opportunity to get away from the frequent religious riots that were then associated with the northern part of the country. The interesting thing was that, each time there was an issue in the nation's politics, such as the rigging of elections or even international incidents such as the perceived persecution of Muslims, some elements in that part of the country vented their anger on foreigners, especially those from Ogadimma's ethnic Igbo tribe. The Igbos were well known for their business acumen and commercial interests in trade and were considered the most mobile people in the country. So Ogadimma's parents and relatives had heaved sighs of relief when they heard of his transfer to Onitsha. No longer would they have to keep their ears constantly on the radio news to learn when the next Maitatsine (a religious sect in the north) riots would happen and, when they did, suffer through the long wait for the letter or telegram announcing that their engineer relative was still alive. Everyone missed the north, though, even with all the troubles. Most especially they missed the bags of onions, rice, and yams that the Ogadimmas usually sent home. *Kwilikwili* was another of the northern delicacies that was missed, especially among the kids. "*Kwilikwili na eme ka mmadu nyuo ahu isi*" ("Kwilikwili Makes One Fart") was one of the favourite folk songs among the kids as they played and had a go at their portions of the ground and baked groundnut paste. A typical sharing of the kwilikwili gift by the neighbourhood kids in the village when the Ogadimmas came home for Christmas would be proceeded by a kind of neighbourhood town crier kid going around the neighbourhood and shouting, "*Umuazi yard, gbanu iririri! Uumuazi yard, gbanu iririri!*" (Kids of the compound, come around! Kids of the compound, come around!) Once kids heard this cry, they would know there were some goodies to be had, and they would all find their way to the source of the announcement. Their parents, though not invited, would wait patiently for them to come back with the goodies. The good kids among them would take theirs home while the ones who exhibited *akpiri* (gluttony) would consume theirs even before getting home. Of course, they would be reprimanded for that. Whether the punishment was to teach them that they must first show their parents anything they had been given by strangers before they ate it, or because they had denied the elders the opportunity to feast of the groundnut paste was known only to the parents.

The transfer of Ogadimma from Onitsha to Owerri came with a promotion, as he was elevated to chief resident engineer (CRE) of his ministry. He was to oversee the construction of the new dual carriageway that led from Onitsha to Owerri, which was considered part of the federal government's integration efforts of the Igbos after the prolonged civil war waged in the region several years previously. This transfer in the summer of 1979 was during the reign of Olusegun Obasanjo, a man believed to have contributed so much to the development of the country and who ruled both as a military head of state and later a civilian president. OBJ, as he was fondly called, was later sent to prison for an alleged attempted coup against another Nigerian leader, General Sani Abacha, in the nineties, and it was from the jail that he was conscripted to become the civilian president of the nation. Unfortunately, that prison experience did not seem to have reflected positively on his disposition because, while he led the country a second time, most of the atrocities in society such as bribery, corruption, and nepotism seemed to exist on even a larger scale than they had prior to his ascending to the throne.

The chief resident engineer's house was located at Aladinma, a serene neighbourhood with tarred roads and bungalows. Specifically, the family's new house was situated on the almighty Road Seventeen, which happened to be the place of residence of the most senior judges in the town. A medium-income location, it boasted various shopping outlets from the small kiosks down the road from Ogadimma's office location to the supermarkets on another exit road towards Wethral Road. Popular among the supermarkets were the Maris and Chanrise supermarkets that sold all kinds of things from groceries to toothpaste and plastic bags to bags of rice. Though it was a small neighbourhood, it also boasted of a post office and even an art centre. The Mbari Cultural Centre boasted several artefacts that told the story of a people and their journey to nationhood. It displayed the peoples *chi* (gods) of the early times before the British destroyed everything and replaced them with their own God, the Almighty. *Aladinma* literally meant "a good land," and the land was indeed fertile and beautiful. It was a great place to raise a family.

Ogadimma was already well known as an uncompromising man

by his peers in the Ministry of Works. He was a man known for not taking bribes, which was contrary to the case within most government establishments. With his arrival to the regional office in Owerri, most of the contractors soon realized it was no longer business as usual. The contractors were so desperate and cunning that they would try to avoid Ogadimma, whom they knew would reject their gifts. Instead, they would send these directly to his house in his absence, and this made Ogadimma give a standing order in his house that on no occasion must any member of the family receive any item from anybody without his authorization. In some cases, when this plan did not work, some of the contractors even resolved to threaten his life.

One night, as Ginika and his sibling were about to go to bed after saying their routine rosary, Ginika alerted his elder brother, Emeka, to the sobbing of their mum as she begged their daddy to let them go and sleep at their uncle's house as a way to avoid an earlier threat by unknown persons who were supposedly angry contractors. The stubborn Ogadimma would not budge and insisted that whoever wanted to assassinate him should come and meet him face to face for a duel with guns. It took the pleading of several of Ogadimma's relatives to get him to sleep outside his house that night, but that was the last time he would give in to such threats. He had a licensed gun and believed he could match any intruder. At that time, armed robbery was not that rampant or sophisticated.

There was a story about how a driver in the ministry, Mr Nwangene, had uprooted a flower Ogadimma had planted himself. Nwangene's excuse was that the flower could kill human beings if eaten. Ogadimma, as the officer in charge, ordered that Nwangene vacate his boy's quarter apartment, which he shared with his two young children and wife. All entreaties to Ogadimma to forgive fell on deaf ears, and it took two days of pleading and the intervention of Reverend Father Mmegwa, a Catholic priest in the estate, for Ogadimma to change his mind. Nwangene's family knew that, even though Ogadimma was severely strict, he had a weakness in his allegiance to the church, and they exploited that weakness successfully. They knew that Reverend

Father Mmegwa could get him to change his mind. To Nwangene's family, the inconvenience of losing the ministry's accommodation was unthinkable. Apart from the fact that the apartments were attached to the office situated at 3 Ngwa Street at Aladinma Housing Estate, which eliminated the need for transportation to and from work, Nwangene's two kids had recently enrolled in the prestigious Aladinma Housing Estate Primary School, a hundred metres from the house, with its large expanse of playground, new buildings, and well-trained teachers. The government-run school was known as the best school in Owerri at the time and was where the governor's kid was educated. This was the same school that Ginika would enrol in a year after the Ogadimmas' arrival to Owerri.

Ogadimma's other known weakness was his love for his wife's cooking. This was so profound that he would not eat any food prepared by another person, not even food prepared by any of the numerous relatives who lived with them. A story was told of how his mother-in-law came to visit, and Ego, the most senior of the relatives living with them, was asked to prepare *onugbu* soup (bitter leaf soup) for dinner that day. The mother-in-law was told about Ogadimma's penchant for Ngozi's food, but she waved it aside and insisted that he be served the onugbu soup Ego had cooked. On his return from work, Ogadimma was served the soup, and he loved it so much that he congratulated Ngozi as usual for delivering the tasty dish. When he was told that Ego had made the soup, Ogadimma sighed and said, "No wonder *nnu adighi ya*" (No wonder there is no salt in it). This caused a burst of laughter from the mother-in-law and Ngozi.

Ogadimma was also known to have clashed with the locals he met in Owerri. This time it was about the correct pronunciation of his surname, which literally meant "it would be well." His father was born during an acute famine in the country, and his grand parents had already faced other challenges of childbirth. It was a big relief when the little baby chose to stay; hence, he was called Ogadimma as a show of their faith that the birth of the child would wipe away years of suffering and pain. That he chose to stay was a miracle, as ten of the earlier children of the grand parents had died of childhood diseases that were all attributed to being *ogbanje* (from the water spirits). With the history behind him, the name Ogadimma meant so much to him and his parents. Unfortunately, the various Igbo dialects prevented his name from being pronounced correctly by the locals in Owerri. They could not pronounce it the exact way the folks from Anambra would pronounce it. On a fateful Monday morning, a driver greeted him, "Good morning, Oga Ogiirimma." "*Ogiirimma nke gi!*" Ogadimma shouted back at him, reminding him that his name was "Oga adi mma," not "Ogiiri." The response was so spontaneous it left all the workers around laughing at the scolded driver, who bowed his head in shame over not knowing how to pronounce Oga's name.

CHAPTER 2

Ginika Goes to School

Ginika's first day at school saw him rushing back home during the break period thinking the school was over for the day only to be taken back to school by his dad's assistant. Ogadimma had just returned from a brief meeting in another office within the complex to behold an excited Ginika cooling down in a chair in his office. Ginika held a bottle of Fanta he had taken from the refrigerator in his dad's office, and he was chilling after a hard day's work at school—at least that's what he thought to himself! Ogadimma simply looked at his watch and sighed, "But it's ten o'clock," he told his son, "and your school could not have been dismissed for the day." Not until Ogadimma's assistant took Ginika back to school did they realize what had happened. When the bell for break had been rung, Ginika had seen the other kids going to a Tuck Shop just outside the school owned by the Durumbas. Ginika had thought they were heading home and thus he'd headed home as well. Ginika hadn't noticed that none of the other kids had their school bags with them.

Primary school was fun for Ginika because lots of time was scheduled for play in the large school field. The school compound was so large that only a portion of it could be fenced off. The other part remained open and sometimes was host to other members of the immediate community who would use it for functions on request and approval by the primary school authorities. A typical school day began with the early arrival of students from all parts of the community. While some, like Ginika, who lived very close to school would walk to school, others who lived far from the school were dropped off by their parents or guardians. Police escorts and orderlies delivered kids of the commissioner and the governor. Everyone was expected to arrive by at least seven thirty in the morning, and latecomers were restricted from entering the school compound until Mrs Nkonye, the headmistress, addressed them on the need to be early and sometimes scolded them for coming late to school. It was in one of those scolding sessions that Ginika learned about the word *snail*. Mrs Nkonye was so furious at the latecomers that she shouted, "Look at how they are walking like snails to school! Will you all run!" This was one of the days that Ginika had come to school late while in primary two, and he kept saying the word *snail* to himself in order to remember it and ask Emeka during the break period what it meant. And reason for this lateness? Toast had been prepared for breakfast, but Ginika would have none of that and insisted on beans mixed with vegetables the way Aunty Fidelia made them with scrambled egg! With no eggs in the house and Aunty Fidelia away to visit her mum in the village, her specialty of mixed vegetable, egg, and beans was a tall order for Ngozi or any other person. It took extensive begging and the threat of missing school that day to get Ginika to agree to something else for breakfast. Mrs Ogbuehi, Ginika's primary two school teacher was surprised that Ginika was late to school that day since she knew he lived a stone's throw from the school. Mrs Ogbuehi's son, Kelechi was also in her class and taunted Ginika for coming late. Kelechi always picked a fight in the belief that his mum would flog anybody who hurt him. To his frequent disappointment, his mum would always ask for details about what caused the quarrel and would punish whoever was at fault, including Kelechi himself.

As part of morning activities at Aladinma Primary School, students were made to line up according to their classes and sing the national anthem. After the national anthem came the morning information discussions. Any willing student was expected to stand in front of the assembly and give some information on any topic of interest or happenings in the state or country in general. The students were encouraged to listen to the news on the radio, or watch it on television for those who had televisions, and their elders were expected to help them understand and prepare the information they were to share. On one occasion, Ginika came out and shared information prepared for him by his immediate elder brother Chinedu who was next to Emeka in age and in another school, Ikenegbu Primary School. Even though Ginika didn't understand the meaning of the information he shared, he did so well with the presentation that he earned a round of applause. This was even though he referred to the governor of Imo State, Chief Onunaka Mbakwe, as "Thief" Onunaka Mbakwe. It was his innocent disposition and the intervention of his brother Emeka that stopped the fight that almost broke out during the break period as the governor's child wanted to teach him a lesson for calling his father a thief, irrespective of whether Ginika understood his information or not. "Ignorance is not an excuse!" he shouted at Emeka as Emeka tried to make him appreciate the fact that it was an innocent mistake on the part of the poor boy who wanted to share something special with his peers.

Chief Mbakwe had initiated the contract that saw the use of big trucks and large steel waste bins for evacuation of wastes around Owerri and other parts of Imo State. Sulo was the name of the refuse removal company, and the name appeared on all of the bins. It was a delight for the kids to watch the operation of the automatic loading of the bins onto the trucks and the jerking of the trucks as they emptied the contents of the bins into the bellies of the trucks. Owerri was then touted as the cleanest state capital city in the whole of Nigeria, and Chief Mbakwe was a celebrated man. It was the delivery of the award for the cleanest state capital city in Nigeria to Chief Mbakwe in Lagos that was the subject of Ginika's presentation, which went thus: "My name is Ginika Ogadimma. I am in primary 2A. My morning information is that the Imo State governor, Thief Onunaka Mbakwe, has received the award for the cleanest state capital city in Nigeria by Alhaji Shehu Shagari, the president of Nigeria. Thank you." This was followed by a rousing round of applause by teachers and Ginika's fellow students. Both those who understood and those that didn't clapped, and Ginika felt like a star as he made his way back to stand in his class assembly line.

After morning information, the students' uniforms were checked for cleanliness. Aladinma Primary School was a public school in the eighties, which meant it was affordable and had some class. There were no private schools then and only a few missionary schools. Parents were expected to sew their kids' uniforms having received the school colour samples from the school authorities and were expected to buy the school badge only from the authorities. The Aladinma Primary School uniform consisted of a white shirt and blue shorts for boys and a white shirt and blue jumper for the girls. The white shirts easily got dirty during a day of play at school. Ginika had two uniforms. He had to wear each one at least twice before it could be washed. This was especially important during the rainy season when the laundry always took longer to dry because of the dampness and the absence of sunlight. However, on some days, he played so hard that his white shirt got dirty, and if he wore it for a second day, he would rank among the dirty students for the day. It was always a tough choice—admitting that he had played too hard at school and asking to change his uniform before it was due, or wearing a dirty shirt and running the risk of being called out in front of the school assembly for wearing a dirty uniform. With time, Ginika devised a way around being pulled out of the assembly by hiding behind students who were wearing clean uniforms. It was always tricky because he had little time to synchronize the exact step of the teacher making the check and his own steps as he moved as close as possible to the next person in front of him so that the checking teacher would overlook him while focusing attention on the person behind him. It worked most times, especially when his shirt was not too dirty, but if his shirt was exceptionally dirty, he was bound to be caught. Not even smiling to woo the teacher to be his friend and thus be favourable in his or her assessment of his uniform would make those teachers refrain from calling him out if his shirt was dirty. Ginika always thought the teachers had no friends as even their own kids were not spared the humiliation of being called out for dirty uniforms.

One of Ginika's most dreadful days in school was the day he took some biscuits from his classmate's bag. Even though he had come to school with his own biscuit and sweet, which had been given to him at home, something came over him as he entered the classroom and saw the protruding red colours from Okon's bag. Two steps from his desk got him close enough to take the red package of Cabin Biscuits and plant it in his own bag before running off to join the morning assembly. It was not difficult for Okon to discover who had taken his biscuits when they came back to class after the morning assembly. No one else came to school with the bright red package; Okon was the only one. Okon reported to Mrs Ogbuehi, who promised to deal with Ginika after school hours. That threat kept Ginika restless the whole day, and he barely paid attention in class as he was thinking of the punishment that awaited him at the end of the school day. Fortunately for him, Mrs Ogbuehi did not flog students; rather, in this case, she only counselled him and let him go without even telling Ogadimma, who was the main threat that Ginika had dreaded. Ginika was ready to do anything, including giving Okon his own biscuits the next day and conceding to any punishment that would not involve telling his father what he did.

By primary three, Ginika was already enlisted among the group of people responsible for cleaning the blackboard. This meant freedom to pass through the school gate across to the "agric" field where *abalidiegwu* leaves were picked. The leaves were ground and used as wet rags to clean the blackboard, leaving it crispy green-black for legible writing by the teachers and students. Alternatively, the students were asked to bring charcoal to school. The charcoal was ground and made into a charcoal paste which was used to wipe the board leaving it crispy black to the writing delight of the teachers and students. The students' uniforms would, of course, get dirty from such an activity, but it was always a source of pride for Ginika to show off at home the fact that he was on the team that cleaned the class blackboard.

Though cleaning the board could be fun, it was not fun when it was done as part of punishment for nutty actions such as noisemaking. Noisemaking in class, especially when the teacher was not around, was a punishable offence. Punishment could be strokes of the cane or a one-week, clean-the-blackboard assignment. When given as a punishment, the task was not that fun anymore since it entailed cleaning two blackboards given that two classes (such as primary 3A and 3B) were normally situated in one room with a wooden board demarcating the classes. The exception was only the primary one class, which was held in one room close to the headmistress's office with boards demarcating all the classes. Aladinma Housing Estate Primary School consisted of two long buildings facing each other. As one entered the school via the main school gate on Ngwa Street, the primary one hall was to the right. A hedge of flowers in a roundabout form was next to the gate before the row of classrooms. Primary three was situated in the middle of the left row of classrooms, and it happened to be the one from which the most noise seemed to always come. There were times when the noise would be so loud that the headmistress would get involved, walking round the classrooms to find out what was going on. Students whose names were not on the list of noisemakers had either kept quiet or were friends of the person assigned by the teacher to make the list of those who made noise while the teacher was out. Of course, the person writing the list never appeared on the list of noisemakers either. For Ginika, the game plan was always to make sure he was a friend to any party in power, especially the person writing the list of noisemakers. There were times when the noisemaking came from almost everybody in the class, but not everybody's name necessarily needed to be feature on the list. The compiler of the noisemakers list could use discretion when drawing up the list. He or she could start by putting down the names of his or her perceived enemies. Sometimes the victims would spill the beans when the teacher came back, insisting that all the class members made noise. In such a case, the class might earn a group punishment, which meant group play anyway as all of them would be expected to go out to fetch the abalidiegwu leaves for the cleaning of the black board.

Making friends for Ginika was always tricky because he always chose kids as small as himself so he could lord things over them or appear to be in control of the relationships. But he would also want at least one big kid among his circle of friends just in case there was a need for some sort of protection from external aggressors like the new bully, Justin, who arrived in school at the start of a new term. Justin had relocated to Owerri from Umuahia with his parents and was stepped down from primary four in his former school to primary three in the Housing Estate Primary School owing to his performance in the interview conducted for new intakes. To exert his influence in the class and among the kids, he beat up a boy on the second day of his attendance and was a terror for other students after that day. Ginika and his friends simply kept their distance even though they vowed they could handle Justin should their paths cross for any reason. That day came, and their paths crossed when one of Ginika's friends, Obi, was responsible for writing down the names of noisemakers. Without fear or favour, Obi put down Justin's name! It was a disastrous move by the boy who was simply doing his job, but now somebody would have to pay during break for Justin's name appearing among the names of noisemakers. Helping and standing by little Obi was a task for all Ginika's friends including the heftiest of them, Nnachi. Unfortunately, even though Nnachi matched Justin in size, his heart was not that strong. Nnachi was already visibly sweating as they gathered outside the class during break. Ginika's friends had thought about how to handle the situation while little Obi was still in the classroom sacrificing his break period because of the uncertainty that awaited him if he went out to play with other kids. It took the intervention of Ginika's elder brother Emeka to resolve the impasse and enable Obi to enjoy his break period that day.

On another occasion, it was Ginika's group against another set of brothers who arrived at Housing Estate Primary School midterm. This time around, Ugo and Ebi came from Lagos. Their parents had transferred them to the south-east of the country to ensure they imbibed the culture of the Igbos, their native culture. Ugo and Ebi had been brought up speaking English as a first language and so could not immediately communicate with the kids at school who spoke Igbo as their first language in most parts of South East Nigeria, especially Owerri. It was surprising to see these boys speaking in an unknown tongue. Some others felt a bit of jealousy at the accents that came with the foreign language. They would shout at Ugo and Ebi, "*Iche na ima asu* English!" (You think you know how to speak English!) to which Ugo would kindly respond, "Speak your own international English let us hear!". "*Ewo supu*" (Speak!), the other kids would shout as they marvelled at the way these new kids spoke the white man's language with so much ease. Even in the jealousy-laced criticism of Ugo and Ebi, it was obvious that the kids all appreciated the way the new kids in town spoke and wished to speak like them. Interestingly, as the days went by, they all became friends with Ugo and Ebi and eventually lost the accents in their spoken English as they blended into the environment.

CHAPTER 3
A Wounded Cow in the School field

Ginika's school compound was so large it could not all be fenced off against trespassers, and once in a while, some third parties used the unfenced part of the school compound for community activities such as friendly neighbourhood football matches. The unfenced portion of the school compound was large enough to accommodate a mini stadium.

One day, the space even played host to a helicopter. No one was sure of who the passenger was or what warranted the big bird to land in the school compound, but it was fun for the kids to rush close to the fence to have a glimpse of a helicopter. Later, rumour had it that the visitor on that day was no other than Chief Arthur Nzeribe, a very wealthy man. No one actually knew what he did for a living. Some said he made a lot of money from selling military hardware and equipment to African countries including Nigeria during the Civil War. Others said he was highly connected to the government, and hence his wealth was unexplained, as was the wealth of many other former government officials. Prior to the landing of the helicopter, kids had only seen drawings and photographs of such aircraft in school textbooks. A few privileged kids may have seen a real one, especially kids like Ugo and Ebi whose parents lived in the big cities. Though all the students were restricted to within the fenced portion of the school while the helicopter was in the unfenced portion, the large breeze from the machine's rotors that accompanied the landing and eventual take off of the helicopter was enough to raise the school uniform of the female students, exposing their multi-coloured underwear to the excitement of the boys, who were subsequently scolded by the females, who called them *ndi iberibe* (naughty boys). The helicopter was really interesting for the kids, and they showed their gratitude by waiving goodbye to the big bird as it rose slowly, its nose bent forward and tail raised as if in a final dance farewell to the teeming crowd cheering at it. Then it departed with a large noise as some of the kids cheered on.

One sunny afternoon, the unfenced premises played host to another unexpected visitor, a wounded cow. Most of the beef consumed in the southern part of the country came from cows transported from the northern part of the country in trailers or other big trucks. Prior to their slaughter, the nomads who took care of the cows, as they awaited buyers, would escort them across the different parts of the city to graze the grasses that were abundant in uninhabited areas or some green areas in neighbourhoods. They sometimes grazed the cows on people's farmland causing damage to food crops such as cassava, melon, maize, and yam. On this occasion, no one knew how this cow came about to be left in the compound without any attendant. On close inspection, it was discovered that the animal may have suffered some kind of injury that prevented it from keeping up with the rest of the herd, and thus it was left behind as the herd moved on. It was about eleven o'clock in the morning when Ginika and the rest of the kids came out on their second break for the day to discover the unthinkable—some people were busy butchering the live cow as it groaned in agony. It looked like a movie, but it was real. A rickety car was parked by the side of the cow while these agents of torture and sadism continued cutting pieces of meat from the dying cow and loading them into their waiting vehicle. Not even the shouting of the school kids would deter them from their dastardly act. Eventually the cow died, and the butchers left, but what annoyed the kids even more was the continued slicing of the meat from the cow the next day by some other parties even though the dead cow's meat had already started to rot and smell. The thought in poor Ginika's mind was, *Who is going to eat the spoilt meat? And why didn't the relevant authorities come and rescue the poor cow in the first place?* Cows produce milk, the children had been taught in school, and so are good and productive animals and should not be subjected to the kind of cruelty they had witnessed.

The watching of the "enemies of cows" was over when the end of break alarm sounded. It was time to go back to their classes. Many of the kids would continue to play until forced to go back to their classes by the teachers. On this occasion, as the students were running and continued their play, one of them, a mixed-race child, fell into a failed portion of the school toilets' soakaway pit. His school uniform was covered with filth from the pit. This got the rest of the kids laughing as they made way to their different classrooms, and the victim, Johnson, was rushed to the toilet by the pursuing teacher for proper cleaning. Though the failed portion of the toilet had been known by the school authorities, no attempt had been made to either repair it or provide barricades to warn the students of the dangers. This incident infuriated the boy's father, who threatened to sue the school authorities for negligence, but he was not known to have carried out the threat eventually. The incident would, however, earn the boy a stigma and nickname among his classmates who would refer to him as Obunshi Aladinma (Janitor for Aladinma).

Obunshi Aladinma turned out to be the best fine arts student in primary three that school year. His painting of a wounded cow won the best painting award in a painting competition organized for the primary three pupils as part of the end-of-year speech and prise-giving day ceremonies. When asked what inspired his painting, he said it was his deep thoughts about the agony of the wounded cow on that day that made him forget himself so much that he fell into the toilet ditch, earning him the nick name Obunshi Aladinma. For Johnson, his nick name was not a stigma or laughing matter; rather, it was a call to do something about the cruelty against animals in the hands of their caretakers. Johnson later studied veterinary medicine at university and continues the crusade against cruelty to domestic animals in Africa to this day.

CHAPTER 4

Romana

Ginika, though a bright boy, sometimes found himself shy and not able to exert himself when duty called. While he was in primary four, he was to take the entrance examinations that would lead to admissions into secondary school. The class teacher asked all students in primary four to indicate whether they were interested in taking the necessary exams. The practice then was that class six students were the rightful candidates, but in some cases, students in lower classes were allowed, especially if the students thought they could scale through the exams. Ginika had already told the teacher he did not want to take the exam when she asked the first day. But he hadn't consulted anybody at home. Unfortunately for him, when he asked Ogadimma, his dad, and his elder sibling Emeka, they were of the view that attempting to pass the exam could actually help him prepare for a more necessary exam in future. So Ginika was in a dilemma over how to give the update to his teacher. It was a sober Ginika who waited until everyone was out of the class on break before he approached the teacher to inform her that his father had changed his mind on the enrolment for the exams. This was not a problem for the teacher, who thought that Ginika had what it took to sit for such an exam. With the preparations for the exams came other senior responsibilities such as the representation of the school in interschool quiz competitions, and this stretched Ginika's schedule even more.

School quiz competitions were very important because the results reflected the level of intelligence of the students to the average man on the street. Not even the school performance in the common entrance examinations enjoyed the kind of publicity these quiz competitions had. As a result, the schools paid a lot of attention to the competitions and made sure they entered only their best students. To the public, the quality of each school was a direct reflection of their performance in the interschool quizzes, which were normally broadcast on NTA Channel 6 Aba, the only TV station at the time in the whole of Imo State. The television broadcast would normally start at four in the afternoon with the national anthem after a display of some vertical rainbow coloured stripes for a couple of minutes and a weird whistling sound. The quiz competitions were usually broadcast on Mondays at five o'clock in the evening and would last for thirty minutes. For the privileged families that had televisions, it was a thrill to see a child's school team in action, and it was every kid's aspiration to be a member of the school delegation. The next day at school would see the quiz team members celebrated by all, and the success of the participants was an achievement that resulted in pride and joy for both the competitors and their teachers.

Ginika's family was privileged to own a standard four-legged, black-and-white, twenty-one-inch television encased in a brown box with a double folding doors. To be part of the quiz team was a major point of pride for Ginika since it meant his father saw him live on stage during the competition as the whole family watched one of the evening broadcasts. The importance of the morning information that the students were encouraged to give in school dawned on everyone as it was obvious that most of the quiz questions related to the information that had been shared during most of the morning assembly meetings to which only a few people payed attention. One of such questions was "In which year was Owerri declared the cleanest city in Nigeria? And who made the declaration?" Ginika quickly jumped up even before the moderator could finish the question. He had delivered that information as "morning information" while he was in primary two. Being aware of current affairs became important for the students. Everyone aspired to know and understand as much as possible beginning with the names of commissioners of the different state ministries and governors of different states of the federation. Sometimes there was a daunting number of names and offices to memorize, especially when African heads of states were included. On one occasion, a child was asked to name the governor of Lagos State, to which he proudly named the president and commander in chief of the armed forces, General Muhamadu Buhari, who had taken over from the civilian government of Shehu Shagari in a coup d'état in 1983. With the military in power, there were constant changes in the state administrators, and this got the poor boy confused over time; however, he got an even harder question—who was the president of Cameroun? He shouted, "Paul Biya!" Paul Biya was a popular name among the students as they used different methods to remember a series of names such as list of African heads of states. Paul's surname —Biya—was pronounced "Beer". Every student giggled at its mention whether in class lessons or during the sessions in which they practiced recalling important names. The students would always add in a shout at the mention of Paul Beer, "Golden Guinea" or "Star". Golden Guinea was the beer of choice then in the area. It was produced by the Imo State government, and a number of civil servants were connected one way or the other to the company. The company had a yellow trademark and flourished well, making huge profits for the government and employing thousands of its citizens directly while a lot more relied on sales indirectly to make a living. This included one of Ginika's uncles who lived in the city of Benin and was one of the major distributors for the company.

One of Ginika's friends, Johnbosco, was also a member of the quiz team, and together they would strategize and ask each other all kinds of questions they anticipated might be included in the coming competitions. Both boys and the rest of the team became the delight of the other students, and everyone wanted to be their friend. Ginika, being the shy one, would always not want to be seen wooed by any girl and would always get tongue-tied during any opportunity to have a discussion with a girl. Johnbosco was at ease about relating to girls and was always quick to open conversations. In fact, he looked forward to meeting girls from other competing primary schools. It was not surprising, since Johnbosco had elder and younger sisters while Ginika had no sister at all at the time and really didn't know what it was like to talk to girls. He knew he enjoyed every bit of their company and wished each rare chat with a girl would never end. No wonder he would come home every day to narrate to Okechukwu, a relative who had just come to live with his family, how beautiful this or that girl was. He would mention all the things he wanted to do with the girls. On one particular occasion, Ginika expressed his love for Nkemjika in a song. However, she was a girl who had not one atom of knowledge that Ginika liked her! Okechukwu and Ginika were seated in the cool of the evening on the asphalt road outside the house when he burst out singing "Nkemjika, Nkemjika, Nkemjika *kamma na uwa*" (Nkemjika, Nkemjika, Nkemjika is best in this world). Okechukwu kept looking at this young man who seemed to have found love so early in life—in primary five!—and kept wondering what was next for him as he seemed to have found all he ever wanted in life. His affection for Nkemjika lasted only a few weeks. Soon Ginika came home with another love story, this time a half-cast girl who sat next to him in class. Ginika's love stories became so frequent that Okechukwu had to caution him against breaking any girl's heart. Ginika's eyes popped out in surprise at the word *heartbreak*. "How does one's heart break because of love?" he asked. "Moreover, I never told any of them I would marry them!" This was his defence.

He had, earlier on, been the talk of the school because of what had happened one day at school. Mr Ojo, the agriculture teacher and the teacher responsible for preparing students for the school matches, was introducing the details of the preparation to the students. But Ginika and a girl called Romana were lost in a side conversation as

the teacher was talking to the class. Not even Mr Ojo's shouting of
"Hey!" (since he didn't know their names) could bring the lost minds
of Ginika and Romana back to the classroom. It took the combined
shouting of "Ginika!" by the rest of the students for Ginika's attention
to come back to the classroom. From that day, Ginika's name changed
to "Ginika Romana". Romana did not mind this. After all, Ginika was
the favourite of every girl in the school, and if she had caused him to
carry her name so what?

One would think Ginika would be finished with the girls after
the Romana incident, but then Ugochi entered the picture. Ugochi, a
beautiful fair-complexioned girl, was also burning in Ginika's heart
even while he was carrying Romana's name as a pseudo surname.
Ugochi sat on the other side of the class divide about four seats behind
Ginika. Ginika was very happy to lend his notes to all who came to
him, especially the girls. He was gradually warming up to talking with
girls; he was catching up to his friend Johnbosco. It was not surprising
on this particular day that Ginika gave a notebook to Ugochi, and the
exchange was glorious to him as he talked with this beauty for real.
So he looked forward to the return of the book for another round of
conversation. Alas, Ugochi was so naive she didn't see her blunder
when she returned the book right where it belonged, in Ginika's bag.
That denied the poor guy the opportunity of having a long-awaited
talk with the damsel. Ginika would not be denied his right and thus
ignored the knowledge that he saw the book right there in his bag. He
went ahead to engage Ugochi in conversation to ask her to return the
book. She told him she had already put it in his bag. Ginika pretended
not to know while asking if she had finished copying what she wanted,
a question with an obvious answer; otherwise, why would she have
returned the book if she hadn't finished? Ugochi became impatient
with this exchange. She was better than Ginika academically and was
just unfortunate to have missed the class session for which she needed
Ginika's notes. But Ginika wanted to use the return of his notebook as
an excuse to have a lovely friendly conversation. He told Okechukwu

that night about this new beautiful girl in their class that he was dying for again, for the hundredth time!

When Ginika was not talking about Romana, Ugochi, or the quiz competition where he expected to exchange some pleasantries with ladies, he was thinking about strategies to join the drama group. The drama group in the school represented everything "Aladinma". The group was run by Johnbosco's younger brother, Uchewuba, and their productions usually portrayed common themes relevant to the small community as part of entertainment during special school occasions, especially the speech and prize-giving days. One of the common plays that attracted Ginika to the group was a play titled *Aku*. It featured the head mistress, Mrs Nkonye, acting as the mother to two boys, Kelvin and Richard, who refused to come out in the middle of the night to help the family gather *aku* during the season, only for the boys to turn up the next day begging for some of the delicacy that had been gathered the previous night. Aku, which are winged termites, are roasted and are a favourite high-protein food in Nigeria. Aku usually take flight during the rainy season. At night they are attracted to streetlights, so most families go out every night to harvest them. They do not fly every night, and there is no way to predict when they will fly, so it behoves people to constantly be on watch for them. The watch entails everyone taking turns to look out for the signs, especially when each person gets up in the night to urinate. Uchewuba acted the part of Kelvin and was so good in the role that Ginika approached him after the event to enquire about joining the drama group. "You have to have the passion to act," Uchewuba told him. "You have to feel it in you and behave as if it is real life. For instance, crying," he continued. "Can you cry convincingly?" He asked Ginika. Ginika however thought that the question was not necessary since he felt Uchewuba had no reason to deny him entry into the group. Ginika believed he was already qualified given the fact that he was a friend of Uchewuba's elder brother.

Unbeknownst to his friends, Ginika's request to join the drama group had little to do with his passion to act or his ability to write scripts as he claimed he could. Ginika was more interested in what went on at the rehearsals. With the higher numbers of girls in the drama group than in the quiz group, Ginika decided the drama group was for him! Ginika eventually joined the drama group and wrote the best plays the group performed. He loved everything to do with drama, and his scripts depicted every aspect of daily life in the small town. One of his scripts, *Kosi*, was presented during the speech and prize-giving day that came after he joined the group.

Unfortunately, Ginika's *Kosi* turned out to be a subject of conflict in the drama group because Uchewuba claimed he wrote and directed the script. The amazing story earned Uchewuba a top prize that year, coupled with the fact that he was the head of the drama group. Prior to the selection of the best drama and scriptwriter, the teacher in charge had approached the heads of the various units including quiz, fine arts, and drama, and asked for nominations. The heads of the groups provided the teacher with the names and winning works and events. For the quiz group, it was easy since everyone knew the pupils who represented the school in each quiz competition. The names of fine arts students were written on the various works of art. For the drama group, everyone knew the actors in each play, but no one actually knew the people who had put together the story behind each play.

Kosi was a story from Ginika's experience with one of their house helpers who happened to come from a poor background. His other two siblings were leaving with other people from their village because his parents could not afford to train them. Kosi, the lead character was so loving and hardworking that his master gave him a free hand and treated him like a son until Kosi changed. The change in Kosi was so bad. He started stealing money from the house and ended up being sent back to the village of his parents. He later regretted his wrongdoings when he saw his other siblings doing well in their lives and were not limited by the fact that their parents were poor.

After the prize for best drama and writer was awarded to Uchewuba, Ginika approached the teacher in charge to complain that he wrote the script. The teacher responded that there was nothing he could do since he could not tell who wrote the script and he could not contradict the head of the drama group and his submission. Ginika then requested that the teacher call Uchewuba so that he could confront him regarding ownership. Uchewuba feigned ignorance when he came to meet the teacher and Ginika. He detailed to the teacher how he had given the script lines to the drama group, and they all liked it and even prophesied it would win an award. Uchewuba even asked the teacher to talk to any member of the group to investigate further. Ginika's eyes turned red when he realized that there was nothing he could do about the situation. On getting home that day, he searched his room to see if he could find the small sheets of paper on which he had written down some of the lines. He could not find the papers, and that was when he gave up his quest to regain his work. Ginika was moody the whole evening and did not have his dinner. It took his parents, especially Ogadimma, to console him. His father pointed out the need for Ginika to keep his work and books tidy in his room. Ogadimma pointed out that, probably, if he had found the script, it would have been evidence he could have taken to the teacher in charge. However, as things stood, he had no evidence. Ginika should just reconcile himself to the fact that his work had been stolen. Ogadimma consoled him and noted that, since he produced one award-winning play, he had the potential to produce more award-winning plays in future, and no one would dare steal them from him. Ogadimma was so vexed by the incident he thought of going to the school to complain to the authorities. He was convinced the script had been written by Ginika because he knew the story the poor boy had depicted. He only changed his mind when his wife pointed out that the confrontation might bring about negative consequences that might outweigh his intensions.

But it was a different Ginika when it came to church matters. Ginika was as dedicated to church matters as he was to his endeavours in school. The Holy Cross Catholic Church where his family worshiped was about double the distance away from home as his primary school. Reverend Father Mmegwa had held his position for a long time. From his diligence in catechism classes to serving as an altar boy, and finally graduating to the choir ministry, Ginika was a well-known figure in the church. The graduation from the altar boy to choir member was a surprising one as Ginika was not really known for his voice except when singing about the new girls he met in school. It took further probing by Okechukwu for Ginika to reveal the real reason he left altar service. A Sunday experience with Reverend Father Mmegwa was all he needed to resign from the Lord's service. This particular Sunday was a thanksgiving Sunday, and the women's organization had come for a special thanksgiving. They dropped an envelope that supposedly contained money in the offering basket. It was not clear how the Reverend Father got to know about the special offering from the women, but to the surprise of the priest, that envelope had grown legs by the time the offerings were counted. A visibly angry priest questioned all the altar boys, both those who were on duty during that service and those who were not. When none of them owned up to taking away the envelop, they were all asked to lie down right there at the altar. Luckily for them, this happened after the congregants had left the church after the Sunday service. For some reason, a scared Ginika and a couple of others were left off the hook. Reverend Father Mmegwa flogged the hell out of the boys as their voices went up in "praise" as he ministered to their buttocks one by one with his *koboko* (cane). A scared Ginika would take the easier way out, opting out of serving as an altar boy so that he would not find himself in that dilemma for any reason.

Primary school remained a fun place for Ginika and his friends. Ginika's family lived within walking distance—a hundred metres—from school until sometime in 1983 when they moved to a new building located inside a private estate called Nkpaji Estate, a new federal housing estate developed by the federal government to address the massive housing deficit at the time. The federal housing estate was then a choice location to live, with well-built similar houses in rows without any block fences to demarcate neighbours or ward off any unwanted intruders. The roads and side drains were always clean and maintained by diligent daily-paid workers who were very satisfied and proud to do their jobs without complaints. There was no police post in the estate since it was crime free at the time, and it would have been a waste of public funds to institute police protection there. The new house and longer distance to commute meant Ginika and his siblings could no longer walk to school; rather, they had to be driven by his father's driver, Emeka, popularly known as Zigizi, a jolly good fellow who respected everyone, even the little ones who didn't seem to have any need for that. It was always fun to ride with Zigizi as goodies were sure to be a bonus on any trip. It was even better for the older ones like Emeka, Ginika's most senior brother. Going on errands to far distances with Zigizi meant profit sharing for any passenger they picked up on the road or equal sharing of any delicacies bought on the road with such proceeds. One example was *okpa*, a favourite food made from babara seeds wrapped in leaves like bean cake. It was not uncommon for Ginika and Emeka to be sent to the village for one thing or another such as transportation of goods to the village in preparation for the yuletide season or to bring Ogadimma's relatives to the city to undergo a medical appointment since the hospitals in Owerri were considered better than the ones in Onitsha at the time by Ogadimma. One wondered at the criteria Ogadimma used to rate the hospitals and their doctors to come to the conclusion that the ones in Owerri were better than those at Onitsha after praising the Onitsha hospitals while living there just a couple of years back. It appeared he confused proximity with professionalism and enhanced this by the number of his classmates who worked in such hospitals. Having attended the prestigious Government College Umuahia, popularly known as Fisher High School, Ogadimma would tell anyone who cared to listen how the school singlehandedly produced the only doctors in the eastern part of the country for a long time before other schools came on board. It was always a war of words at functions when he would start his Umuahian rhetoric and get other scholars bored with his Umuahia ideas. That was if he was not challenged by the alumni of other old schools in the South East such as Methodist College Uzuakoli.

With Zigizi, going to school in the morning was also fun. Since the Ogadimma family lived in an estate, other kids would join in the car that took Ginika and his brothers to school as well. Most times it was always tight since the vehicle meant to carry five passengers was used to carrying up to ten neighbouring children who all went to the same school. It was sometimes a problem sorting out who would ride in the front seat and who would ride in back in order to be able to pack all the kids into the car. Later, an additional car was provided in order to prevent the tight packing of the kids. The additional car brought its own problems as the quarrel among the kids shifted from who would sit in front to who would sit in the new car. The commute to school also meant keeping to the time of departure for the driver and the kids. It could be a struggle sometimes getting all the kids ready on time, and every school departure was always a time for crying for a lot of the kids over one thing or the other. If one was not crying because his or her preference for yellow stockings was overruled by an aunty, it was because of a lost HB pencil or that another kid gave an *ntoo*—an eye glare—to him or her. For Ginika, being in senior primary class meant he needed to be in school early enough to do some morning classroom duties such as sweeping the floor or watering the flowers in front of the class before the morning assembly began. And that was why he never found it funny when there was a delay for any reason. It was so bad that he would complain bitterly in his mind or to anyone who would not tattle on him. To him, it was because the drivers had finished going to their own school that they did not bother about whether they arrived early or not!

It was worse when Ginika heard the drivers discuss some topics that were irrelevant to him, such as upcoming national elections. In a particular case, Nigeria had then transitioned from a military to a civilian administration and was about to make its first transition from a civilian to a civilian administration with all the intrigue and blackmail associated with the campaigns. The same political discussions the drivers engaged in before taking Ginika and company to school would continue in the school with their teachers during any spare time they found either during break or assembly time in the morning. The outlook of each candidate both at the national and state levels was always in focus. For Imo State, which was governed by incumbent Chief Sam Onunaka Mbakwe at the time, it was a tough fight between the chief and one Collins Obi with the rest of contenders being very lightweight politically and not even part of the discussion among interest groups. While Chief Sam Mbakwe was of the Nigerian Peoples Party (NPP), Collins Obi was of the National Party of Nigeria (NPN).

Even with Ginika's distaste for political discussions among his elders, it was not long before the bug caught up with him, and he joined in the chorus of the different slogans of the different major political parties, NPP and NPN.

The NPP slogan was *"Ebe ka anyi ga abinye aka? Ebe esere mmaadu. Ebe ka anyi ga abinye aka? Ebe esere mmaadu."* This can be translated: "Where would we thumb print? Where we see a human as symbol." This chant referred to the symbol of the party for voting purposes so that voters should note the right party symbol when they got to the booths to vote.

The NPN slogan was *"Ebe ka anyi ga abinye aka? Ebe esere ulo na Oka abuo. Ebe ka anyi ga abinye aka? Ebe esere ulo na Oka abuo."* Similarly, the NPN chant referred to their party symbol, which directed people to where a house and two cobs of corn were drawn. Corn, or maize, was one of the staple foods of Nigeria and the symbol represented the fact that the party was ready to feed the nation. The party supporters would follow up the singing with a particular reference to their candidate Collins Obi shouting "Collins Obi oh, aye iye! Collins Obi oh, aye iye, *owu onye ga achi* Imo State. Collins Obi, NPN *ga achi nu ndi Imo. Owu onye ga achi anyi o,* Collins Obi NPN *ga achi nu ndi imo.*

A landslide victory brought Mbakwe back to the government house. The busy Ngwa Street, where Collins Obi lived and which was coincidentally where Ogadimma's office was located, became less busy as the reality of the election results settled in.

CHAPTER 5

Government College Umuahia

It was not surprising that Ginika ended up at Government College Umuahia for his secondary school, having been indoctrinated by the rhetoric of Ogadimma for so long. With the common entrance exams into the secondary schools, he faced a choice between multiple schools in the Owerri capital city area or the longer distance to Umuahia away from home. No hard and fast rule was to bear in his final choice, but a lot of his friends chose to stay in the schools in Owerri while some went to the Federal Government College Okigwe, another distant school from Owerri. The kids who obtained admission to the federal government colleges were particularly thought to be the most brilliant ones, and it was not surprising when other kids saw them as being snobs out of envy for their highly prized schools. The examinations for entrance into the federal government colleges were conducted just like the ones for the state schools, but admission to the federal government colleges required an extra step in the form of a face-to-face oral interview. Preparing for the interview was similar to preparing for a job interview; instructors gave students lessons on etiquette such as not sitting down once you approach the interview panel unless you are asked to do so.

Federal Government College Okigwe was a mixed school, and one needed to go to the school at Okigwe to be interviewed. The Federal

Government Girls College Owerri was an all-girls school situated in the capital city of Owerri. Going to the federal government colleges was every kid's dream at the time as there were no other schools apart from them and the state colleges. As with the primary schools, there were no private secondary schools. Hence some children started from primary four to try their luck at securing admission to these prestigious colleges, and sometimes people were lucky enough to transit straight to college from primary five or even four.

Ginika's attempt had started as far back as in his primary four and continued until he found himself in Government College Umuahia. Not even already being in a state college would deter him from one more try, even at the risk of losing a year of study if he secured the admission. After passing the first phase of the entrance while at Government College Umuahia, he attended the face-to-face interview session at Okigwe and waited for the results. It was as if Ginika's life was hanging in the balance; he had attended only a term at Government College Umuahia. With the shocking experience of the few weeks at his secondary school, Ginika needed this change of school more than anything in the world. On the day Ogadimma returned and informed Ginika he had not made the list for those admitted into Federal Government College Okigwe, all hell broke loose. From his countenance, anyone looking at him would think it would be better for the ground to open so that Ginika could simply jump in and end the nightmare that awaited him if he had to go back to Umuahia. Sleeping and waking up was difficult for those few days after the announcement because the thought of going back to the bullying and fetching water from a distant stream that marked entrance to the so-called secondary school was never what the young Ginika had bargained for. Not even pleading from his aunts, Fidelia, Ego, and Rita, could calm Ginika down. Aunty Rita, a close relative of the Ogadimma's, had been around at the time the result was relayed to Ginika, and she saw how he took the news in bad faith. She counselled Ginika, reminding him that it might be God at work in not letting him get the admission because He might have other plans for him. Ginika would hear none of this, and he continued with his wailing. Finally, Ginika accepted the reality of Umuahia as a secondary school for life since he had exhausted his chances at the federal government college attempt and had to make the best of Umuahia.

No doubt, Government College Umuahia was a prestigious school in its own right, boasting notable alumni such as Chinua Achebe, a renowned writer and author of *Things fall Apart*; Ken Saro-Wiwa; Chukwuemeka Ike; and others. Ogadimma also had done well in the glory days of Umuahia and probably thought the school was the same or at least close to what it had been when he attended the school in the fifties and sixties. Alas! This was the *eighties* and not just any eighties. It was the eighties of the military with all the neglect of public institutions and infrastructure. The setting at the college could be both intimidating and encouraging on a first visit. After driving through the main gate, visitors passed along a paved road lined on both sides by beautiful trees. It was just like driving into a university. There was a row of teachers' quarters to the left and a wire fence to the right demarcating the school from the immediate village. A five-hundred-metre drive brought visitors to the principal's house on the right just as the road met a wide roundabout at the junction with Fisher Hall. Mounted on a podium in front of the building was the sculpture of Robert Fisher, the first principal and founder of the school. It was said that the building had been donated to the school by its past students as part of the alumni contributions to the school. These associations were very helpful for the development of schools, especially with the current neglect of public schools by the governments. Turning left at this roundabout, visitors encountered the main school area, while turning right they encountered the senior teachers' quarters. The amount of vegetation in the compound was impressive; there were lots of mango trees lining up the roads. These trees would later turn out to be the resting place of Ginika and most other students during their leisure times. Also, the fruit of the trees augmented the poor-quality food served in the dining hall.

On his first day at Umuahia, Ginika entered his dormitory with all the new stuff that had been bought for him, including a black box that contained his school uniform as well as boarding house uniforms, bed sheets, pink bed-ends that reflected the colours of Kent House. This was the oldest of the houses in the school. It was built with raw bricks and had a roof known as "send down the rain" in modern Nigerian building parlance. Kent House was closest to the dining hall, and this gave Ginika a bit of a warm feeling, especially as he could perceive the aroma of the dish to be served that afternoon as he settled into his new home. Just as it was with every other kid starting off newly at Umuahia, it did not take more than two minutes after the departure of Ogadimma and his wife, Ngozi, for Ginika to burst into a thunderous cry that shocked even his mates while the senior boys looked on with pity and sympathetic smiles as they were used to the drama that followed such drop-offs. It took the intervention of a student known as Favour, who turned out to be designated as Ginika's "magi", to calm him down. A magi was a senior who was served by a junior student called a fag. The new students simply used the terms they learned on arrival without asking questions. As far as they were concerned, magi meant lord. That assumption was indeed correct as the word derived from Latin and was used in the context of "wise men", which reflected the status of the seniors in the school. *Fagging* also was a correct English word though the students simply used the term as handed over. Fagging was a traditional practice in British boarding schools in which younger pupils were required to act as personal servants to senior boys. It was sometimes associated with sexual abuse by those senior boys. The casual and incorrect use of the words can best be illustrated by a new student's response when he was asked who was the owner of the plate of food he was carrying in the dining hall. He said, "My magi please, am fagging it." There was a great deal of laughter by those in the area. It always was a symbiotic relationship between a magi and his fag, with the fag making sure the magi's clothes were washed and ironed, fetching water for a bath from the stream, safeguarding and bringing back the magi's food from the dining hall. All of this could contribute to developing some skills to be able to "deliver". There were times when a dining hall master or school prefect would insist on sharing the food of everyone who did not attend the dining hall to eat. At such times, duty then required the fag to do everything possible to hide his magi's food from the prying eyes of the masters who wanted to share such food. Fags could put the food on their laps under the table while eating. They could also hold the food under the table with one hand. They came up with many ingenious tricks to prove to their magis that they looked after their well-being. Ginika was not new to such tricks as his experience hiding from teachers looking for pupils with dirty clothes at the housing estate primary school had equipped him well for such occasions. On the other hand, the magi had the responsibility of protecting the fag against any aggressive senior students, and the fags of prefects were better off in this regard than those of yoo men, who were students in senior classes but not designated as school prefects. Life was thus repeating itself in phases as Ginika remembered Nnachi and the cluster of friends at Aladinma Housing Estate Primary School who protected their circle of friends from aggressors.

Favour was the assistant house prefect of Kent House, so he had some powers of protection for his fags, including Ginika, Mark, and Uchenna. Mark and Uchenna were two classes ahead of Ginika, and that left Ginika doing the worst of the chores such as washing the plates after meals and passing the plates in the dining hall before the sharing of food. Passing the plates meant keeping the empty plate turned upside down on the tables designated for each house. There was a designated time for passing plates before the sharing of food, and the passing of plates ended just before the start of sharing. Anyone who did not pass his plate at the right time ran the risk of missing his food. It was customary for Ginika and his fellow fags to wash and pass their plates for the morning meals just after returning from the stream. Afternoon meal plates were passed at break periods at around ten in the morning, and evening meal plates were passed after stream just before seven when food sharing started.

Life at Government College was stressful and brutal but fun for

Ginika. He and the other kids were almost 99 per cent sure of getting flogged every day by the prefects for one thing or another, and for trespasses they may not be aware of. For instance, entering the house common room and finding out that a student *makarred* (defecated, using the so-called Umuahian language) in the room meant for house prayers! The house prefect then insisted that the perpetrator must be found or everyone in the house would have to take strokes of the cane, including his classmates since he was the prefect. This was one of the surprising aspects of life in this college—the authority of students to flog their classmates simply because such a student was a school prefect! On such occasions, Ginika wondered about the kinds of persons who committed such crimes and the real purpose for the crimes. Was it to ensure all house members got punished? This would be the case since it would not be because of lack of designated toilets in the school. The possibility of other students from other houses committing the crime was not ruled out either. On lucky days, the presence of the *makar* was noticed early as the house members came into the common room before the house prefect, and thus they were able to act quickly to remove the filth. The house prefect then only perceived the bad odour as he entered the common room. Without the evidence of the physical makar, he could not do anything.

It was a regular sight to be "five-toeing" in the school, meaning that one of the student's sandals had been seized by senior students or prefects for some wrongdoing or as a guarantee that the "victim" would do something. Such seizures normally were evident all around the school, and the teachers payed no attention; in fact, they accepted it as part of the Umuahian tradition. Be it in the school assembly hall or classrooms, students could be seen walking as if they had some physical disability with their unequal height arising from having a sandal on one foot and none on the other. The image became more pathetic in *uguru* (harmattan) season when the sight of the student provoked so much pity because the five-toeing would be accompanied by the whitish nature of the student's skin as the dry weather took its toll on the poor student.

Part of inculcating the Umuahian tradition was the obligation to memorize the different house and school anthems. The expiration of a grace period for new students to memorize the house and school anthems was another milestone that guaranteed strokes of cane for the new students who had not accomplished the task. The house anthem of Kent House had four stanzas; the first was sung thus:

Oh God perpetual father of Kent,

Through thee thy beloved house shine as one,

Through thee the glories of Kent abound,

From generation to generation.

The students would always remember the first and probably the second stanzas, but when it came to the third and fourth, they struggled and exploded into loud cries as they realized the consequence of their failure—the long cane dangling over their heads. Sometimes, the confidence exhibited in reciting the first and second stanzas could influence the house or presiding prefect to allow the student pass the test without the need for the last two stanzas, or the students would be encouraged to memorize them in case of such need. It was also not uncommon for some new students to be protected from the dangers of flogging by their very powerful magis who might come to such gatherings to ensure their candidates were bypassed for such tests, or they might be so powerful that even without their physical presence, their fags were not touched. Such school anthems turned out to be the pride of the students when they eventually left Umuahia as they continued to repeat the songs at their alumni meetings to the admiration of any visiting guests.

Morning chores for Ginika started when he woke at about 3.30 to 4.00 in the morning to fetch water from the stream. The time depended on the kitchen roster. Different houses were assigned specific days to fetch water for the general use of the school kitchen, and on the day a particular house was to fetch, all the eligible students got up extra early to ensure they would finish fetching for the school kitchen before going to bathe in the stream while fetching water back for their magis to use for their own baths. Once Ginika and the rest of the boys were back, the next thing they had to do was their house morning work. Ginika had to sweep a long area behind the dormitory before going for breakfast and then morning assembly. Sweeping the area was not a big deal for Ginika as he had mastered the technique to quickly complete the task in a few minutes. If it hadn't been for the mango tree at the middle of the area, Ginika would have had no need to do the sweeping in the mornings. He devised a routine for doing the sweeping late in the evening so that the area remained relatively clean in the morning and required only a little touch-up to ensure it was within the acceptable limits of being clean. However, during the dry season, this was not possible as the evening winds took a toll on the mango tree and it would make a mess of all Ginika's earlier evening efforts. The rainy season was pretty much in line with the strategy because the area stayed fairly clean after he swept it in the evening. In the morning, the light coating of dew simply needed a light brush of the broom. To survive in Umuahia, Ginika realized quickly that he had to be imaginative and devise schemes to be ahead of the numerous tasks and chores required of the average student.

Because Ginika came from a federal civil servant parents' background and had lived in the relatively urban Owerri capital city of Imo State, he was already familiar with some spoken English, unlike some of his newly acquired friends who had come from more remote parts of the state. The older students, who had once been in the shoes of the new students, made fun of the kids who struggled, usually easily forgetting their own struggles when they first started school. Take Okempku, one of Ginika's close friends in Simpson House, for example. A tall, handsome boy, he never disappointed in making the seniors laugh at his murder of the English language. It was told that, one night, he was returning from the dining hall after the evening meal when Kenneth, a form-five student in his house, flashed a torch light at him. To the surprise and laughter of Okempku's mates, he shouted, "Who pour me that light?" This turned out to be one of the most-remembered slogans of his time at school.

Such incidents again reminded Ginika of the Ugo and Ebi scenarios at Housing Estate Primary School when Ginika and his friends were the local kids who were treated to some correct usage of the Queen's English from the Eko boys who had just arrived from Lagos. On one occasion, Okempku was being dealt with by a senior student for not washing his plates and doing other chores he had requested of the poor boy. Because Okempku's magi was not a prefect, it was difficult for him to protect Okempku from such abuse and bullying by other senior boys, and Okempku ended up being everybody's fag since anyone could send him on errands without the risk of having any pushback from his magi. Okempku could no longer take it from one boy called Nkeodi. He burst out, "You told me to lie down, I *lie* down! You told me to kneel down, I *kneel* down! Am I a slave trade?" This caused a burst of laughter among the students, and so finally, Nkeodi had no choice but to leave the poor boy alone.

It was interesting how Ginika quickly adapted to the school food, which he initially found tasteless when compared to the *ecumba* from home. Ecumba generally refers to cooked food brought from home by parents during the school visiting days or at any other time that might warrant visits from parents or guardians. This food was alternatively called imported food to indicate that it was not made in the school. For wise kids like Ginika who might not be privileged to receive regular visits from home, unlike some other kids, it was a good idea to become friends with those who received regular visits. That way they could be guaranteed some measure of imported treats. With time, every kid got so accustomed to the school food that they struggled to get extra portions, especially when the food of absentee students was to be shared in the dining hall. It was common to find kids from rich homes in conspiracy with school prefects. They would give money to the prefects to spend at *bukas* (restaurants) outside the school premises.

Prefects were above the laws and could not be punished by other prefects when caught eating outside the school. These prefects, in turn, would bestow upon the rich kids the food of absentee students they had confiscated for the purpose of sharing in the dining hall. Students who had prefect friends also were guaranteed some extra food, and it might be so much that they could share with friends and housemates. In very extreme cases, such as the visit to the dining hall by the school principal, Mr Amadi, a tall, handsome, and soft-spoken man, even absentee prefects' food could be shared. That meant more food for everyone since they normally received larger portion than ordinary students or their class mates that were "yoo men."

Another story that relates to the need and love for food by students involved an occasion when a boy was found in the night at around ten o'clock scraping the food basin for leftover porridge, when others were about rounding up from the night prep (reading). Nkechukwu was a known food lover and a dirty boy at that. He was always willing to jump any queue in his quest for extra food, especially when extra and absentee plates were been shared. Even when everyone felt reluctant to be given food from an absentee prefect's plate because of the risk of been dealt with by the prefect outside the dining hall, Nkechukwu didn't give a damn. His motto was eat first and face the consequences later. Normally when a fellow prefect or dining master took an absentee prefect's food for sharing, the prefect's fag would watch out for the person the food was given to and make an attempt to get the food back from the person. On some occasions, the fag might successfully get the food back and take it back to the house for the magi. In some other cases, especially when the food fell into the hands of people like Nkechukwu, the food was gone for good as he would start scarfing down the food immediately. Nkechukwu was not alone in his love for food. Another student, one of Ginika's close friends, was nicknamed Skoolfoodifu (meaning school food has seen something) after the boy demonstrated his loyalty to and uncommon love for school food by being the number-one person to be sighted at the dining hall for consecutive weeks and who was always carrying several plates of food for different seniors he served. Apart from opportunities of getting extra food by the sharing of absentee students' food, serving an *un-ukposious* senior was a plus for every junior student. Un-ukposious seniors were those who did not eat very much. Their fags where always guaranteed some leftovers. The ukposious seniors would not leave anything for their fags.

Ginika's magi, Favour, was un-ukposious and a prefect, which meant he got a large portion of food. However, he had three fags at his service, which meant he had too many mouths to feed. Ginika found it always difficult getting anything extra from Favour's leftovers. Sometimes he was lucky when Mark and Uchenna, his fellow fags, played at being big boys and let him have the remnants from Favour's food. Other times he was not that lucky and had little or nothing in addition to his normal ration from the dining hall.

Ginika later found another means of getting extra food while he was at Umuahia. He explored his scheming skills to survive in the challenging Umuahian environment and made friends among the pantry workers who usually had access to more food than the rest of the students since they distributed the food to the different houses. Becoming a friend to a pantry worker could guarantee a student a lifetime of luxury in school food. And if a student could not befriend a pantry worker, he or she could try to engage the cooks directly. Ginika struck gold in his second year at Umuahia when he suddenly ran into Obinna and Kelechi Ozungbo, who had just transferred to Umuahia from their previous schools. For this they were termed "white shirts", or rather Obinna was termed a white shirt while Kelechi was not because he was in class one while Obinna was in class three. They somehow got to know one of the cooks, a woman who was from their village. From then on, their lives did not remain the same as far as school food was concerned. Ginika knew Obinna and Kelechi from Owerri, and even though they had not attended Aladinma Housing Estate Primary School with Ginika, they were contemporaries in the local church in Aladinma where Reverend Father Mmegwa presided, and so they bonded immediately at college in Umuahia. For Ginika, this friendship made up for missing all of his numerous friends like Johnbosco and the rest who now went to Government College Owerri for their secondary school education. Seeing them was only now possible during school breaks when they would attempt to catch up on happenings as much as possible. Anytime they needed the extra food or wanted a taste of some better food, Obinna and Kelechi would deliver a covered plastic bowl at an appropriate time and would then collect it at another precise time to avoid any eyebrows being raised by other cooks or prefects in charge of the dining hall. For Ginika, it was a question of timing the timers and watching out for when Obinna and Kelechi would make their moves. Ginika had to know when the eagle had landed. On several occasions, however, they would call Ginika to join the party, and he even occasionally participated in the delivering and collecting of the container. At some point, the cook started treating Ginika as part of the family.

Some of the food was quite tasty, especially *akamu* (pap from corn) and *akara* (fried bean cake). Students' favourite food continued to be porridge beans with yam slices. For this, the rich kids were willing to bribe the heavens to get extra portion. Soups could be good or bad depending on the cook and type of soup. One day Ginika overheard the dining hall master apologizing to the Kent House master, Mr Obi, who had come on a routine dining check in the evening, for what had happened in the afternoon of that day. The students were given porridge with yam in the morning, and by afternoon the remaining porridge was used as a thickener for the *egusi* (melon) soup that was served with the *garri* in the afternoon. When Ginika heard this, his suspicion was confirmed of what they had all heard about—the egusi soup had been too tick even though it was tasty as usual to the poor lads.

Food was so important that distribution even became political. Houses that had the privilege of producing the dining hall prefects were sure to get larger portions of the shared food in the large basins used for the distribution of the cooked food from the kitchen. Pantry workers responsible for sharing also favoured their houses.

Normally there was a sharing formula just like any sharing formula adopted by Nigeria or any other country, and population was the key indicator of the sharing ratio. The dining hall prefect was in charge of implementing the food sharing formula. He would list the houses and their ranks in the sharing while the pantry workers did the actually portioning. Sometimes the prefects on duty could also influence the amount of food that was apportioned to a house; a prefect's house was positioned to benefit anytime that prefect was on duty. Prefects on duty took turns to go round to the houses to ensure students took an afternoon nap. They also conducted the morning assembly and organized the dining hall during meals. A major activity at mealtime was saying prayers before and after meals. A simple prayer was said by the prefect on duty, but with a lot of drama. He would start by asking all the students to stand up, and then he would shout, "Shall we pray?" The students would reply, "Oh yes!" Next, they would recite a simple prayer: "For the food we are about to take we thank thee, Oh Lord." Or: "For the food we have taken, we thank thee, oh Lord." Nothing more, nothing less. The prefects also had to check the cutlery. Umuahia prided itself on inculcating dining etiquette into the curriculum. It was just as important as polishing the students' spoken English to improve the poor quality evident with the class-one students. Everyone was expected to come to the refectory with a complete set of cutlery—a fork and a knife. When the prefect shouted "Sets!" before a meal, students would raise their cutlery high so that the prefect could see it when he made his rounds. Those who did not have complete sets had their incomplete sets confiscated. They suffered the added risk of having to share their food depending on the mood of the prefect on duty. Before the pre-meal prayers, everyone would set his cutlery in the proper places around their food—the fork on the left and the knife on the right. While eating, they held their forks in their left hands and their knives in their right hands. This method was used even with garri, which was awkward for Ginika and the rest of his mates since they were used to eating garri with their hands back home. It took a while before they mastered the art of dining with forks

45

and knives, but then they started enjoying it so much they became experts. They could even mould garri with their knives and dip it into their soup bowls and swallow, all with only a table knife. Ginika had an embarrassing moment before he mastered the technique on a day he was asked by Ogadimma to join a group of old boys, Ogadimma's alumni colleagues, travelling back to Owerri. The old boys had come to Umuahia for one of their meetings, and since Ginika was due in Owerri for a medical check-up, Ogadimma used the opportunity to get one of his friends to give Ginika a ride back home to Owerri. With the old boys' meeting over, Ginika followed the assigned old boy and the rest to a hotel in the town where they were scheduled to have lunch before the final departure. Lunch was brought for Ginika, and to his amazement, his lunch consisted of a whole chicken with a little rice and stew to go with it. With a little smile across his face, Ginika went to work immediately using his newfound skills just as the old boys were all doing their own thing. To Ginika's surprise, it was not as easy as he thought to demolish the huge chicken. The leader of the delegation saw what was happening to poor Ginika and intervened, advising him to use his fingers if the chicken proved stubborn.

Another aspect of school food in Government College Umuahia in the eighties was army food. It was the best food Umuahia could offer. As part of paramilitary training, a group of soldiers were posted to the school to help train the students as cadets. In fact, some students were chosen to go on to the Nigerian Defence Academy as a result of their outstanding performance in the cadet program at Umuahia. The same school kitchen prepared food for the three military men in charge of the training. Their food was prepared separately from that of the rest of the students, and it tasted far better because they had more seasonings. To get any of this army food, students had to be connected to the kitchen through the cooks, high-level pantry workers, dining prefects, or the army soldiers themselves.

For Ginika, entry into the group of those privileged to have a taste of army food came by sheer luck through his next magi after Favour, who had graduated from the school after writing his senior school certificate exams. Unfortunately, this opportunity also lured Ginika into the dark world of college sex. Sexual relationships had remained an imagined sweet experience for Ginika after his fantasizing about almost every pretty girl at Aladinma. One would think that, upon coming to Umuahia, a boys-only college, his feelings of romance would die a natural death, but that turned out not to be the case. It all started with visits to the streams where the local girls would always shout out warnings when they were approaching. They did that to give the boys the opportunity to dress quickly before the girls arrived. The girls could then fetch water and leave so the boys could continue their play, diving into the water naked and swimming in the shallow water. It was always fun for the boys to compare their penises to determine whose was the largest and to know who was circumcised and who was not. A particular infection they called scroaches often afflicted the students and was thought to result from the dirty stream water causing inflammation of the penis and causing a sweet itching sensation on the genitals. It was not uncommon to have the local girls arrive so suddenly that the boys were not able to get their clothes on. When this happened, they had to stay down in the water, hiding their little penises under the water until the girls departed. Obinna had a crush on one of those local girls, and Ginika even overheard him say the girl was from Owerri. For this reason, Ginika saw the girl as his sister and was always delighted to see her. Eventually, he also developed a secret crush on her, just as he'd had on girls in his Aladinma days. The only problem this time around was that he could see the girls only in the evenings during the water fetching period. Even then, it was for only a few moments. They would pass each other without speaking since there were no books to borrow or any forum for exchange of pleasantries. Thus, the love remained contentedly in Ginika's heart.

With Favour gone, Mobi became Ginika's next magi, and he treated Ginika nicely. Ginika had more privileges now as the fag of a dining hall prefect. This gave him access to unlimited amounts of bread as well as packets of milk, sugar, and Bornvita, a drink made from cocoa. He could have army food whenever he wanted in addition to the regular school food, which he now gave out as favours to his friends including Ediri and Adebayo, who were both in Erekosima House, and he did not need the food fraternity of Obinna and Kelechi anymore since he now had direct access to food as they did. Mobi was so nice to Ginika. Even though he had another fag, he preferred having Ginika stay in his prefect's allocated room while the other fag stayed in the dormitory. No one knew what was going on behind closed doors between Ginika and Mobi when they stayed in the same room, which was furnished with bunk beds. Mobi would ask Ginika to come down to the lower bunk, and they both would lie together naked. Mobi would fondle Ginika's genitals and asked Ginika to do the same. They would both have hard-ons as they lay together, talking. It was not surprising, then, when Ginika, knowing what this meant, decided he was no longer going to serve Mobi as a fag, even at the risk of losing all the goodies that came with being the fag of a dining hall prefect. Interestingly, no one suspected what had been going on, not even Lekan, Mobi's very good friend and fellow Scripture Union (SU) member. Mobi and Lekan would normally take Ginika along to the SU fellowship close to the upper-six classroom area where they would sing songs and praise God, even though they knew Ginika was a Catholic. Eventually, the crises of junior boys' abuse by senior students came to the forefront as Ezebuilo, a teacher who was touted to have passed through the same school, spilled the beans. Ezebuilo, one hot, bright afternoon, put up a notice in the teachers' common room alleging that it was a pity that the assistant school prefect was a homosexual.

The word *homosexual* was strange to Ginika; he had never heard it before. It was not until the story unfolded further that Ginika realized what it meant and what people were involved. The assistant school prefect, a revered senior boy, had four fags, and the story was that he was having sexual affairs with all four boys. He was later stripped of his position, and the fags withdrew their fagging services. Meanwhile, little attention was paid to the possibility that other seniors might be doing the same thing with their fags.

Other sexual escapades for Ginika were in the form of relationships with girls from Holy Rosary Girls' Secondary School in Umuahia where school debates were often held. There were always after-debate parties, which were the main reason for the boys joining the debating society. It was the only way they would have a chance to dance with the girls from the opposing schools. Interestingly, Ginika's school never debated with a boy's school. It was interesting how the debating society would not choose other boys' schools to debate; they chose only girls' schools, or they would insist that the debate would be held in a girls' school when other boys' schools were involved. The boys in the debating society were always known to be very conscious and careful about how they dressed, and this made sense since it meant possibility of attracting members of the opposite sex. On some occasions, the girls also came over to Government College, and it was then time for the boys to show off their powers. Those who were prefects were fond of dishing out orders to the junior students to the admiration of the visiting girls.

Ginika later discovered that the homosexual acts he had witnessed and participated in were not restricted to Government College or boys' schools alone. While exchanging banter during holidays with his Aladinma friends, he discovered a worrying trend among several other schools which, for some strange reason, was never discussed in public. Everyone except parents pretended it did not exist. Welcome to Chidinma's world of *supe*, a term girls used to describe a lesbian relationship. Chidinma, just like every other Aladinma kid, entered Government Girls Secondary school Owerri—nicknamed Ojingbo. She was an innocent little girl when she entered, expecting to make the best grades and enter university. She had been one of the brightest kids in Aladinma, constantly appearing in quiz competitions and favoured by teachers. For Chidinma, what started as a sisterly relationship, with constant attention showered on her by a so-called senior, Odinaka, later transformed into an immoral sexual relationship. She probably thought no one else knew. Also, she probably did not know that what she did was bad. Chidinma was lucky to drop the habit after Odinaka graduated and left the school. Some other kids, however, found it difficult to drop the habit after it had taken hold. For Chidinma, even discussing her experiences with Ginika and their friends was difficult as she felt ashamed when she realized the bad nature of the act and the dangers it posed to her and some other of her friends, whom she feared were into the same activities. And Chidinma was not alone in this suffering of ignorant secondary school children. Here is Nneka's story. She attended another secondary school in a remote part of the state. For Nneka, it was not supe that was her problem; rather, it was the father next door! The school, which used to be a mission school, was adopted by the government during the military takeover, and the government continued to administer the school while a church, which was supposedly the original owners, retained ownership of a building next to the school. The students attended the church because it was close to school, and they carried out functions as assigned to them by the father in charge. Nneka was so devoted to the church that she would attend both morning and evening masses to the envy of her classmates, who felt jealous that she was so close to God. But they didn't know that Nneka was rather closer to Father Linus than she was to God. Not until everyone started exposing undesirable activities that were happening in their different schools did Nneka drop the bombshell, and then all eyes turned on her as the worst of them all. They found out they were mistaken when people at Amachree Seminary School dropped their own atomic bomb. Nneka had the privilege of a normal heterosexual relationship with Father Linus; some other boys at Amachree's did not!

Neatness was one thing Umuahians never compromised on, from the daily clean uniforms for the morning assembly to the Saturday inspection and parade that demanded completely white attire. In Aladinma, Ginika had developed skills for hiding when he was wearing dirty uniforms, but at Umuahia he was expected to display more self-regulation. Also, he had the advantage of wearing brown khaki shorts as a uniform. Dirt didn't show up as much on this colour, which meant it was difficult to tell when his uniform was dirty. With the shorts, he wore a pink shirt on formal occasions and a brown check shirt for every day, which was so amenable to hiding dirt that Ginika did not have to worry much. However, there were occasions on which dirty students were called out for some strokes of the cane for disgracing their houses, and that was one of the numerous reasons that one was usually flogged every day at Umuahia. Notwithstanding the unique dirt-hiding quality of the school uniforms, some students were known to be very dirty all the time, not even taking their baths often enough. One such student was called Afor. He was a smallish boy whose parents lived in Lagos. Afor would always five-toe for one reason or another and would happily give anyone a very compelling reason for why he was five-toeing. Laziness was, however, the major reason for Afor always being dirty. He earned a bad reputation among the prefects, who would then always pick on him. Back at home, he would tell them, his mummy, elder sisters, and house help did all his washing, and he would brag among his friends. The friends would, however, rebuke him for being such a mummy's boy after so many years and even after developing *aji amu* (pubic hairs). Afor suddenly realized he could no longer be excused as a small boy. Ginika would boast he started washing his own clothes when he was in primary four and had been doing so ever since. He even helped out washing the toilets and bathtubs in the house. It turned out that the trend of hard work and early initiation into house chores was evident among the kids who were from the South East, while those from Lagos were mostly the lazy ones like Afor, though that was not necessarily the case with all the kids.

Whether a student came from Lagos or the South East was no one's business when it came to Saturday's morning inspection and parade. Inspection and parade were opportunities for assuring the cleanliness of the school houses and dormitories. Reminders about the weekly Saturday event would normally start on Wednesday and climax on the Friday night as the relevant prefects on duty drummed it into the ears of every student. While bouncing around in the dining hall, the prefects would shout, "For this Saturday's inspection and parade, it is extra compulsory as I am on duty! If you like travel to Oboro, I will be there. If you like travel to Ibeku, I will be there!" This referred to the school's neighbouring villages, which would not be hiding places for those planning to absent themselves. These announcements drove fear into the heart of everyone who planned to hide from the exercise for whatever reason. The main reason for wanting to be absent was the possibility that the school or house prefect of house that came in last might choose to punish the house mates. Punishment might include fetching water for the kitchen or cutting the grass after their canvas or other items were confiscated. It was a position everyone prayed to avoid.

For Ginika and the rest of the Kent House crew, avoiding punishment meant hard work during preparations, which started immediately after the evening meal on Friday. No schoolwork or night reading was done on Friday nights; everybody went straight to the house common room for prayers and sharing the work. Groups would be detailed to wash the seats and tables in their section of the dining hall; remove cobwebs from the dormitories; wash the bucket toilets, which were later converted to pit toilets; and sweep the dormitories. The washing of the dining tables could be tedious because of the many *pampam* (gari stains) that stuck to them in the course of the week's meals. It meant using plenty of buckets of water and detergent and scrubbing with the bristles of brooms, since there were no brushes available for the scrubbing. The Friday night work could also be an avenue for settling scores as the person in charge of assigning the work, who may not necessarily be the house prefect or his deputy, could give the hard work, such as toilet washing, to his perceived enemy. Flowers might also be cut on Friday afternoon or evening. With the main work done on Friday night, the rest of the work was reserved for the morning, especially the sweeping and the raking of the lawns. No clothing could be spread outside on the flower hedges during the inspection and parade, and once the inspection started at the ringing of a bell, everyone was expected to stand at his duty post until the inspectors came and examined the area and students. Inspectors were normally prefects and teachers and, on some occasions, the school principal. All the inspectors would be given a set of marking criteria and what to look out for including the condition of students' clothing and fingernails, neatness of bedding, cleanliness of the rooms, and so forth. After the house inspection, it would be time for the parade, and everyone would go to the field opposite the administrative block for the full parade and the singing of the school anthem. It was usually a glorious sight to behold with all the students in their immaculate white shorts and shirts and their respective prefects all standing by their various house groups. Next would be the announcement of the results followed by the joys and tears of the winners and losers, which filled the air until the next inspection and parade. On rare occasions, when the old boys came for meetings at the school, it was fun having them do the inspection themselves. It took most of them down memory as they remembered when they were young and adventurous. The inspection and parade were prone to politics as most things in Umuahia. The number of prefects from a particular house could play a substantial role in scores that the house were assigned, especially if those prefects were on duty. The prefects also had a substantial say in the overall weight of the scores and could influence the outcome, at least so Ginika and his friends thought. There was always a trophy for the wining house, which they kept until the next inspection and parade.

Government college Umuahia, despite all the school's traditions and peculiarities, did not lose focus of the main reason the students attended the institution. Reading was already part of the tradition with scheduled prep times. The curriculum followed the direction of the government. Ginika was taught subjects like music, French, introductory technology, and the Hausa language. These were termed exceptional subjects. Mr Anosike taught the music class and ensured the students developed interest in the subject. He would always wear a particular pair of trousers that Ginika found funny because he would always hold up the trousers with his right hand and then his left hand. He never wore a belt! Mr Anosike looked every inch a disciplinarian who would not take any nonsense behaviour from students in his class. If students talked about G clef and F clef, Mr Anosike would be their friend any day, which meant they could also visit him in his house. And he might give them the opportunity to pluck some mangoes or oranges from his well-endowed garden. The only problem was that his house was quite far from the main school, and students had to be desperate for fruit to go all that way. They usually went there only when the rest of the other fruit trees closer to school were depleted. Ginika would always remember Mr Anosike because he had achieved eighteen out of the possible twenty marks in the music practical test on the school piano. The test entailed playing a particular song, and Ginika, having practiced in his mind, since they did not have the luxury of practicing on the piano, did so well in the test that he never forgot the tune he played that day. Starting from a particular key his tune went thus; 133, 133, 255, 232, 133, 133 2321; 531, 531, 234, 313, 531, 531, 2321. Mr Anosike would always play the piano during special occasions at the school such as visits from the old boys and special combined church services when both Catholics and Protestants were expected to worship in the school assembly hall. It was always impressive seeing Mr Anosike nod his head as he tapped those precious keys to the delight of all the students, teachers, and old boys. Ginika secretly wished to be like him one day. Mr Anosike had the sort of carriage that earned him the respect of everyone in the school including Mr Amadi, the principal.

The "etre rich" teacher, the French teacher who bagged the nickname as a result of her first lesson, which left Ginika and his class mates giggling for the rest of the day, was so tiny that Ginika and his friends wondered how a human being could be that thin. This happened in his second year, and as if the school heard his thoughts about his second-year French teacher, in their third year, their French teacher was a very fat woman who spoke through her nose because she had just come back from the United States where she had been called an African American. She was quite kind, though, and was loved by the students.

Hausa was offered as a second Nigerian language, and even though it was not compulsory, Ginika had a go at it even though he was Igbo and knew it would be difficult for him. It was challenging, but he was determined to understand the language. He believed it could be instrumental in opening doors in the future, and it might even help him understand other people's cultures and possibly other subjects like social studies that dealt with those cultures. Moreover, with the family having lived in the north it was an opportunity for Ginika to catch up on the things he may have missed now that they no longer lived there. The learning of Hausa should have culminated in his taking the subject in his junior secondary school exam. He had forged a friendship with Musa, a Hausa boy who helped Ginika with assignments and classwork. However, Ginika knew he could not guarantee success in the subject, and he chickened out at the last minute so he could remain in his comfort zone, the Igbo language. At the height of his Hausa lessons, Ginika could write letters in Hausa as required even though it meant memorizing a large part of the letter, which he did not understand.

Fine arts was another subject Ginika enjoyed. Mr Ojo, the fine arts master, wore his hair in an afro that made him stand out in any group. He reminded Ginika of his agriculture teacher in primary school. He was a serious-minded teacher, and his glasses seemed to focus on every detail when he was at work creating one of his sculptures in the arts studio. The arts studio was located to the far east of the administrative blocks behind the upper six classes. One could feel the serenity of the location with a large mango tree in front of the studio and numerous shrubs behind the building. Mr Ojo's office was located in an inner room of the studio, and in the outer area were all sorts of materials used in developing different kinds of artwork. Mr Ojo usually worked with a chisel and a hammer on large tree trunks. No one would be able to tell what sculptural form Mr Ojo was making until he had spent several days slowly chipping at the wood. He would start each project by positioning a large trunk of wood on a slab. The faces would always appear first after a couple of days' work to the delight of Ginika and his friends, who would then start speculating on what the action of the body would be. Mr Ojo would normally keep the main action of the sculpture to himself and allow the speculation to go on. He would become excited at the giggling from the kids in forms two and three who had come to do their practicals. Over time, Mr Ojo's sculpture would become more predictable; it would be, for example, the body of an adult sitting down and thinking with his arms to his cheek, or it would be a woman carrying her daughter on her back or carrying a pot on her way to the stream. It was not long before Ginika and his friends discovered that Mr Ojo actually drew pictures of his sculptures before he created them even before he began chipping away the wood. This seemed to explain the magic to the boys.

The fine arts classes were held in the normal classrooms, and the practicals were held in the studio mainly on Fridays. Sculpture, painting, and drawing were the main subjects. Mr Ojo would always tell the students, "You need to use your imagination." He repeated that thought almost in every class. So, soon the students gave him the nickname "Mr Imagination". Ginika took to drawing and would draw all sorts of things including his family and cartoons of anyone he fancied such as his first French teacher, whom he would draw with her tiny waist. He would draw a broomstick next to her to enhance the point of her thinness. Drawing was fun, but it also brought troubled times for Ginika because some of his enemies would sometimes report his cartoons to Mr Ojo, who would scold him while admiring the excellent examples of art. Ginika would always stand his ground, though, insisting he had done nothing wrong but had simply used his imagination as instructed by Mr Ojo. Onumkpu, another student in the same class, was also very good at drawing and liked drawing trees, animals, and anything that depicted the environment in a good light. To Onumkpu, the environment was everything, and he admired it so much while using his imagination to paint pictures of what the ideal environment should be like, with animals and humans co-habiting peacefully without any interference from either party or encroachment on each other's territories. Lions featured most frequently in his art, and he occasionally drew pictures of Sampson tearing the mouth of a lion as described in the Bible. With Ginika's cartoons and depiction of women and their different shapes and sizes, the question from his classmates was, "Why does Onumkpu imagine the environment while Ginika imagines women?" The friends attributed Ginika's behaviour to the fact that he loved girls so he was using his imagination to develop one in a school where there were none! For some other students in the class, drawing guns and cowboys was the norm; they wanted to depict the heroes they had seen in favourite films they had watched at home or in school.

Ginika never knew that some people had televisions at school. They were mainly kept in the rooms of the house prefects. He discovered this only after he met Agina, the house prefect for Fisher House, who was in his upper-six class preparatory to taking his advanced certificate exams while Ginika was in year two. It was after one evening meal that Ginika heard someone call him as he was leaving the dining hall and hurrying back to the house to drop his plates and head straight to the common room for night prayers. He needed to hurry in order to avoid giving anybody excuses to flog him for tardiness. Agina called out, and Ginika turned and looked at him uninterestedly until Agina introduced himself as Ginika's relative. He said he had heard there was a son of Ogadimma's at Government College, and he had made it a point to find out who he was, and that had taken him quite some time. Not until he told Ginika that he was the house prefect for Fisher House did Ginika relax during the discussion with the realization that Agina could easily protect him from any strokes of the cane he might be entitled to for arriving late for the night prayers. And true to that prediction, Agina came in handy for Ginika, shielding him from further aggressors in the school. This was even more protection than he could have received from his numerous magis because the word easily spread around school that Agina was Ginika's elder brother from the village. Thus no one dared mess with Ginika as they would have to deal with a response from several quarters including the Kent House master who took Ginika as his own son.

Ginika would go to Mr Obi's house anytime and feel relaxed and have meals to the surprise and jealousy of other Kent housemates to the extent that they would attribute to Ginika any leaking of house information that they would rather not have Mr Obi know about. Unfortunately for Ginika, though he did not tell Mr Obi anything, as the man had his own sources and means of keeping his ear to the ground, the housemates had no other clue as to the source of the leak and thus held Ginika responsible.

Even with the protection from prefects and the housemaster, Ginika had a bad experience one night. He could not believe his eyes. It was a Thursday night; school was to close the next day, Friday. Ginika had a complete set of provisions he had saved so he could take it back home with him the next day. His miserly attitude was at its height. His provisions included a packet of sugar, a tin of powdered Nido milk, a tin of Bornvita beverage, and a packet each of Nasco Cornflakes and Cabin Biscuits. Ginika was excited that night until one "old boy" (an alumnus of the college) entered the dormitory and asked everyone to open their lockers. Since old boys were highly respected and obeyed, Ginika obliged, and he was asked to open up the provisions so that the old boy could take some. This was difficult for Ginika though he had no option but to oblige the old boy who had come on his own authority and not on the authority of any old boy association. Thus, the so-called old boy was actually an impostor, and he had connived with some other senior students to deprive younger ones of their property. However, one student from Niger House who had fallen victim to these tricks would have none of that and quickly made a report to the police at their station just behind the school assembly hall. Ginika was later called as an additional witness to the crime and was at the police station until about midnight where the police drilled the so-called old boy into a confession and a promise to replace all the items he had collected from the students.

CHAPTER 6

Federal Housing

Ogadimma moved with his family from Aladinma where he had settled on arrival to Owerri from Onitsha to a new federal government housing estate development meant to cater for low-income, mid-level civil servants in the early eighties. The new estate boasted good tarred roads, a mission primary school, and some green areas. At the time the Ogadimmas moved in, most of the houses in the estate had no fences, and there was no need for them as there was little or no crime in the community. The federal housing was about one or two kilometres from Aladinma, and this meant that Ginika and his brothers had to be transported to school every day. Federal housing also meant new friends and playmates.

The Ogadimmas settled in a large gated estate called Nkpaji Estate within the federal housing estate. Nkpaji Estate had been built by Ogadimma, by then a well-known prudent and diligent civil engineer. He built the Estate with funds that were excesses from construction projects. Those were times when people could rely on civil servants to do the right things to the benefit of the country. Nkpaji Estate was one of the numerous estates Ogadimma built over the course of his career as a senior engineer with the Ministry of Works. These projects benefitted so many senior and junior staff members alike. Nkpaji Estate had a lawn tennis court and a standby generator, which lay idle most of the time because NEPA, the electricity power company, was at its best at the time. The generator would, in future, become the main source of power when NEPA collapsed due to decay in the system. The houses were later sold on an owner-occupier basis by the federal government and would later become a source of litigation between some senior and junior staff members. The senior staff members claimed that the junior quarters were part of their entitlement. This bewildered the junior staff members, and eventually Ogadimma became involved in the conflict to safeguard the entitlement of the junior staff members who were involved.

With the move to federal housing, the first routine change was the driving of kids to school, which Zigizi, the driver, handled with alternate arrangements when necessary. For Ogadimma, life as a civil servant working in Owerri was fulfilling. A typical daily routine started with breakfast in the morning before going to work. He would return home in the afternoon for lunch with no traffic congestion to delay his travel. For Ginika and his siblings, after school meant play, lessons in the evening, and play again. With no concrete barriers or fences demarcating the house lots, Ginika and all his friends had the freedom to roam around not just Nkpaji Estate but the wider federal housing estate from one friend's house to the other.

With lots of time to play, Ginika found it hard to concentrate on his schoolwork. This resulted in neglect of assignments until he was reminded at home by aunties or flogged in school for neglect of his homework. Lessons were a part of the preparation for taking the common entrance examination that qualified students for entrance into secondary school.

Ginika and his friends attended lesson at Teacher Anthony's place at Shell Camp quarters close to the government house. This was about three kilometres from home, and Ginika and his friends who were also children of civil servants would trek to the lesson location every day and trek back after the classes. Teacher Anthony was a well-respected and intelligent teacher, known all over the city for his diligence in helping prepare kids for their common entrance examination. Rumour had it then that Teacher Anthony's brand-new white Volkswagen Beetle car was bought for him by a parent who was highly impressed by his kid's performance after attending Teacher Anthony's preparatory classes. It was not surprising to see so many kids in attendance at Teacher Anthony's evening classes. There were not even enough seats for all who attended. Some had to stay outside while others would go outside and play football as a result of the frustration of not finding a seat. Those not playing football would wander around the numerous vocational activities that went on around the Shell Camp Primary School which was situated within the premises of Alvan Ikoku College of Education. The most interesting place were the music rooms, which were close to the classroom used by Teacher Anthony. The beautiful tunes that originated from those rooms were enough to attract any inquisitive mind, and Ginika would sometimes find himself admiring the wonders of these majestic instruments that sent out such beautiful tunes that made him feel good. He would later have the opportunity to actually lay his hands on one such instrument when he went to secondary school at Umuahia under the masterly hands of Mr Anosike. For some reason, it looked like the music room in Alvan endeared Ginika's heart to music at Government College Umuahia and also influenced his fondness for Mr Anosike, the music teacher.

One interesting thing about Teacher Anthony's teaching method was that he began with first principles. He made sure that the students understood the basics of the subject and could therefore think for themselves when the questions were twisted in any form. He also gave lots of assignments to ensure the students properly understood the context. He was the toast of all kids from different parts of the city when they marched at any event to commemorate Independence Day at the state stadium. The governor would normally watch the school children marching by on these occasions. Shell Camp Primary School always came in at the top during marching parades because of the extensive training that could only come from the strong hands of Teacher Anthony. He was a tall, slim man with a large voice that seemed to be specially made that way because God knew he would have the large responsibility of teaching very large classes in an era where the use of microphones was not in vogue. Ginika would not see such crowds as there were in Teacher Anthony's classes again until his university days. Teacher Anthony was so good at the preparation for common entrance examination that he would administer mock exams to his students aimed at getting them ready for the actual exams. The mock exams were meant to prepare them not only for understanding the subject matter but also to test their exam-writing skills since he understood that, in most cases, understanding the subject matter would account only for 70 per cent of the kids' performance in the examination. He understood that it was important for the kids to train on the amount of time they should spend answering any given question. They needed to be able to make quick assessments and judgments on the difficulty of a question and make a call on when to leave any stubborn question and move on to the next one. Another important exam-taking technique shared by Teacher Anthony was to quickly scan the questions and understand where the bulk of the marks lay so that more energy could be expended on those questions. These were the things that made Teacher Anthony's lessons outstanding. Everyone in Owerri knew he had achieved the results to prove his abilities as most of his students ended up attending the federal government colleges or most of the best schools available. He was known for demanding discipline during his classes. The large crowd and no loudspeakers meant the class needed to be quiet in order for everyone to hear what he was saying. And if, at any point in time, he found any kid talking while he was talking, it was typical of him to ask the kid, "What was my last word?" And God have mercy on a child who had not been listening and hence could not reveal Teacher Anthony's last word. This became somewhat of joke among the kids, and they used to mimic Teacher Anthony or call attention to anyone disturbing a lesson or something that had to be focused on.

For Ginika, Teacher Anthony's lessons were fun as they allowed him and his friends to make the long walk to Shell Camp from federal housing with all the play on the way, which resulted in their late arrival most of the time, which meant they had to stand at the window or go off to play. For this reason, and to his embarrassment, the mock examination began without Ginika knowing about it. This was doubly bad because his father had made payment for the mock examination that Ginika did not make. He couldn't have known about the payment because he was always out playing with friends. Playing the smart kid, Ginika, when he realized what was happening, tore a piece of paper and wrote a set of questions he planned to show his mum at home as an illustration of what they had done at the lesson that day. Unfortunately for Ginika and his group, they did not realize they returned home too early from class, and this raised suspicion at home causing further questions to be asked. Ginika thought he was ahead of the game and brought out his so-called lesson notes and assignments to show anyone who might be in doubt about the genuineness of their lesson attendance for the day. Unbeknownst to him, his mother was ready to go to great lengths to find out what caused their earlier-than-usual arrival that day. She suddenly asked Dume, his friend, to bring his own notes so she could compare them to Ginika's. Shocked and jittery, Ginika immediately realized they had been busted. He started crying and agreed to confess. In a matter of minutes, Ginika and company were bundled into the car and driven straight to Shell Camp where their mock exams had been paid for, and they were sent into the class for the exams. That marked the end of playing football or wandering during lessons for Ginika as he could not afford such an embarrassment again.

CHAPTER 7
University Days Are Here

"Have you finished? Have you finished?" Stanley kept asking Dume and Ginika as he raised his paper in pride for being the first to finish the multiple-choice practice Joint Admissions and Matriculations Board (JAMB) test question papers they were working on. Entry into university was based on a nationwide test for all secondary schools. There was also the prerequisite of five credits in the General Certificate of Exams (GCE) or the Senior Secondary School Certificate (SSCE). To study certain science subjects at university, such as engineering or medicine, students were expected to have credits in mathematics and English as part of their five credits. As part of preparations for the JAMB test, parents of secondary school students paid for their children to attended all sorts of extra classes both in their schools and during holidays.

It was during such a holiday that Ginika and his friends battled in a mock test as Uju, Ginika's younger sister, watched. Uju was not impressed with the performance of Ginika, since he was not among the first to finish. But she wouldn't say anything while his friends were there in order not to embarrass the poor boy. As soon as the friends were gone, she started laughing at Ginika, who would normally boast to her about how good he was at school and how everyone looked up to him. It was no sweat for Ginika as their Mickey Mouse exam was over that evening, but that performance did not deter him as he insisted that it was only a mock exam and did not define who he was and did not lower his confidence level for the forthcoming examinations. This was, however, only to clear the doubts in Uju's mind because Ginika was indeed worried at his performance in relation to that of his friends who seemed to have gone ahead of him in the preparations, perhaps because of the pace and strategy of their different schools. But that argument did not hold water because they had all attended the same lessons presented by Teacher Anthony while in primary school and had learned the same exam-taking skills. They were expected to have developed further in their different secondary schools, and none of them had reason to slack in the trial runs for their JAMB tests. To improve his performance, Ginika acquired more past-question papers in addition to what he already had and doubled his efforts at solving the questions. To him the questions were pretty easy, but he realized that passing the JAMB test was not about knowing the solutions but being able to provide those solutions in a reasonable time. Therefore, his further mock exams concentrated on timing himself to finish in good time and marking the scripts to see how many correct answers he had achieved. He recalled Teacher Anthony's techniques all the way back to his primary school days. He found that his performance improved with every consecutive self-test, and this improved his confidence level. At one point, he drafted Uju to become his official time keeper in a bid to simulate the real exam experience, and he used a totally different past-question paper he had not worked on before to provide himself the flavour of surprise. Part of the improvement in strategy required knowing the right time to allocate to each question and knowing when to move on if he had no clue to the solution of any particular question.

The preparations for the JAMB test followed the same mock exams in school along with paid extra class with Mr D. No one in Government College then actually knew the full meaning of the "D" in Mr D's name. They speculated it meant "Duru", but not much further thought was given to it, and the students were not bothered much to ask the teacher himself since they were comfortable calling him Mr D. He was a very large and tall, dark man, always smiling and ready to chat with any student at whatever level. He was touted to come from Owerri and had an accent similar to that of those who came from the area. That was the same area the staff people who mispronounced Ogadimma's name came from. Mr D was also touted to be an old boy of Government College Umuahia, and this relationship fuelled his commitment to ensuring the students did very well in their external exams. Some others thought that he was, in fact, an old boy of Government College Owerri and not Umuahia. It was interesting to see him walk to class with his briefcase, which he carried all the time, and his well-ironed trousers and clean shoes. Mr D had read engineering at university, and that explained the flare he had for mathematics, physics, and technical drawing. These were the main subjects he delivered to his students. He always boasted how excellent all his past students performed both in the secondary school certificate examinations and the JAMB test. He actually had the facts and figures to show anyone who doubted him. Chidi Ofoegbu was in Unilag, a short name for the University of Lagos in the South West of Nigeria. Ken Nnamani was in Unijos, and Nkenaso was in Uniben— "my alma mater" he would boast. Or was it Nnanna, Kelvin, Clarence, Odu, and the rest of the kids in Federal University of Technology Owerri (FUTO)? The list was endless.

Ginika and his friends each paid forty naira to attend Mr D's extra classes, an amount equivalent to about ten dollars in 1990. The amount was termed expensive, but nothing compared to the fear of not making the JAMB test at the first sitting. Older students who had taken Mr D's classes testified that they had passed on their first attempts. At the senior class level, school ended at about two in the afternoon, and Mr D's classes started exactly at four with a revision of the previous day's work or any assignments. Understanding the concepts for Mr D meant starting from the first principles and building up one step at a time. He would make sure every student in the class followed the steps. This was the same strategy Teacher

Anthony had used in the primary school for Ginika and his mates. A favourite approach was to use acronyms to help students memorize concepts in any subject. For example, in mathematics, SOH-CAH-TOA represented the sign of angles; CAH referred to the fact that the cosine of any angle is the length of the side adjacent to that angle divided by the hypotenuse of the triangle. Mr D was so dedicated that, if it was possible, he was ready to teach each student in his own mother tongue to make sure he understood.

Thus it was no surprise at all that, when the results of both the SSCE and JAMB tests were published, Mr D's students again made him proud and added to the list of candidates he could use for future boasting and wooing of prospective candidates for his extra lessons. Ginika did not miss out in the party; he passed all his papers just as his friends had back at Owerri, Dume and Stanley.

It was a proud Ginika who came home to the embraces of Ogadimma and Ngozi who, by the way, expected nothing less having given Ginika the required support in terms of encouragement while at home and the necessary fees for the extra classes while he was at college. Ogadimma knew the importance of Ginika passing his exams at the first sitting and was willing to support his son in any way possible including providing the money for the extra classes while he was in school, which some other parents were not willing or able to do. To such parents, it was morally wrong for the schools to accommodate such extra classes and a testimony to the acceptance of school authorities that they were doing a bad job at teaching the students during their normal class hours. Some parents even insinuated in some cases that teachers deliberately under-taught the students in order to create the need for supplementary lessons for which they could earn money in addition to their normal salary. The genuineness of such claims was not lost on Ogadimma, but he was willing to give the school the benefit of the doubt so long as the extra classes delivered what he wanted—a seamless admission into university. He did not want a repeat of the crying and wailing that accompanied Ginika's failure to secure admission into the Federal Government

College Okigwe. Ginika's aunties Fidelia, Ego, and Rita, who had been at hand to help cuddle the poor crying kid, were all married and living in their own homes. It was difficult thinking about who would play that role if Ginika once again failed admission. In addition to that was the suspicion and heavy speculation that people were fond of "fixing" their JAMB scores. This fixing had become a new addition to the JAMB lexicon and was used to describe a situation in which parents or relevant parties arranged for a student's JAMB scores to be manipulated right at the headquarters of the JAMB office at Ikoyi in Lagos. The word on the street was that the perpetrators of the deal were always in connivance with the computer room personnel who manipulated the results in the system. Though no one owned up to having influenced his or her JAMB scores, it was obvious that something was happening given the outrageous scores reported to have been made by students whose less-than-sterling academic performance records were in the public domain. Jealousy was also not ruled out as class rivals peddled rumours of their rivals being involved in the scheme simply because they scored higher than they did in the examination.

Thus, it was a delighted Ogadimma who spontaneously threw a congratulatory success party for Ginika and his friends, something he had never done before. Normally, achieving passing grades at school, to Ogadimma, was a duty any kid owed his parents for providing the fees. He did not see the reason for any special celebration at the end of school terms or when kids did exceptionally well, such as taking the first position in their class. This was in sharp contrast to the parents of some of Ginika's friends, who would always promise them one thing or another to encourage them to work for good positions in their class. A typical gift would be a bicycle, a trip to a fun spot in town, or some fancy toy. Though Ginika and his siblings had all those things, they had not received them as rewards for schoolwork; rather, the items had come naturally because kids are entitled to have toys or to go to fun places in order to remain children.

The party took place right there at the Nkpaji Estate residence of

Ogadimma. All of Ginika's friends attended who had just qualified to enter university. Also in attendance were his friends from Government College Umuahia who lived in Owerri, such as Obinna and Kelechi. And to prove that the boy had come of age, they were asked to invite some girls who were their peers in the neighbourhood. This was unprecedented and meant that Ogadimma realized that Ginika had come of age because he was going into a life with no direct supervision! Prior to that, Ogadimma never dared to see any of his sons with any girl he did not know. This knowledge included knowing the girls' parents and the nature of the relationships. It all had to be spelled out, and he would tolerate no games hidden from the eyes of the public. The kids were not, for example, allowed to go into rooms alone; rather, they were expected to stay in the sitting room for all their discussions, which mostly should centre on holiday schoolwork. Ngozi was even worse! A girl dared not come to her house to ask about any of her sons. On one occasion, Olachi, Emeka's girlfriend, came to look for him while he was away. Unfortunately, Chinedu was playing a new song released by Bobby Brown so loud in their room that he did not hear the bell ring, and by the time he heard, it was already too late as their mum had reached the door already to see who the visitor was. Chinedu had no choice but to stay by their room door and listen to the conversation between their mum and Olachi.

Olachi, expecting to see any of the boys come out from the sitting room door, was shocked to see their mum and could only mumble the words *"Ana m acho Emeka"* (I am looking for Emeka). When Ngozi asked her *"Onye ka ina acho?"* (Who are you looking for?), Olachi wished the ground would open at that moment so she could disappear, as Emeka's mum took a second guess at her and wondered why the little girl should be running after her son instead of staying in her own father's house. After some long seconds, she asked her *"Ina achoro ya gini, nwoke na nwanyi ana akwu?"* (Why are you looking for him? Do boys and girls hang out together?) It was a shamed Olachi who told Emeka's mum, as a cover-up, that she had come to borrow a novel from Emeka. While this was going on, Chinedu was by the door listening and enjoying fun and laughter knowing their mum and how embarrassed she could make their male visitors not to talk of females. He was also not just listening for the sake of fun but to also be ready to collaborate any story or lies that Olachi would tell to make it look real to their mum knowing that she would call on him to take over the conversion with Olachi once she satisfied herself on the reason for the visit. Once their mum was out of the way, it was an excited Chinedu who hailed Olachi for being smart enough to quickly think of how to divert their mum's attention.

After the JAMB scores had been released and after the house party thrown by Ogadimma, there came the waiting for the university admission letters. Several weeks after many of Ginika's peers received their university admission letters, Ogadimma became worried and quickly drafted his assistant in the office to go to the university to find out what might be the problem as Ginika's several visits had not yielded any tangible results. The admission process in Nigerian universities then began when students received notification of their JAMB results. Then there would be a letter from the candidate's first choice of university if he met their subject cut-off mark for merit or non-merit depending on the available spaces. In cases where a large number of students applied for a specific course, students were declined because of lack of space. Then the students could apply for admission to his or her second choice school. A student could request the same course or any with a lower qualifying JAMB score. There was also the issue of the national quota system or catchment area system, which was designed to ensure that students from educationally disadvantaged states in the federation also got a chance to be admitted to study their choice of course.

Ginika had chosen the University of Port Harcourt as his first choice and engineering as course of study. Engineering then was very competitive; every student classified as intelligent aimed to get into university to read engineering, medicine, or law for those inclined in the arts. Ogadimma, as an engineer, also wanted to see his son read engineering, so the pressure was on to get into the preferred course and university without a problem. Luckily, Ginika's JAMB score of 229 was above the merit score of 218 for his chosen engineering field, and this gave his dad a comfortable feeling. However, this was no watertight case, as in Nigeria then, anything was possible. There were known cases of people paying a lot of money to buy admission spaces for their children or wards even if the students had not attained the minimum required scores on their JAMB tests. Such actions meant that some qualified students were denied admission to make way for the "money miss road" candidates. Money miss road refers to money bags in a society that wasted money because they obviously made the money from fraudulent activities.

The concern and pressure to have Ginika's admission sorted out even with his good JAMB score increased when Ogbonna, Ginika's friend, received his admission letter. Ogbonna had been in the drama group with Ginika in primary school. He had featured as Richard in *Aku*, the play that was Ginika's best script. Ogbonna received admission to read medicine, which was one of the most prestigious courses at the University of Nigeria Nsuka. From their days in primary school, Ogbonna had told anyone who cared to know that he was going to be a doctor. The only problem with Ogbonna's desire to be a doctor was that he hated drugs and would cry each time he was ill because he knew he would have to take some medicine. His parents knew his hatred for drugs had no boundaries; he would do anything to avoid taking drugs. Asking him to take medicine while no adults were present was not an option because he was known to have thrown the drugs away while claiming he had taken them. When reminded that he would not make a good doctor since he could not be trusted to practice what he would preach as a doctor, his answer was always that theory and practice are never the same. Ogbonna saw his reading medicine at the university in Nigeria as the first steppingstone to his dream of practicing medicine in the United States of America. He had heard that doctors were paid big money in the US, and he wanted to get part of that money. In fact, that was said to be one of the boasting lines Ogbonna had used on one of the girls in the drama group. Unlike

Johnbosco, their friend, who was a known smooth talker, Ogbonna was quiet and reserved. He looked intelligent, but no one knew how some of the girls fell in love with him until it was revealed that he had told them fictious stories about how he was going to study medicine in university, go to America, and grow dollars on trees—enough dollars to buy the girls cars and big houses for their parents.

The increased pressure with the trickling in of admission letters to Ginika's peers brought Uncle Chuky into the picture. Uncle Chuky was a jolly good fellow, well loved by his peers and fellow young engineers in the Ministry of Works where Ogadimma held sway. He was the person Ogadimma drafted to find out what was wrong with Ginika's admission letter from the university. Chuky came from the same local government area as Ogadimma and had related with the family as if he was a close relative, and all Ogadimma's household treated him as such. So it was not a surprise that he was drafted into this task that would see him giving it his best if only to please his boss. In Nigeria, then, it was not abnormal to see bosses sending younger colleagues on errands outside official business. Such errands could even be seen as better assignments in terms of performance rating than the actual official responsibilities since those performance ratings were usually subjective and depended on the boss. So to Chuky, it was time to impress Ogadimma, and he had better get it right.

Ginika got ready the morning he was supposed to go to Port Harcourt with Chuky, but he quickly took ill, initially complaining of headache and then stomach ache as well. He finally had to be rushed straight to the hospital, and the trip to the university was aborted until he recovered. Apparently, a case of food poisoning had taken its toll on young Ginika after he attended a JAMB success party similar to the one Ogadimma had thrown for him. He was reported to have dealt well with the assorted foods on display at the party and boasted to friends who had not attended the party how the guests had been served with *orishirishi*, meaning all kinds of food. Ginika was said to have had an appetite for everything on the table, and he had been adventurous with the different foods on the menu to the delight and sometimes surprise of his friends who were picky about their choices, having been brought up with the basic Nigerian food such as rice and garri. This party was held at the house of one of Ginika's friends whose parents had relocated from abroad and were known to live like *oyibos* (expatriates) with cooks and all sorts of domestic servants wearing uniforms while working in the home and being at the beck and call of the lady of the house. These were the few privileged top-of-the-range kids who were known as *ajebutter*, a term used to describe them and the fact that they had everything going on for them beause of wealthy parents. There were others also referred to as *ajebutter*, but the term sure had ranges, or as they would say then "there is ajebutter, and there is ajebutter", a saying that highlighted the subtle differences. There were then some other kids with a small amount of family privilege who were referred to as *ajekpako* meaning that they did not qualify as ajebutter but were simply pretending to be among the privileged class.

Four days after the initial planned trip to Port Harcourt, Ginika was well enough to make the trip, and so he departed with Uncle Chuky early in the morning immediately after breakfast. They travelled in Ogadimma's official car with his driver. The trip from Owerri to Port Harcourt took about an hour and a half, and it took another twenty minutes from Port Harcourt to the university town of Choba via Rumuokwuta due to the bad nature of the East-West Road at the time. On arrival to the school, uncle Chuky went directly to the engineering department where Ginika had been going frequenting, without success, over the past few weeks. He engaged the averagely built young man they met at the department, explained the circumstances of their visit, and pleaded for any help he could provide to make sure his younger brother, as he referred to Ginika, got his admission letter. The young officer at the department then referred them to the admissions officer, who was at another of the university sites called Delta Park. When they arrived at the admissions office, it was a troubled Uncle Chuky who slowly turned and asked Ginika "What is happening here?" as if both of them had not just arrived on the scene at the same time. The commotion was disturbing as the crowd in the office kept shoving, pushing, and shouting at every available person attending them. The desperation and frustration was so evident that Uncle Chuky immediately understood why poor Ginika had not made any headway when he had come down to Port Harcourt alone. Some other people who were probably tired of the pushing game were hanging around and discussing the situation with friends or sitting down on the green grass lawns around the area. Uncle Chuky imagined that poor Ginika had been one of those hanging around on his previous visits.

Uncle Chuky knew he had to devise a strategy to make sense of the chaos, but first he needed to get through the madness at the door and into the admission office before he could even talk to any of the officers. The queue into the office was too long. The small spaces by the door were filled with other people who would rather jump the queue and test how far they could go in an attempt to get a chance to enter the office. They were booed by the orderly ones in the queue and threatened by the respective school security officers who were not armed and could not do much to deter them. The queue was largely made up of students, and because Uncle Chuky was well dressed and respectful looking, one of the university security officer noticed him as he approached the side door leading to the admission office. The security officer immediately approached him, bowing down while smiling and greeting him. He asked, "Oga, good afternoon, sir. What can we do for you sir?"

Uncle Chuky, who had experience working in the ministry, was aware of the meaning of the greeting and the man's body language and was ready to play the game. He quickly told the security officer he wanted to see the admission officer. The officer told him the students were the people seeing the officer at that time, and they were in the queue as Uncle Chuky could see, but he promised to let the admission officer know about Uncle Chuky as soon as he took a breather. He would inform the admission officer that there was someone other than a student waiting for him. Uncle Chuky thanked him and quickly thrust a five-naira note into the security officer's hand. The man bowed lower than he had initially as the students in the queue shouted, "*Anya huru deal nwere share, oh!*" This meant that they wanted a share in the money Uncle Chuky had handed over. The security guy shouted back, "No shaking!"

Not very long after the exchange, the security man shouted, "Oga, Oga go see you now." Uncle Chuky said thanks as he meandered his way through the small opening by the door and walked into the admission officer's office. The officer was a lanky, tall man. He smiled at Uncle Chuky immediately and apologized for the chaos around the office. They quickly addressed the reason for the visit. The admission officer advised Ginika to write an application to his office requesting his admission letter. He should explain that he had scored more than the required merit score for his choice of study at the university. It was an excited Uncle Chuky who smiled immediately and thanked the officer for the assistance while offering him lunch that afternoon, to which the officer agreed.

At lunch, the admission officer and Uncle Chuky talked over the whole admission process, the lapses and subsequent hassles the poor students endured in getting what was due them. Part of the problem turned out to be that most of the processing was still manual, and there were piles of paperwork that had to be sorted out for each case. No wonder the school and admission office would rather first focus on the students who found time to come down to the school. The plan was then to shift attention to the other people who were not on site when the queue went down. This was the cause of the long wait that Ogadimma and Ginika had become so worried about. Some other schools that were ahead in terms of computerization of their systems were better off and did not have the problem that Ginika's chosen school had. That was the case of the Univeristy of Nigeria Nsuka, which had wasted no time in issuing an admission letter to Ogbonna. With gratitude for the lunch provided, the admission officer took over the writing of the application on behalf of Ginika since he thought he was in a better position to word the letter to the standard template other people had used. Uncle Chuky was grateful for this as it saved him time that would have been dedicated to correction if Ginika had written the application himself. Haven written the application right there at the lunch table, the party then went back together to the admissions officer's desk where he acknowledged the receipt of his own hand-written letter and asked Uncle Chuky to send Ginika back to the school the following week to pick up the admission letter. As promised, the letter was ready when Ginika went the following week. After he picked up the admission letter, he headed home and showed his father. Uncle Chuky was proud to have delivered when duty called.

CHAPTER 8

Jambito

Setting off that early morning from Arugo Park at Owerri for the one-and-a-half-hour trip to Port Harcourt to start his university education, Ginika was excited as he listened carefully as his elder brother Emeka advised him on some strategies that could help him survive the university environment. "You have to be careful about the friends you keep," he said. "And most especially, you have to study hard in the early part of your stay in the university." He pointed out that, in most cases, year-one university students were so excited about the new freedom that came with being on their own in the university campus that they ended up being influenced by bad students and neglected their studies, the primary purpose of their being in school. The worst-case scenarios were some intelligent students who ended up playing in their early years, a circumstance Ginika later understood was termed "jonsing" in the school. By the time they realized what was happening, they had already obtained low grade-point averages (GPA) and their quest to improve led to futility and they ended up having university grades that did not meet with their actual potential. This point continued to ring a bell in Ginika's brain all through his stay at university as he indeed saw his friends struggle through the issue. While some of the friends who had the issue were really "jonsers", some others did not do well because of circumstances beyond their control such as starting school late due to admission process delays or due to ill health.

On arrival at school, Ginika followed other "Jambitos", as the new students were known, through the rigorous registration process after paying the school and accommodation fees that amounted to a total of 110 naira, about $30 at the 1990 exchange rate. The accommodation fee was 90 naira out of that sum. It was interesting that the new system Ginika found himself in did not provide any direction like Ginika was used to in secondary school. However, as diehard as he was, his survival instinct kicked in again as he devised a means to follow through in this new, unrestricted world. A smart strategy was to make sure he identified a group of other students he met during the registration process and follow them closely in all that they did including locating their lecture rooms and departmental office and obtaining the relevant lecture timetables. They heard gossip from the year-two students they met. They learned which lecturers to watch out for; for example, those who were termed wicked or mean to students. They also learned which lecturers were fatherly and could be approached when they had any problems.

Ginika's first bad experience in this new environment was realizing that five people would be sharing the little room to which he had been assigned. He hadn't heard of how students were cramped into hostels at Nigerian universities. He was relieved when he heard they were only five allocated to the room at the "barracks" hostel. He found the name funny and wondered why it was nicknamed such. He thought it was probably because it was a little off location from the rest of the hostels and had lots of bush around it.

He learned another survival challenge in the school—again it referred to accommodation. He soon discovered that the actual number of people who would be using his room would, in fact, be double the number he initially thought. Due to the limited living space available in the university-owned hostels, the policy had been to allocate school accommodation to only the first- and final-year students. The rest of the students were expected to fend for themselves. These other students rented rooms outside the university premises or, in some cases, bought university-allocated beds from the rightful owners or shared beds with the rightful owners. Because of their proximity to lecture rooms, the accommodations on school premises had a better guarantee of electricity than areas in the neighbouring villages where the students without school accommodations were expected to rent rooms. The demand for the university accommodations became so high that the black market prices (since it was considered illegal to sell one's accommodation) became so high that the children of civil servants such as Ginika and other poor children found it very expensive after their first year to find school-owned hostel accommodations. To this end, the deal for the Jambitos was to share their accommodation with someone studying medicine who was in his or her second year. There was an agreement: when medical student reached third year, they were entitled to accommodation like final-year students. The medical students then shared their accommodations with the Jambitos. Alternatively, they shared with someone in a year prior to the final year depending on the course of study of the person at the university since the number of years differed for science and engineering courses (four years for sciences and five for engineering courses).

Ginika shared with a medical student who was in year two. Unfortunately for him, he was allocated to a double bunk behind the door with another Jambito. The other senior students were allocated the other three corners of their small room. The corners were each delineated by canvas dividers that could be closed with a zipper. With the dividers in place, when students entered the room, they could not see what was going on in another student's corner. With the allocation of Ginika and a second Jambito to a double bunk behind the door and the fact that both Ginika and the other Jambito offered to also share with students in other years for future accommodation guarantees, the space the four of them shared was then so small and uncomfortable they could not all sleep at the same time! The double bunk was a six-spring bed that could take only one person on the bottom bunk and another on the top bunk. The remaining floor space by the side of the bed was covered by a rug and was the sleeping space for the third person. That left the fourth person to continue reading into the night until he could switch positions with one of the other three students. It was rough for the four students, but that arrangement was the only way they could survive the difficult circumstances. In some way, it benefitted them academically since it meant they read more than some other students who had the luxury of sleeping all through the night.

The tight nature of their accommodations also meant that they could not entertain many female visitors in their corner space due to the embarrassment it could cause. That also helped them to concentrate on their studies. Only genuine girls who were willing to share knowledge and would not mind or laugh at the circumstance of their friends visited.

The extent and implication of liberty granted by the university environment dawned on Ginika one hot afternoon when he came into his hostel room to have a nap before dashing out for the afternoon lectures. He heard some strange murmuring and groaning as if someone was crying softly in the corner. Ginika did not think he was hearing correctly, so he put his ears close to the dark curtain. Before he knew it, the bed started rocking harder with increased groaning, hissing, and sounds that suggested some kissing was going on. Then he started hearing low-pitched voices and actual words: "Love me, baby. Love me, baby. I love you more than anything, baby. Oh, f**k me, love me." Ginika listened to the cries and the expressions of deep love between the lovebirds, and he was surprised when his penis hardened as he thought of the pleasure they were experiencing. He giggled at the sudden stop in motion from behind the curtain as the couple realized they had company.

To the surprise of Ginika, he now understood the efforts made by the older students to keep their corners neat and ensure a closed space where they could have sex undisturbed. This was also why students had to be driven out of the bathrooms when the girlfriends of the older students needed to take a bath after some of these escapades or even in the mornings. Young Ginika continued to wonder how boys could bring in girls to sleep over in their hostels and even wondered about the type of girls who accepted such offers. He felt they were the real Jonsers and felt sorry for them as they jeopardized their stay and studies. He did not believe that, one day, he too might be involved in such activities.

When Ginika thought about real Jonsers, his mind would always go to Piper, a handsome, hairy dude who always charmed the girls. Piper paraded with the choicest girls in school and would always leave the hostel as others left in the morning only to return a couple of minutes or an hour later and stay indoors until other students returned from their lectures. No one took notice initially because he never encountered the same people as the roommates returned from classes. He would always claim their classes ended first. Unfortunately, the fact that Piper never had a course mate who came to share any study materials did not occur to anyone. However, he would identify some course mates he met as he visited different lecture halls as he wandered about during lecture hours without actually attending any lectures. Ginika was amazed to learn later that Piper was not enrolled in any course of study and was just pretending to be a student. Piper had deceived his parents, who lived in faraway Lagos, into thinking that he had received admission into the university, and he continued to extort money from them. It happened that he had not made the merit admission list, and he hoped he would eventually get on the supplementary list during the admission process. This was why he took the necessary funds from his parents and bid them farewell on his journey to the university. He was disappointed when the final supplementary list came out. Not ready to go back home and face the shame among his friends, he decided to hang out in school while pursuing another attempt at his JAMB test and the so-called preliminary studies. This was a bridging one-year program at the university through which successful candidates for admission into the preliminary studies were offered admission into several courses of study after they completed their preliminary studies. That was how Piper and many others like him kept hanging out with real students pretending to be genuine. In some cases, they deceived the real students. Their choices of pastimes were things such as going to parties or clubs and participating in unauthorized demonstrations or cult activities. These were not in the best interest of those who were pursuing serious academic studies and who were determined to make good grades to guarantee them good jobs at the end of their studies.

This situation sounded an alarm in Ginika's brain, reminding him of Emeka's advice at Arugo Park and an Igbo adage he had heard Ogadimma use several times: *"Oke soro ngwere maa mmiri, mmiri ko oke oga ako ngwere."* This means that, if the rat jumps into water with the lizard, if the water drains from the smooth body of the lizard, would it drain from the hairy body of the rat? This illustrated the point that, if the children of poor civil servants like Ginika followed the example of Piper or other students from very wealthy homes who played at school and thus missed the whole purpose of going to school, then when the time came, they might face consequences that might not be applicable to the children from the rich homes? The rich kids might have their parents buy jobs for them or they might even take up positions in their already established family businesses. And this was why Ginika cut off ties with an expatriate friend of his called Laide.

Ginika met Laide at a restaurant one afternoon, and they struck up a conversation having seen each other in a lecture hall some minutes before. Laide's mother was Nigerian, and his dad was Lebanese. They were so wealthy that Laide drove a Peugeot 505 at school to the admiration of some poor kids like Ginika. Laide had a beautiful girlfriend who was also a half-caste like him. Following their chat at the restaurant, Laide and Ginika became friends and would always sit together during lectures. They became friends with another male engineering student, Charly, who was also a half-caste. However, Charly suddenly stopped hanging out with them.

Though Laide appeared very serious during lectures, he seldom came to school even though he lived not far from school, and he had a car. He always gave one reason or another for having to be in Port Harcourt and so must miss out on important lectures to the distaste of Ginika, who could not understand the boy. Not too long after the friendship began, Ginika was smart to dissociate himself from the boy as he appeared to be a bad influence, not taking his lectures seriously and always relying on Ginika or any other of their classmates to do his assignments for him. Interestingly, Laide quit school later without anybody's knowledge and without giving any reason for leaving. Ginika thanked God he had been smart enough to realize in time that Laide was not the kind of friend he needed as a student.

Matriculation for the Jambitos was held a few weeks into the start of studies that semester. It was such a busy day, with long queues of cars on all the roads leading to the university, that people found it difficult to get to both the hostels and the arena, the venue for the ceremony at the Abuja campus. It was a glorious day. The students, parents, and guardians who were able to make it to the arena were taking pictures with the students in their matriculation gowns, which they had hired from the university for a fee. The picture taking took place immediately after the official induction ceremonies were over. Others who could not make it to the arena had their wards wait for them at their different hostels for the after-ceremony parties. Parents brought coolers of food to share with the students and their friends. Though Ogadimma and Ngozi could not make it, Ginika's friends back at Owerri, who then had gone to the Federal University of Technology Owerri and University of Nigeria Nsuka, came down with Ginika's sister, and they had a swell time together enjoying the merriment that went on all around the barracks hostel. They also visited other hostels where some of their friends resided. Some other friends from Owerri studying at the University of Port Harcourt and knew it was Ginika's matriculation day came around for food and pictures as well.

For some families with wards in the school, matriculation was not a joke or a minor event, and they took time to prepare all kinds of dishes to share. They even invited cultural dancers to accompany them to the hostel where they would perform to the admiration of other hostel members. Some people even had the whole event covered by both public television stations and private video recordings to the surprise of fellow Jambitos who continued to parade themselves around the vicinity so as to be caught on camera! Group pictures, loud music, cultural displays, and noise from the excited students continued all over the barracks and other hostels into the evening when the visitors finally left. The loud music continued into midnight.

Sunday was a day of thanksgiving for some of the students who attended church and a morning for extra sleep hours for those who didn't. The liberty afforded by the university environment meant that some students who did not like going to church at home had the freedom to stay away. Some other smart ones knew the importance of church in achieving their goals in school. For Ginika, this was another survival strategy he could not overlook. He would get himself embedded in church activities so that he would be fully occupied when he had little schoolwork to do. Moreover, he was not close to any lecturers at school, and he did not have any relatives nearby, and he needed the comfort of a true family that only the church could provide. Attending Mass and receiving Holy Communion were regular activities for him because he wanted to make sure he was always in a state of grace, which was the precondition for receiving Holy Communion. An announcement by the officiating catechist was always made before the start of the distribution of Holy Communion by the officiating priest.

One thing worried Ginika during the service, though, and that was the question of discrimination by the church when it came to Holy Communion against those who were not from that church. He thought Christ was the same for all people. Apart from the announcement of the requirement to be in a state of grace, an additional requirement and second part of the announcement was that only the members of that particular church were invited to approach the alter for communion. He noted, however, that all attendees were asked to contribute to the offering without any discrimination of any kind. This scene would play out every Sunday to Ginika's discontent. He would, in some instances, not make any contribution to the second round of offering called second collection, sighting the excuse in his heart that only those who had taken part in Holy Communion should partake in the second collection. His complaint with the church did not end there. He also had issue with the clever way he thought people were being blackmailed into giving their offering in some other churches. People were asked to go to the alter line by line as the seating arrangement in pews warranted. He felt vulnerable on days when he had no money for offering. He felt he was being blackmailed to stand up and walk to the alter to give something. If he remained seated, he would feel ashamed that others would see he was the only one sitting down while others went to the altar. This was even though, when he was small, he had been told that, if he had nothing to give in church, he could still go to the altar and simply put his clutched fist into the offering box to signify that he had given his heart. He felt this was not honourable and would rather sit in his pew whenever he had no offering.

As part of Ginika's commitment and activities in church, he got close to Otte, a beautiful and kind-hearted woman, who led the Veritas Society, which was dedicated to providing support and encouragement to students in the faith. The society had branches in all of the universities in the country. The overseeing head in Lagos was called Anna, an expatriate who sometimes visited Port Harcourt to have discussion for encouragement of the students. This association gave Ginika the feeling of family when he was away from home, and this was what he so dearly desired. Ogadimma and Ngozi were glad when they heard of Ginika's church activities.

Lectures, reading, assignments, and examinations were the main activities for Ginika during his stay at university before he considered anything else including, religion, sports, and recreation.

Lectures were held at different venues including Ofrima Hall at the Abuja campus and the engineering classrooms at the Choba campus about two kilometres from Abuja campus. The lecture halls at Ofrima were new. The seating arrangements were like those in movie theatres; students could see the lecturer from anywhere in the room. However, overcrowding was the order of the day as the students outnumbered the capacity of the hall. This led to situations in which many students ended up standing through the lectures. Those who were even less fortunate stayed outside the hall listening to the voice of the lecturer and missing any illustrations on the board. This meant that serous students had to arrive way ahead of the scheduled time in order to get a seat. However, in most cases, lectures were held back to back and students had to rush from one lecture hall to the next to try to grab a seat. It was the weakest among them who suffered. The smart females in some cases relied on their male classmates to secure front-row seats for them. When one of the students was asked to describe her experience in the crowded classrooms, she said she had just discovered what sardines go through.

Arriving on time for early-morning lectures was critical for students, especially those who lived far from the lecture halls. For example, since Ginika lived in the barracks in Choba, he and his friends had to arrive very early at Abuja if they wanted to get front row-seats for the lecture that started at seven o'clock in the morning. This meant getting up early, having their baths, and rushing to get *okadas* (motor bike taxis) to drive them to school. In most cases, the okadas might not be up and running that early. In that case, students had to walk the couple of miles to Abuja campus in the cold of the morning. However, the trekking was always worth it as far as Ginika was concerned.

For some of the smarter and more brilliant female students, survival meant making friends with the males either for the purpose of sharing knowledge, working on their assignments, or attempting to procure better seating positions in class. For guys like Ginika, such relationships were healthy and symbiotic. The partnerships were real company for the likes of Ginika, who right from his primary school days in Aladinma, had enjoyed, albeit shyly, the company of the opposite sex. This time around, he enjoyed it even more. He was made to read even more as the females requested more after-class readings and meetings to discuss concepts taught in class or more reading time at the library to the delight of Ginika. This worked well for Ginika given the poor hostel conditions in the barracks, which meant he was always out of the hostel and reading somewhere with one or more of his female classmates. Soon his roommates got to know all of the girls to such extent that he was always informed well ahead of time before the females knocked at their room door. On sighting approaching ladies (most of whom his friends already knew by name) in the hostel corridor, one of his busybody hostel mates would giggle, whisper, or even shout as the pretty girls came to look for Ginika. Sometimes this was done to the embarrassment of the poor girls who, however, refused to be intimidated by the boys.

For the students in the hostels, it was always a bet to see who could pull the most beautiful and highest number of girls to the hostels for whatever reasons, and Ginika eventually occupied the top spot. His female friends came for honest, good reasons, and Ginika was the envy of some others who got visits only from their girlfriends for immoral reasons. Ginika would carry his engineering drawing board and go with some of the females to their hostels to teach them technical drawing or help them out with their assignments to the chagrin of his friends who called him "car washer", a term they used to connote the fact that he was helping out another person's girlfriend. He was not perturbed. He got nothing in return, not even a kiss or a pat on the back.

The poor boy sometimes felt embarrassed, but he was, in fact, helpless because he could not say no to any girl who requested his help with her technical drawing. For some reason, he could not explain himself. He felt they were friends, and he had no reason to decline helping the girls, but when someone asked him why he had to go all the way to the girls' hostel to offer this help, Ginika was speechless. The suspicion was that Ginika felt that going to the girls' hostel meant he would be noticed by other girls while doing the engineering drawing coaching. He would be assumed to be very intelligent and thus capable of attracting the attention of other girls who came around the table where he would be discussing the work with his female classmate. This could possibly increase his potential clients and subsequently visitors to his barracks hostel to help him maintain his rating as the guy who pulled the most girls to the hostel. Ginika would not refute this suspicion and continued his coaching classes as though nothing was wrong. Indeed, he was getting better at his engineering drawing with every coaching session he gave; his relationship with the girls he helped seemed symbiotic enough.

The reading and library sessions would always pay off when it came to the examinations for Ginika and his friends. With the solid work done during the semester in terms of reading and diligence in his assignments, the exams usually appeared to be a fulfilment of all righteousness. He was bound to always be very successful and always finish ahead of the stipulated exam time. The strategy for them lay in the review of all past examination questions related to any particular course. Ginika and his friends came to realize that, most times, the lecturers repeated the questions from exams that had been administered in previous years. The lecturers would seldom develop new questions; students always noted that the lecturers could, indeed, be lazy in terms of thinking up new questions. This applied to all courses to the surprise of the students. There were a few lecturers who provided fresh questions, though, and could even go the extra mile of producing different questions for different students during the same examination. One particular instructor, a physics professor, gave each student a different set of questions to minimize the possibility of their copying each other or attempting any "expo" as it was termed. During one of the examinations, Ginika and one of his female friends sat close together only for the lecturer to separate them. The young graduate lecturer thought that the female friend would start pleading with him to reinstate her to her supposed advantage position close to Ginika, without knowing that the female friend was an authority on her very own in the subject! To the young lecturer, the fact that the girl was very pretty suggested she was probably parasitic to the young man. He did not understand that every engineering student, whether male or female, had what it took to pursue the course and only sometimes appeared dull because of jonsing, but none of Ginika's friends were a part of that. On realizing what the lecturer was trying to do, both Ginika and the girl just smiled at each other as they whispered the word *olodo* and made a face at the lecturer when he looked away.

Though Ginika was very smart and did well in his examinations, he had a weakness during those examinations. He always wrote very fast, aiming to finish far ahead of the stipulated time, and he would sometimes not review his answers exhaustively before submitting his papers. Though this worked for him most times as he tried hard to be very diligent as he worked his way through the questions, some other times it did not. He and his friends would argue about the right answers when they reviewed the questions after the exams. Sometimes, to his disappointment, he would then realize that he had left something undone, something he might have noticed had he used the extra time he had to go through his answers a second or third time.

Some other students who may not have done their homework and studied well for the examinations would always look for the intelligent ones to latch onto when it came to examinations. They sometimes solicited the cooperation of the intelligent students to leave their answer sheets wide open so they could see them and copy easily. They could also even go to the extent of paying them large sums of money to be allowed free "giraffe" access to their answers so they could copy. And if those options would not work, they could import "mercenaries" to help them write the examinations. These mercenaries were intelligent students who had done the courses before and passed them. They could even apply their work to courses they had not done before. They had the capacity to simply read the material and write the examination successfully. It was a source of pride for such students that they boasted they could even read French and do mercenaries' jobs on it to the admiration of their fellow student customers. The mercenary's job was a dangerous one as anyone caught by the school authorities was liable to be expelled from the school after an indictment from a panel set up to investigate such cases.

Thus, it was a do-or-die affair when an attempt was made to arrest such imposters. This sort of cheating became so rampant that the school authorities had to start posting security agents around school examination halls to deter students from bringing in mercenaries. This action did not deter those desperate to cheat as they devised other means to beat the system instead of devoting their energy to studying.

Those who were not interested in cheating during their examinations would leak the question papers before examination day. They would do this by becoming friends with the lecturer, if he was a young man. Through this friendship, they could obtain the papers. If it were an older lecturer, they would make friends with his children who would then help them to extract copies of the examination questions from their parents without their knowledge. In all these cases, a lot of money change hands. If they were not able to obtain the questions before the examination, some students would attempt to have their answer sheets replaced by lecturer friends or through the kids of the older ones. And if all that effort failed, they would resort to the almighty "sorting", paying the lecturers for extra unmerited marks. The level of sorting depended on the original performance of the candidate. If a student's grades were just under passing, it would take less money to bring him into the pass region. If he was completely failing, then he would have to cough up more money. Sorting remuneration was not limited to cash alone as females were rumoured to offer sex in return for extra marks, and sometimes they even blackmailed their professors into doing it. There were stories of lecturers asking the girls out. If a girl declined the request, the examination could be used as payback. The lecturer would deliberately fail the student so that she would come and beg him for a better grade. He would then insist on a relationship and sex before he passed her. This was so bad that many female students had to stay an extra year in the university because the "mean" lecturers continued to fail them until they agreed or God intervened. Surprisingly, the students would not get a reprieve if they reported such wayward behaviour because a lot of the lecturers were involved in the practice. Those who were not would feel uncomfortable confronting their colleagues on the subject.

One of Ginika's friends ran into such trouble with a lecturer, an ugly man called Mbong, who was old enough to be her father. Ginika heard about how Mbong had been harassing Inem for a long time. He heard this from his friends one day when they were going to town for a party. Everyone felt sorry for poor Inem, as they all knew they could do nothing concerning her case given that the lecturer in question was an old and powerful man on the faculty. The man in question was so ugly, Inem wondered how she could even face him in bed if she were to even accept and succumb to his blackmail. Moreover, her boyfriend had heard of the trouble. All of their friends were strategizing ways to get the old man to back off; they even engaged the help of a senior friend of theirs who was a lawyer. Ginika, who did not understand the extent of the situation, was surprised one day when Inem sat close to him in an examination for which this ugly old man was one of the invigilators. Whether he was asked to invigilate or he invited himself because of his zeal to embarrass or deal with Inem no one could say, but to Ginika's shock, this old and shameless man came to Inem's desk and asked her to get up. He took her to another corner in the room to complete her examination for no obvious reason.

For the girls who did not mind sorting lecturers with sex, the arrangement was a jolly good ride to good grades as they flexed their muscles with their friendship with those lecturers and even threatened other students with failure if they crossed their paths. It was not unheard of to find a student failing just because he or she had issues with such girls. The girls would use their friendships with these lecturers to ask the lecturer to fail their classmates in their exams simply because they had quarrelled, and the lecturers would oblige them.

In fact, it was rumoured that some of the lecturers appointed certain agents who collected sorting money from the students who were interested in sorting for better grades. The interesting thing was that those lecturers would make their examinations highly difficult and sometimes beyond the scope of what they had actually taught. This strategy was a bid to ensure that a lot more students failed, and the candidates for sorting increased, leaving Ginika to wonder whether the lecturers did not realize that they were indeed the ones who failed. This was why he was convinced that, if the students could not pass the examinations, the teachers had failed in their bid to impact the knowledge. For these sinister reasons, these lecturers would release their results several months after the exams were taken so that their agents would have time to contact them and collect enough sorting money.

The more professional lecturers who did not indulge in such crimes against students were always able to release their results within three weeks after the examinations were taken depending on the number in the class. Some professors, like physics Professor Ewveraye, had been known to release results within two days of the examination. Professor Ewveraye was known to assign three different sets of exam questions to ensure no two people sitting together answered the same questions. This totally eliminated cheating during the examination. The release of his results within two days of the examinations also meant there was no avenue for any student begging for better marks or substitution of papers by his children or malpractice of any kind. Professor Ewveraye was so efficient that he would dedicate time to discuss every student's paper with him or her, highlighting mistakes and advising about what the student needed to do to improve.

Cheating on examinations had turned into a way of life for some students, but nothing prepared Ginika for what he was about to go through during his final year at the university. With the University of Port Harcourt in the oil city, the engineering students always had the privilege of writing scholarship examinations. The scholarships were awarded to qualifying students by the oil companies operating in the city. The first set of examinations was conducted at the beginning of their studies, and winning students had their school fees paid for the duration of their studies. It was always a thing of joy to be successful with the examination. Ginika, being a civil servant's kid, looked forward to winning one to the scholarships in his first year at the school. However, he did not make the first-round list, and so he looked forward to another opportunity. The opportunity came again during their final year when the stakes were even higher. This time around, the scholarship was for postgraduate studies overseas. This would be a life-changing experience for Ginika. The first qualification criterion was already in the bag for him—his cumulative grade point average (GPA). To qualify for the first round of the examination, each final-year student needed to have made a minimum of 3.5 cumulative grade points. This was the first time Ginika appreciated the fact that all his efforts and diligence had not been in vain. With his GPA comfortable at 4.1 at the time, he knew the sky was looking blue and rosy. The next examination for the scholarship required a written essay, and that was where things started getting ugly, even though Ginika did not see the dangers at the time.

The qualifying students were asked to write a five-page essay on any topic of their choice and submit their work within five days. They were to submit two typed copies of their essays for a so-called blind review panel. They were not to write their names on the papers to prevent any bias on the part of the reviewers. The format was provided, and the students submitted their essays as required. All participating students were warned to keep a copy of their essay for their own use. Unfortunately, that information was not complete. The copies the students kept for themselves were required to identify the owners of the winning entries. Two days after submission, the winning entries were announced. The best essay was the one titled "My Ojo and the Bleeding Cow". There were other two runner-up entries, and the panel ended up selecting five of the essays for the next stage, but the overjoyed Ginika already jumped up at hearing the winning title knowing it was his. However, that was where the trouble started because the title was not his until he proved it was by providing the matching "owners" copy.

Unbeknownst to Ginika, some of the students had already started planning how they would make sure the potential winners like him would be schemed out of the preliminary screening for the university scholarship. The bad guys found a loophole in the blind review method of the process and exploited it.

Ginika had taken precautions to safeguard his "owners" copy. He had kept it in the overhead locker in his room. This was in a different hostel from the barracks where he had lived during his early years. He shared this room in block C with two other final-year students, and they all had invited in squatters who were students who had accommodated them in their earlier years. One of them was a member of a church referred to as Olummba Olumba. One was an engineering student just like Ginika. The third was a geologist called Pamela, a light-skinned boy. Pam, as he was fondly called, had mainly engineering students as friends, and they had all heard about Ginika and his diligent schoolwork. One of Pamela's engineering friends, however, took note that Ginika never locked his cubicle as others did. That singular mistake caused Ginika a great fortune. With the race for the Shell Scholarship on, the bad guys in Ginika's set looked for every avenue to deter him from emerging the winner. To advance their cause, they secured the help of one of Pamela's friends. The task was easy—simply confiscate Ginika's "owners" copy of the essay he submitted for the scholarship competition. It took the mercenary several hours before he could locate the work tucked inside one of Ginika's handouts at the bottom of the pile of papers in the overhead locker on top of the wardrobe. The wardrobe was to the right of the entrance to Ginika's cubicle. The overhead locker was on top of the wardrobe but faced in a ninety degree direction to the door of the wardrobe. Both the top of the wardrobe and the inside of the overhead locker contained piles of papers, and Ginika had made sure to hide the material from the prying eyes of anyone as if he had a premonition of what could happen.

Immediately after hearing the result of the essay competition, Ginika ran back to his room with excitement, shouting to the top of his voice a recent song he had come to like. The song went thus:

When Jesus says yes, nobody can say no;

When Jesus says yes, nobody can say no;

Ginika had his own version of that song in which he had changed the second line to confirm that Jesus had already said yes. He changed the second line to;

Now Jesus has said yes, nobody can say no;

Jesus has said *yes!* Ginika kept saying this to himself as he made his way to the bottomless overhead locker! He knew precisely where he kept the material and went straight to the position. He stretched his hand and worked it down to the bottom of the pile of papers and quietly drew out the last paper at the bottom of the pile, confident it was his copy of the almighty final round of the selection process. He was still in the "Jesus has said *yes* " mood, humming the song as he closed his eyes in the process of extracting the precious material. He slowly opened his eyes to behold his passport to a greater and better future with a smile. He froze as he saw what looked like a scrap of notes he had used in his exam preparation. Thinking it was a mistake, he drew the seat close to him and climbed up to move the piles of paper and extract the correct paper he was looking for. He did not find what he was looking for and thus had to bring down the entire pile. He laid the papers on the bed and started searching through them, throwing down one after the other. He was sure of where he had kept the essay, but as he continued to search, his heart suddenly started to beat hard. He became anxious and started tearing the whole corner down. He pulled the pile on the top of the wardrobe down as he continued frantically to search for his matching "owners" copy, which seemed to have taken flight. As he was searching, Pamela and a couple of his engineering friends came in. They started congratulating him and said they heard he was one of the people who had passed the second screening of the competition. Pamela started getting worried when Ginika would not respond to their greeting, and he had to take a peep into Ginika's corner. He was shocked at what he saw—paper lying everywhere on the bed and the floor. "Ginika, are you OK?" he enquired.

"I cannot find my matching copy! I cannot find my matching copy," he responded again absentmindedly as he continued his long search for his future that would never be!

"Wait! Wait!" Pamela responded. "Are you sure you kept it in this room? You may have taken it to some other place. Think of the places you may have gone since you wrote it." A wounded Ginika was speechless as he put his hand on his waist as sweat poured down his cheeks. Pamela pitied him as he suggested there might be other options to secure his right to the material. Pamela suggested that they go to the business centre where Ginika had typed the work. It was possible the business centre could still have a copy and could print a copy for him. That seemed to be a logical and possible solution to the problem. However, before they could get to the business centre, the operators had closed for the day, and a defeated Ginika had to walk back to his room accompanied by Pamela who tried to encourage him.

That night, Ginika was so restless he stayed awake until very late in the night. He almost shed tears that night but hung on the little hope that all might not be lost since there was a chance he could still recover his "owners" copy. But time was running out! He had twenty-four hours to provide it or the screening team would simply move on to round two of the process with the remaining four who had won the essay competition. This little hope kept him encouraged as he drifted away into a deep sleep that evening. While asleep, he remembered his encounter with Uchewuba in primary school. Uchewuba's face kept flashing during the dream as Ginika recalled the episode that led to the loss of his right to his drama script of *Kosi*. In the dream, Uchewuba tormented him, shouting at him that no matter how careful he was, he was a loser and would lose again even if he had been careful to keep a backup hard evidence this time. Ginika started crying in the dream, begging him to help him this time recover his "owners" copy. He continued begging and thought he was getting a favourable response from his tormentor as he saw Uchewuba's countenance soften. It was at that point that he woke up feeling as dejected as he'd felt in the dream. He did not know what to make of it, but believed he would experience the best outcome under the circumstances.

As early as six o'clock, Ginika was already in front of the business centre waiting for the attendants. As the other shops continued to open, a restless Ginika enquired from the shop's neighbour about the whereabouts of the business centre's employees. He was told they were supposed to have opened by then; it was strange they were not there. They were usually the first to open in that arena, a young boy told Ginika. Ginika asked for their number and called the line. A young lady answered the phone and pleaded that she was on her way. They had been looking for the key to the shop since the previous night; hence their inability to resume business as early as usual. They had just found it before Ginika called. About thirty long minutes later, which seemed like an eternity to Ginika, the lady arrived and opened the shop. "Do we have your work here?" The lady asked Ginika. It was obvious Ginika was worried, and that immediately affected the young lady as her tone suggested she was already beginning to pity Ginika. He told her his story, and the search began. There were about ten computers in the shop, and the lady did not know where to start the search. Ginika recalled the seat and particular computer he had used when he came to type the work, and the lady started on that one, checking all the folders that contained clients' work. By the time she had gone through all ten computers in the shop, she had not found Ginika's file. His desperation increased. Ginika went back to his room feeling sad, and this time insisted that someone must have stolen the paper from his room since there was no way the paper could have grown legs. He mentioned his fears to Pamela when he came back from the business centre. Unfortunately, with his room covered in the papers from the previous day's search, there was no way of knowing whether someone had entered his corner to take anything away.

Pamela felt pity for Ginika and asked his engineering friends whether they had seen anyone strange enter the room at any time over the past couple of days. The answer was negative, and while they were all brainstorming of what to do, a thought occurred to Pamela that there might still be a glimmer of hope at the business centre. "I think you had better go back to the business centre and ask them to check their recycle bin to see, if by chance, the material can still be recovered." That was a possibility, and Ginika responded quickly. He dashed again to the business centre. The lady he had met earlier was handy to help him with anything he wanted. Unfortunately, employees had cleared all the recycle bins the previous day as part of their routine in an effort to manage their computer memory space. That seemed to be the end of the road for Ginika as he walked back to his room. By the end of that day, he did not find the copy, and the other four who had made it to the second stage progressed to the final stage. Ginika cried that night the same way he had cried when he missed entrance into the federal government college. This time, though, as a big boy, he cried to himself with no auntie by his side and no Ogadimma to pity a son in distress.

CHAPTER 9
Ndele

Ginika struggled through university keeping his head high and avoiding trouble from all corners to the best of his ability. As a civil servant's kid, he knew his limitations and background, the trust reposed in him, and the responsibilities awaiting him after school. Money was always a problem; there was never enough. He managed and was grateful for the amount he got. There were certain types of feeding schemes that were adopted by the students from humble backgrounds. The rich kids had more than enough to eat each meal. The feeding formulas of the less-privileged kids, however, were 1-0-1, 0-1-1, or even 0-1-0, each "1" representing when a student could afford a meal—either in the morning, afternoon, or night. For Ginika, working out a formula was part of the discipline required to make it at university as the limited funds made him frugal in his expenses.

Keeping away from trouble meant avoiding places like student demonstrations, which usually erupted for several reasons such as lack of water, unsanitary conditions of the hostels, and hikes in school fees. The demonstrations would always start non-violently with bonfires and blocking of the East-West Road, a federal government highway that linked the western part of Nigeria to the South . Vehicles would then be screened as they were allowed to pass. This caused gridlock and subsequent chaos in the area that often led school authorities to invite the government security agencies to maintain order and disperse the protesting students. The students would, in turn, see this as a slight from the school authorities whom they expected would come out and address them and the issues they had raised. Depending on the head of the team from the security agency and the approach he deployed, students might be cajoled into dispersing. If his pleading failed to achieve this objective, he would use force, and things might easily get out of hand. The whole scenario could change and quickly degenerate into a full-blown riot with the breaking of bottles, the smashing of vehicle wind-screens, the chanting of war songs for which the name of the vice chancellor would mostly be the subject of the rhythm. One professor, Akpakpa, was unlucky enough to preside over the university during one of the riots to which the chanting was "Akpakpa is a goat, oh! Akpakpa is a goat, oh! Give us water!" The chanting students would carry fresh leaves as they forced the cars plying the East-West Road to attach them to their cars as a sign of peace and solidarity for safe passage. In extreme cases, the police would release tear gas to disperse the students and even shoot bullets into the air. The bullets could occasionally hit students, fuelling the demonstrations further and requiring reinforcements from the security agency. Within hours, the school authorities would announce the closure of the school and ask every student to leave the hostels with the threat and follow through of the arrest of defaulting students. During such riots, Ginika would always stay put in his hostel resisting the strong temptation to go out to participate in the fun of the chaos, jumping about, and chanting war songs. To him anything was possible with those demonstrations, and anyone could be a victim of a stray bullet from the rampaging security agents; hence, it was better to stay far away from the mayhem.

During one such riot, Ginika came to the school campus only to encounter the rampaging students. He asked the reason for the demonstration and was told it was because school authorities had told students to dismantle the curtains that defined the cubicles in the hostels. The students refused, and to show their anger with the directive, they took to the streets in protest as usual. Prior to the directive, the school authorities were worried that the use of the curtains was not tidy, and they made the rooms stuffy. There were reported occasions during which some students who allegedly belonged to secret cults hid guns in their rooms without any detection. There was also the issue of keeping female students in the rooms with round-the-clock sessions of sex to the disregard and disrespect of other roommates. To a large extent, the demonstration was all about the last excuse because the wild boys saw their lifestyle and that of their companions threatened, so they took up the fight to protect their interest. Ginika was not living in the hostel then as he had sold his own accommodation having received one as a final-year student. The riot was of no concern to him until the following week when school authorities released the names of students who had been suspended for their roles in the riot.

Ginika was studying in class at Choba campus when a friend told him that his name was on the list of students suspended by the school authorities as a result of their participation in the riot. He immediately ran out and confirmed with some other students who had also seen the list. He quickly dashed to the student affairs office notice board on the Choba campus and confirmed the story, to his surprise. Several inquiries later confirmed the reason for his name being on the list, and his strategy to get the suspension revoked began. It happened that, since the riot over the weekend was due to the displeasure of the students over the school authority's directive to dismantle the cubicle curtains, the authorities simply assumed that it was the most senior students who were officially allocated bed spaces in the hostels who were responsible for the riots. They thus suspended all the final-year students in a particular hostel block where they thought the riots had started. Unfortunately, that was the one to which Ginika had been allocated and which he had sold.

It was a confused Ginika who attended classes over the two weeks during which the issue lasted while he attended all kinds of meetings and engagements with everyone he thought could help. It was ludicrous that he was about to be suspended when he was just about to leave school after toiling all the past years. The worst thing was that students would not even be given certificates for a university education for their past years of work; they all stood to lose out on all those years if the suspension was not lifted. Having had a good record all through his stay in school, Ginika wondered what Ogadimma would say if he heard about this. Coincidentally, there were other students who had the same problem and who had parents who were highly connected with the state government. These students got their parents and the state government to intervene. Ginika had already hinted Mrs Otte, who was his spiritual director and mentor at school, and she calmed him down and advised him that the issue should not worry him as she knew the suspension would be lifted in a short time. This did not satisfy Ginika; he then approached one of his senior lecturers and asked the old man to intervene. On hearing the full details of how Ginika's name got into the suspension list, the man wiped his glasses, looked at him, and told him point black that he had left his shadow at the hostel and that was why he had been roped into the mess. To Ginika, it was a case of being between the devil and the deep blue sea. If he accepted that he lived in the hostel, he was one of the students who was primed for the riot. If he argued that he had given his bed space away, the school would take offence because students had been warned not to give away their bed spaces, and he would have to prove that he had not sold the space, as that would be the default assumption and would get him into another kind of trouble. Thus he maintained the argument that he had not sold the bed space, but had given it to a friend.

After a week passed with no resolution in sight, Ginika knew it was time to get Ogadimma to intervene, so he took off to Owerri that weekend to inform Ogadimma of the mess in which he had found himself. It was tough to explain the incident and get Ogadimma to come down to school, but he eventually did that while pretending to be crying over such a dire situation. Ogadimma agreed, came to the school the next Monday, and went to the vice chancellor's office to have an audience with him.

Meanwhile, as the issue dragged on, one of Ginika's friends, who happened to be in Ginika's Veritas society in church and whose mum worked in the vice chancellor's office, had hinted her mum about Ginika's case. Ginika later believed she had intervened even before Ogadimma came to see the vice chancellor. Thus, as Ogadimma and Ginika waited outside the vice chancellor's office to be ushered in to see him, his friend's mum came out and asked if he was Ginika. Ginika nodded in confirmation. She further asked if the older man seated next to him was Ginika's father. Ginika nodded again as she smiled and shook Ogadimma's hand, expressing her sympathy for what had transpired over the past week. She confirmed to Ogadimma that things had been sorted out. She made a promise to Ogadimma that the suspension would be lifted before the end of the week, and that there was no need to see the vice chancellor on the matter. Ogadimma thanked her graciously as he got up to leave. True to the information from Ginika's friend's mum, the suspension was lifted by the end of the week, and Ginika went for a thanksgiving at the Sunday church service having worked through the shadow of death of his university education.

With the end of his struggles came the "call-up" letter for the National Youth Service Corps (NYSC). This is the national service program that requires every university graduate to undergo a compulsory one year of service to the country with some paramilitary training at the beginning of the program. It was always a delight to receive the call-up letter, and every final-year student without any academic problems hindering his or her graduation looked forward to it. Unfortunately, some students with outstanding academic problems sometimes obtained phony call-up letters in a bid to deceive their parents and fellow students that they had actually finished their program without any problem. Their deception could be detected later either at the orientation camps or places of primary assignment. In some extreme cases, these students faked both the call-up letters and success letters which where temporary university certificates only to be found out in the future by employers. In some instances, the young people went quietly back to school and took the relevant courses to complete their studies. There were situations in which the students were known to have stolen success letters forcing a particular school to recall all the school's success letters by informing all the NYSC orientation camps.

Ginika was lucky and got posted to Rivers State where he had been schooled. He was grateful as he did not want to experience the horrible stories he had heard about Youth Corps as the NYSC participants were called. Their three weeks orientation camp took place at Ndele, a village several kilometres from Port Harcourt. Ndele was a great place with lots of fun games, paramilitary training, and free money because each participant was paid an allowance as soon as they entered the camp. The first month's allowance was 3,800 naira (about ten dollars) and was paid right there at the camp; subsequently each received a monthly allowance. Soldiers were detailed to provide paramilitary training, and discipline was instilled in the participants including strict restrictions on behaviour while they were in the camp. There were other camp rules to which all were expected to conform. A "mammy" market was available in camp so people could buy supplementary items including additional food for those who did not like the watery beans and other food cooked for the Youth Corp members. Sanitary conditions were initially good but quickly deteriorated as the days went by and the capacity of the systems did not cope.

Then came the love birds who hooked up quickly in camp; they shared hot romances as they enjoyed the serenity of the environment and accompanied each other during the several work-outs or marathon races organized during the period. Others were jealous because they had not been able to hook up with someone easily. Some of the guys had girlfriends back in school to whom they had most likely promised they would always remain faithful. But it was easy for them to be carried away with the lust offered by daily reality.

The girls showed so much flesh as they were dressed beautifully in their white shorts and T-shirts. And their breasts dangled as they jumped up and down during the exercises. The boys were no doubt in for some trouble. With the ladies' nipples all waving at the boys, no one blamed anyone who fell for the beauties. The genuine decent relationships were encouraged by the government that had set up the program, promising to pay fifty thousand naira to any couple that eventually got married during their NYSC period. The objective of the incentive was, indeed, to encourage intercultural marriage in the country, which would encourage a more unified country. This was a policy introduced in the seventies, a period after Nigeria emerged from a bitter Civil War and was searching for a way to integrate its citizens.

The NYSC had its merits and faults. Apart from enabling integration in the country, it offered opportunities for participants to explore other regions of the country and make them aware of other people's cultures and the opportunities that abounded in those places. The graduates from the southern parts of the country were exposed to the dry and arid savannahs of the northern parts and got to enjoy food delicacies from such areas. It was not out of place to hear some people who served in the northern parts come back to the southern parts a few months later speaking Hausa, the dominant language in the north. It was also not out of place for some northerners to opt to stay in the more economically vibrant south after their service years.

As with everything else in Nigeria, there were some negative stories surrounding the NYSC. There were tales of individuals attempting to fix their postings; some of them succeeded. They did this by going to the NYSC headquarters in Abuja and paying to influence the state to send them where they would like to be posted. This was against the plans of the policy. Consideration was officially given only to married couples who needed to reside in the same state as their spouses during the service year. These couples were supposed to inform the NYSC right from the time they were in school before the dispatch of their postings by NYSC. Anyone who did not do that would normally have to wait until after the orientation camp before effecting a posting change, and that could be very challenging. There were instances of pregnant women giving birth in camp during orientation. Some of them would subsequently be exempted from the exercises unless they opted to continue.

Not only was there payment for preferential posting to states of choice for the NYSC, there was also pay for preferential posting to companies of choice for those in the heavily industrialized states like Lagos or Rivers. At one time, most companies, including banks, leveraged on the cheap labour the NYSC candidates offered to maximize their output with the possibility of offering the candidates who performed well full-time employment after their service years. This prompted a scheme in which NYSC candidates sought to influence the companies they were posted to right from the orientation camps. Some with the right connections would get letters from these companies addressed to the state NYSC asking that the candidates be posted to them. The NYSC would have no choice but to oblige the companies since their overall objective was to ensure the candidates all got placement for the national assignment.

Some state governments complained about the disenfranchisement of their citizens from employment due to the NYSC posting policy. It went thus: since the objective of the NYSC was to have students serve in regions far away from their regions of origin, it turned out that the students from the more industrialized states were posted outside their lucrative regions to the states that offered fewer opportunities. Given the likelihood of companies employing people after their service years, more of the candidates from the states that offered fewer opportunities were hired for full employment after the service year to the detriment of the indigenes when they returned after their service year. This angered some state governments to the extent that they instituted policies that dictated that NYSC members had to be posted to schools to teach; governments did not think their indigenes should lose out after their service years. The policy turned out to be a good one in the sense that it provided opportunities to boost the availability of teachers to handle the teaming population, but it was born out of a bad objective of retaining positions for their so-called indigenes, a position that contradicted the aim and objective of the NYSC.

Ginika had fun at the camp participating in the numerous games and exercises and making sure he had the pictures to tell the story for posterity. It was usual to have some corps members simply pose and take pictures even when they were not engaged in a particular activity. Climbing ropes, running distances, and all sorts of paramilitary exercises were the order of the day.

For those who were religious, the evenings offered an opportunity to get together and have fun the way they wanted. Ginika found solace in Corpers Loveworld, a unit of the Believers Loveworld, a Pentecostal church. Evening was a time of praise and worship, and Ginika and his friends never missed a night, enjoying the preaching, testimonies, and other activities. To Ginika's amazement, Ihemba, his very good friend from the university, rendered a soul-touching song one night that made Ginika admire him so much. Out of nowhere, Ihemba was called out to give his testimony as usual, and he began by singing a song. To the delight of everyone and most especially Ginika his song went thus:

> I have made you so small in my eyes,
> Oh Lord, forgive me.
>
> I have believed in a lie, that you are unable to help me.
>
> But now, Oh Lord, I see my wrong. Feel my heart and show yourself strong.
>
> And in my heart and in my song, oh Lord, be magnified. Oh Lord, be magnified.

Be magnified, Oh Lord. You are highly exalted, and
there is nothing, you can't do, oh Lord. My eyes are
on You. Be magnified, oh Lord. Be magnified.

By the time Ihemba was finished, Ginika was already shedding
tears of joy and grace for the wonderful rendition from Ihemba; it was
a memory he cherished so much that he would blog about it in the
future to the delight of those who could connect to that night.

As a civil servant's kid with few or no "connections" in the
Nigerian context, Ginika depended on God for all things including
the NYSC posting to a place of primary assignment after the
orientation camp. He was happy to have been posted to the Pipeline
and Product Marketing Company (PPMC) an arm of the Nigerian
National Petroleum Corporation. The PPMC office was the division
of the NNPC that pumped the refined petroleum products from the
Port Harcourt refinery via pipelines to the other petroleum products
depots around the country, first to Aba, then to Enugu and Markudi
in the northern part of the country. The PPMC was located in a town
called Okrika. As if history was trying to repeat itself, the management
of the PPMC was not ready to absorb the NYSC candidates posted
to the place to the amazement of Ginika. He had thought that, as a
government agency, the company was duty bound to honour postings
from a fellow government agency. Mirroring the intervention from
Uncle Chuky, whom Ogadimma had sent to the university when the
university would not issue Ginika his admission letter, Ginika had to
seek the intervention of Mr Wonwon, a friend of Ogadimma's who
happened to be a senior engineer with the neighbouring NNPC-
owned refinery. It took a call from My Wonwon to the officer in charge
at PPMC to influence the company officials to admit the NYSC
candidates posted to them that year. To the surprise of young Ginika,
Mr Wonwon called up Ajeyinka who was the area manager for PPMC
at the time and told him he had a candidate posted to his organization,
and that he wanted him absorbed. With Ajayinka complaining about
the fact that PPMC was not ready to start taking corpers, Wonwon,

apparently very friendly with Ajayinka, jokingly offered Ajeyinka a replacement slot in his own organization (the refinery) if the need arose. It was interesting for Ginika to learn how chief executives traded common NYSC positions. It got Ginika thinking of what could have been his fate if there had been no Wonwon to intervene on his behalf for a position he had been posted to by the NYSC. Thus, PPMC eventually offered Ginika and the other candidates posted to it places in the organization in which they could undergo their national youth service year, a period that provided Ginika with some industrial and organizational experience.

CHAPTER 10

My Dear Okrika

A story made the rounds that the Okrikas fought their battles at night, an impression that remained in Ginika's mind throughout his working life in the area. He usually would dream of the darkness filled with moving creatures in the form of human warriors, crawling, hiding, manoeuvring, and defending their positions as they fought any encroaching imaginary enemies. The Okrikas were known to be brave fighters, but it was doubtful that there had been any recent happenings that closely matched Ginika's imaginings. He was consoled by the fact that he had business only with Okrika during the day, leaving out the stories of the night adventures to the gods.

He came close to exploring the night life of Okrika one day during his sojourn at PPMC. A plant operator was unavailable because he was bereaved after the loss of a close family member. His supervisor did not know of his absence in time to make adequate arrangements for a replacement late in the evening. The supervisor's only option was to detail one of the national Youth Corp members to cover the operator's duties for that night. Ginika was considered as part of the leadership of the NYSC members and an engineer who could adapt quickly to the dictates of the all-night job.

Prior to that, rumour had it that the operators who worked at night at the area office of the PPMC had a swell time. They got involved in all kinds of deals that fetched them extra income apart from their normal salaries. The talk on the corridor was that, as quiet as the office and officers may seem in the day, the hawks came alive in the night when all the other workers had gone home. The operators in the area office at Okrika were responsible for the pumping of the products and liaising with their colleagues at the Port Harcourt refinery. The PPMC pumping room operators were required to do fiscalization of the storage tanks that sat in the refinery compound to confirm the volume of products in them.

Exposing the secrets of the underworld PPMC operators was the height of the experience of the night shift for Sola, an NYSC member who eventually covered the duties of the bereaved operator. After the first night, Sola's friends were shocked and wondered why on earth he would opt to continue on the night shift. This was surprising after all the pity that his fellow Corp members had for him after he became the unfortunate one who had to work the whole night in Okrika and suffer the risk of being attacked by the well-known and talked about Okrika war lords who specialized in night struggles. Little did his friends know that Sola had been initiated into the sweet and dangerous underworld of the night operators of PPMC. The job was so lucrative they would not mind remaining on the night shift for longer periods of time than expected. To the amazement of other Corp members, Sola soon started spending large amounts of money. Other Corp members insisted on exploring Okrika's night secrets by asking that they be put on the night shift. Sola was forced to divulge the secret deals when he was threatened by others, especially Ginika, who insisted on knowing what was going on because Sola had stopped attending other daytime NYSC Corp members' meetings and the normal Friday community service days. *Bunkering* was the word, to the wild amazement of Ginika and the few privileged others. But how could that be? Naive NYSC Corp members wanted to know. They could not understand how such a word could be used for a government establishment that was responsible for fighting the oil pipeline vandals that always made the PPMC pipeline shut down intermittently.

Sola summarized their secret night operations to the bewildered Corp members. He pointed out that the taps used for sampling at the pumping stations were used not only for sampling the products to determine the quality; they were also used to fill out large numbers of jerry cans and other containers that the operators and everyone present in the location during the routine area office night party brought. These included the gatemen and the recently baptized Sola. They sold the stolen goods to waiting accomplices outside the premises and did this in the dead of the night when other staff members had gone home to their families. A well-organized and coordinated operation, it started with the buyers positioning themselves in accommodations secured around the office in the neighbourhood. At about eight o'clock, the greedy operators got down to business with the sampling, only that this time, it was sampling for themselves! Within a short time, the team finished their shipment and were back to work as if nothing had happened, checking pipeline pressures, calling the operators at the Aba depot to confirm they had started receiving products, tabulating the arrival time and rate readings on logs, and making all sorts of calculations to confirm that quantities of products being pumped were corresponding to what was been delivered at the Aba end. As usual, the quantities pumped and received never aligned, but the difference was normally attributed to bunkering, a technical term that meant operational losses to management but private pocket gains to the initiated PPMC Okrika night-shift workers.

Ginika would continue to do his duties, enjoying his life as a Corp member and doing his best to deliver on the leadership of the members, as he was selected to be the coordinator of all the Corp members at PPMC.

This was not the first time Ginika would have something to do with Okrika. From his early university industrial attachment days at the Port Harcourt refinery, he was already used to the place. His morning routine to work those IT days remained the same even during his youth service. They had a cool bus ride from Mgbuoba, a local suburb in the Port Harcourt city, to the refinery. The trip took about an hour, and most of the occupants completed their night's sleep on the bus. Once the bus stopped inside the complex, Ginika proceeded immediately to the refinery gate to have a breakfast of roasted plantains and fish before walking down to PPMC, five minutes away. He normally would go for one unripe, which he had heard provided iron, and one ripe for good flavour before the day's work started. As destiny brought him back to the land of Okrika to do his national youth service, he was sure to give his all to the town he had come to believe and cherish, a town where he "almost" met his "missing rib". During his youth service year, he met Sam, an older NYSC batch member one morning. He whispered to him that she was "the one". As God would have it, He had put everything in place to make sure Ginika's heart's desire manifested.

The youth service at Okrika did not only "almost" bring Ginika his missing rib but also gave him his first award in life, and a national one at that. He was given an NYSC award for outstanding performance during the service year. As the leader of the NYSC Corp members at PPMC, he organized fellow members to raise funds to construct a bus stop at the refinery junction at Eleme, a neighbouring town to Okrika. They started by formulating a plan that entailed making initial contributions from their meagre 3,800-naira allowance and the additional 2,500 naira that the PPMC management paid them. With the seed money, they proceeded to engage all the PPMC staff in their plans and solicited their financial support. The staff was motivated and gave generously to the cause. But it was not all about money. There was paperwork to be done, and it was necessary to acquire certain permits from the local government, among other tasks. Committees were set up to pursue these goals, and once the permissions were given, the engineers among them made the drawing for the proposed bus stop. Soon, work commenced. Corp members carried out the excavation and masonry jobs that were involved as part of their community service. The project almost ran into financial difficulties at one point, but the ingenuity of the members saved the day. The team resorted to getting the motorists who plied the route to contribute to the development of the project, practically begging the motorists as they drove past, sometimes during rainstorms. It was fun for the members because they enjoyed the chit-chat and encouragement from motorists, including members of the staff of PPMC. The motorists saw the progress of the project, the dedication of the members, and were led to donate more to their course even after making their initial contributions with which the project took off.

Many years later, Ginika would smile to himself when his hope of seeing the landmark was dashed as he passed the site. He was consoled, however, by the fact that they had contributed their quota at the time, which gave way to better things. The bus stop project was located at the right-hand turn into the road that led to the refinery on the Eleme-Ogoni Road portion of the famous East-West Road.

One of the beautiful memories Ginika would keep always about Okrika was the road from Aba Road in Port Harcourt to the refinery, which was in excellent condition and made for a better sleep during their morning bus rides. To put it in national perspective, it was a road that led to the location of many strategic national assets including two refineries, Old and New Port Harcourt refineries; the PPMC loading depot; the PPMC area office; the PPMC jetty; Eleme Petrochemicals; Onne Oil and gas-free trade zone. This road also led to Ogoni, the homeland of Ken Saro-Wiwa, the internationally acclaimed scholar and late leader of Movement for the Survival of Ogoni People (MOSSOP), who happened to have attended Government College Umuahia, the same secondary school Ginika attended. This road was also part of the East-West Road.

Okrika and NYSC both reminded Ginika of the wayward nature of some leaders of society, people the younger ones would ordinarily look up to for advice and guidance. On one of the days that the Ginika's NYSC team was working at the bus stop construction site, an elegant, good-looking man stopped just opposite the construction site and alighted from his car to the admiration of the Corp members. Thinking that the guy was impressed with the work and thus wanted to provide some necessary support as other road users had been doing, the excited youths started smiling at the guy, hoping that he would support their cause. The gentleman walked to the team and congratulated them on the task and promised to help, informing the youths that he was indeed the local government chairman of the area. All the members became excited, thinking that the much-awaited messiah had arrived at last. After hanging around the construction site for a short time and admiring the results of the labour of the NYSC members, the man publicly announced to the team that he would support the cause with a sum of a hundred thousand naira. He asked Ginika, the leader, to go to his office the next Monday morning to collect the money. The team shouted "Chairman! Chairman!" as the gentleman walked back to his car across the road. The team was so excited that they had finally gotten all the necessary finance they required to finish the project and maybe even some extra for a well-deserved party after the project. They therefore opted to stop begging for contributions from the motorists because they believed they had collected enough for that day.

Ginika could not sleep that Friday night. The promised money was the answer to their dreams. They would get to finish and commission that project before they concluded their national youth service. Their project would not be added to the list of numerous abandoned projects that littered the country, started by administrations who expected their successors to finish them, only to discover that the new administrations had different priorities, thus wasting the public funds already committed to their predecessor's projects. So dreams coming true was all that Ginika had in his mind that weekend. On Monday when the sun rose, he quickly dashed to the chairman's office to collect the promised money.

The one-hour bus ride from Port Harcourt city centre to Okrirka seemed to Ginika to take seven hours as he contemplated going to the chairman's office before proceeding to PPMC, his place of primary assignment. He quickly obtained permission from his supervisor and headed straight to the chairman's office. This was not the first time he had visited the local government secretariat, having gone through the rigors of getting the permits at the initiation of the bus stop project. On enquiring at the chairman's office, he was asked to wait for some time, as the chairman was busy with some people who turned out later to be the councillors, the parliamentary arm of the local government. After the councillors left, some other people entered, and Ginika was ushered into the office with them. He was asked to take a seat a little farther away from the working desk of the chairman where he conferred with the group that had entered with Ginika. Ginika, from a distance, could not hear exactly what they were discussing, but he was sure it was not that confidential as all he heard was "My Chairman" at the mention of any interesting point in their discussion. At some point, Ginika fell asleep, but he woke up suddenly, wiped his eyes, and pretended he was on high alert waiting for his turn to engage the chairman and probably shout his own "My Chairman".

Finally, a continuous, loud chorus of "Mr Chairman", "My Chairman", "Your Excellency", signalled to Ginika that the meeting between the chairman and the group was over. As they all filed out of the office carrying some heavy nylon bags that looked like stashes of money, they were all smiles. They looked like people who had just won a lottery. Poor Ginika—after waiting for over two hours, he was called to the working desk of the chairman. The chairman enquired after the progress of the work on the bus stop. Ginika informed him that work was progressing, and they expected to finish once he took delivery of the promised one hundred thousand naira. But delivery was not to be, at least that day. The chairman informed Ginika, to his surprise, that the local government allocation had not been released and he would have to come back another day to confirm and process the promise of one hundred thousand naira. This was a rude shock to Ginika, as it was totally not expected. On the previous Friday, the chairman had categorically asked him to come on Monday to collect the money. Ginika knew he'd heard him correctly. There had been no mention of anything like dependency on the release of any local government allocation, whether state or federal.

These politicians are all liars, he thought to himself. *This man came to our worksite and encouraged us, only to dash our hopes right here and now.* What was he to tell his fellow Corp members when he got to the office? What was he to tell the NYSC supervisor at the local Okrika NYSC secretariat who had heard of the promised donation by the chairman? In fact, this supervisor would eventually fight with Ginika for the custody of the money, threatening to not recommend him to the state secretariat for the merited national award for having done so much with so little. And why did those councillors not have to wait until the monthly allocation came before taking away those heavy nylon bags that he could swear contained money? For whatever reason those councillors had been given that money, Ginika felt that their cause must have been more important to the community.

Ginika was shocked when the chairman finally revealed his real motive for inviting him to his office. Smiling sheepishly like a little boy, this gentleman, whom Ginika had previously held in high esteem until he started belittling himself, even went further than he had done already. He asked Ginika for the name of the female Corp member with big buttocks who was part of Ginika's project team—the one of average height who had been sitting close to the pole on that Friday, a little fair in complexion, he continued.

"Shelly," Ginika said. "Must be Shelly. There is another Corp member who fits that description, but she did not participate in the community service that Friday."

The chairman said, "Please can you give her my card when you get back?" Ginika agreed, wanting to do anything the chairman wanted so he would fulfil his promise of a hundred thousand naira to the team. That explained things for Ginika. The politeness and interest that the chairman had shown them that day was unlike what he had heard about politicians. They would always do only things that would favour them. In this case, the guy was using his office and position to woo a Corp member while making promises to poor youths who looked up to him as a leader. One thing that was on Ginika's mind was that he would make sure he extracted that money from the chairman, whatever it took. If he had made that promise as a way of impressing his yet-to-be-chased girlfriend, then good luck with his chasing, but he must fulfil his promise. Ginika eventually gave Shelly the chairman's card and never asked what she did with it or whether she was interested in the guy.

Exposure to environmental degradation was another memory Ginika acquired during his sojourn to Okrika. As part of the operations of PPMC, the staff was expected to inspect some of the sea vessels that were used to transport low-pour fuel oil (LPFO) at the PPMC jetty. This product was a product of the distillation process of hydrocarbon from the refinery. Such inspections necessitated visits to the jetty about two to three kilometres away from the office. On one such occasion, Ginika was among the team that went for the inspection, and the experience opened his eyes to the disturbing world of environmental degradation by the petroleum industry in the Niger Delta. Prior to that moment, he, like every other Nigerian, had been hearing the cries of prominent environmental activists such as late Ken Saro-Wiwa. Like most Nigerians who lived in areas that were remote from the activities of the oil and gas industry, Ginika was naive about the issues being discussed and at times thought that Ken and those like him were just out to discredit the government or the oil companies.

As the team made their way over a local bridge that led to the jetty, Ginika first took note of the muddy and oily nature of the beach. There was no sign of any fish or crabs, and there should have been many in evidence. He remembered his days at Government College Umuahia and what it was like fetching water from the stream. He remembered the fun of seeing the little fish swimming in the shallows as the kids made dashes to catch some. So why were there no fish in this large body of water? This was the question that ran through his mind. There were not even any boats in the vicinity, and this was supposed to be a fishing settlement. This troubled his young mind so much that he questioned the standards and operations that might have led to such destruction of the environment. Could this have been caused by the operations at the jetty? Of course it had been, as there was no other operation at the location that could have contributed to the issue. The confusing part was that the operations Ginika's team went to inspect carried on so smoothly that he wondered at the possibility of the degradation coming from such professionally run operation. He kept on theorizing about the source of this destruction. He had heard about the bunkering and puncturing of pipelines by vandals. Could it be that the degradation was caused by the activities of the vandals who most times came from the area? This did not add up, because no one would deliberately destroy his own home in a bid to make quick and dirty money. That was the only time that Ginika visited the jetty; he cleverly avoided by one excuse or the other any further opportunities to go there. This was a bid to save him from the embarrassment of revisiting the troubling sight.

— CHAPTER 11 —
The New World Called the Internet Age

Ginika completed his national service in 1999. The passing-out parade was held at the Port Harcourt township stadium with the serving state governor Peter Odili in attendance. Peter Odili was a well-known and generous governor, and as the saying went then "you cannot come into the presence of Peter Odili and go empty-handed." True to the saying, the over three thousand Corp members did not go empty-handed as the generous governor gave each of the passing-out Corp members an additional sum of two thousand naira. With the announcement of the donation, the Corp members all jumped up and shouted in jubilation and appreciation of the governor. Ginika was happy for the extra cash, which they all believed they would need given that the monthly stipend during the service year was over and no one was guaranteed immediate employment.

He remembered the day he'd visited the local government chairman's office to collect the bus stop project fund. He remembered the councillors who had left the office carrying nylon bags that most certainly had contained cash. And he wondered whether this was what governance was about—the person holding the common purse sharing it with whomsoever he or she desired. To Ginika, there were so many things to be done that could be achieved if all the money that had been shared were used more wisely. Still, he did not reject the small share he had been given. It appeared to him that leaders such as Peter Odili did not have many ideas and projects to support with the finances accruable to the state; hence, their legacy of sharing money. Did he not realize that these same people who were rejoicing and thanking him for donating millions and buses here and there, as the case was, were the same people who would castigate him for not doing anything during his time in office? Unfortunately, there was nothing Ginika could do but endeavour to collect his own part of the national cake according to Odili and move on.

After the passing out, it was time to move on to other things, especially a job search. Then it was scary to hear about the unemployment rate in the country. A lot of the NYSC members who had passed out from PPMC continued to go to the office in the hope that the management might give them contract jobs so they could be doing something until permanent jobs became available. Most times, the so-called permanent jobs never came, and these guys would continue to constitute a nuisance in the office to the annoyance of staff. Sometimes a few were lucky to secure contract jobs, and then the fear that went with such appointments would set in because the employment was based on the management in place at the time with every possibility that the contract would not be renewed once a person's benefactor left office. Ginika did not bother going back to PPMC. To him, the next phase was clear: get a job or go back to school.

Looking for a job meant visiting all the companies in town and dropping off his curriculum vitae. He also made sure he read the Tuesday edition of *The Guardian*, a newspaper edition that was dedicated to advertisements of job vacancies. However, going to town and reading the Tuesday edition of *The Guardian* required money. The alternative was to join the "free readers' club", a gathering of people at the vendors who had the sole aim of browsing through the newspaper headlines for free. With regard to the job adverts that were contained in the newspapers, applicants had to have the addresses of the companies so they could send their CVs. This meant it was better to buy the paper and take it home so they could send to as many as possible.

Ginika sent applications to the companies that had job openings for which he was qualified and also to those that had openings for which he was at the boundary of qualification. Sometimes he even applied for jobs for which he knew very well he was not qualified. He was hoping for a miracle. The Tuesday edition of *The Guardian* became the hottest newspaper in town, and every ex–Corp member who was searching for a job looked out for it. They tried to figure out the exact time the paper would be delivered in Port Harcourt, given that it was printed in Lagos.

The search continued even as some of the ex–Corp member friends of Ginika got weary of the delay in their ability to secure a job. The little cash most of them had saved was running out, and most decided to conserve by not buying their favourite paper; rather, they would look out for those who had bought it, perhaps family friends whose dads would normally buy it. They all kept their ears to the ground, and news of any interesting advert always spread like wildfire among them. With the passage of time, frustration started setting in as most of the job seekers resigned themselves to fate. Some blamed the system of nepotism and cronyism for their troubles at not securing a job. Ginika believed strongly that the newspaper adverts were genuine. He believed that companies were still interested in securing the services of intelligent graduates who would add value even though they might also have provisions for public relations for their stakeholders.

Meanwhile, some of Ginika's friends had already secured jobs after their service year. Most of them were those who had been promised retention by their employers before they left for their year of service. These Corp members were already sure of jobs even before finishing their youth service. One of those was Ihemba. He was one of the few lucky ones who had a choice. He had to choose between serving in an oil company, which was everybody's dream, and serving in a bank that had promised to retain him after his youth service. He chose the latter to the surprise of friends. His friends believed that the possibility of his being retained at the oil company was also there even though it was not as explicit as the banking offer. To Ihemba, a bird in the hand was worth more than a thousand in the bush; in fact, a bird in the hand was the only bird, as a lot of Ginika's friends would later find out. With the dynamics of the working environment and uncertainties in the economy, no one was sure of anything. With Ihemba securing a job, Ginika was sure not to go hungry at any time. He had a solid backup plan in the likes of Ihemba and a number of other classmates who had been lucky to secure jobs immediately after service. Some others who had rich parents flew out of the country to continue their studies at postgraduate levels in the United Kingdom and the United States. There were a few others who had not-so-rich parents but who had been able to secure scholarships for their postgraduate studies abroad. This reminded Ginika of the Shell scholarship he had narrowly missed, or which had been stolen from him, in fact. The loss of his "owners copy" essay during the second round of the Shell scholarship competition remained a wound in his heart that would not be healed. One of his friends who had secured a scholarship to study abroad was Ogbonna.

Ogbonna had always had a dream of going to practice medicine in the United States. Ogbonna went to University of Nigeria Nsuka and graduated with a degree in medicine, and he was lucky to secure a postgraduate scholarship. Interestingly, it was also a Shell scholarship given to non-oil-producing states that Ogbonna had won. He had gone through the same selection exercise that entailed essay writing. Ogbonna did not wait to do the compulsory NYSC since the scholarship could not be deferred and he was not sure of being that lucky the next year if he elected to enter the NYSC immediately. This happened the same year Ginika finished his national youth service NSYC.

With the tight working schedule and little time after work to fraternize, Ihemba helped Ginika to open an email account, a new service that was just penetrating the Nigerian society at that time. Not everyone knew about email, and the few who did know about it did not have any access because it required paying huge amounts of money for an hour's worth of service at the very few cyber cafes available. Ginika first read about email through the Jehovah's Witnesses weekly magazine called *Awake*. With little to do while waiting for two o'clock for the routine walk to the junction to buy the Tuesday edition of *The Guardian*, Ginika kept himself engaged with all the reading material in the house. He found *Awake* pretty useful and a good source of information on current trends. The illustrations used to describe the internet in the version of *Awake* he read described the internet as a fast-moving gateway of information. The picture depicted a tube-like form with rainbow colours and groups of people with books flying through the tube. The picture fascinated Ginika so much that he became highly interested in this new phenomenon.

For one to write an email, one required the email address of another person, and since most of Ginika's friends did not have email accounts then, the service was almost useless to him because there was no other person to write an email to except Ihemba. That notwithstanding, Ginika had to make the best out of it. He wrote Ihemba as often as he could, considering he had to pay for time and had to have patience to stand in the increasingly long queues at the few cyber cafés as the awareness continued to grow among the populace and job seekers. At one time, it became a hip thing as youths tended to show off their acquisition of email accounts. It was common to hear folks say to the other "*Iji email m*" (Do you have my email?) as if email was an object one could put in a pocket.

With time, the email bug caught up with everybody, and Ginika did not have the problem of whom to write an email to anymore. The revolution even helped him in his communication with his girlfriend, whom he had earlier met at PPMC. He had had very little communication with her after the service year due to the slow postal service. Communication with his girlfriend would evolve from hard copy letter writing to intermittent phone calls and finally to email. Their phone calls were especially interesting. This was before the advent of mobile telephones, and the only place Ginika's girlfriend could receive or make calls was at the NITEL office, the national phone company. So she would leave school and take an approximately ten-minute motor ride to the NITEL office, queue in the long line, and wait to talk to Ginika, who would be so excited at the other end that sometimes she could not even hear what he was saying except "love you, love you, "love you" as if those words were headed for extinction or he was scared someone else was saying the same thing to the girl and so he wanted to make sure he said it more than whoever that was. And the girl would respond "love you too" every time Ginika said it, reassuring the poor young man of her love and loyalty to him.

It was not only scouting for Tuesday's edition of *The Guardian* and writing to his girlfriend that kept Ginika going while searching for a job. He had other things on his mind, including ensuring he kept faith with his brethren at the church, partaking in the activities of the Believer's Loveworld, a branch of Christ Embassy Church he had been involved with at the orientation camp at Ndele. Being involved meant attending the numerous meetings held at different hotel locations and churches as well as helping out in the organization of the crusades that the church held in Port Harcourt. Ginika was impressed by the boldness of the leaders in taking on projects that would initially look so gigantic and not within reach of the group. But surprisingly, with careful planning, engagement, and prayers, the plans always manifested results to the admiration of Ginika. He felt he had come into contact with another set of powers as a human being. To Ginika, being born again meant he had powers to accomplish whatever his heart set out to do through the guidance and support of the Holy Spirit.

It was while he was with Believers Loveworld that Ginika got to know what it was like to have an all-night session of prayer. He would initially imagine how it was possible for someone to stay awake all night praying even though he had had experience with his friends staying awake all night clubbing during his university school days at the Dreams night clubs at Rumuola, a location in the Port Harcourt city centre. The all-night prayers became a new frontier for Ginika.

The session would usually start with meetings, then songs, prayers, and more songs. Ginika would not want the meeting to end; he dreaded the rising of the sun in the morning as they enjoyed the sweet presence of the Holy spirit as He ministered to them one after the other and as their leader spoke the living word, encouraging and firing up their spirits to the things of God.

The church meetings were not all about prayers. They had fun engaging in other activities that helped their careers afterwards. One such activity was the development of printed fliers to publicize any of their programs. The team would gather in an apartment and work on PowerPoint presentations that could be printed. Everyone would contribute to the design or the development of catchy phrases to go in the fliers. Ginika, for one, had a flair for developing catchy phrases to the admiration of Nnachi, the very tall and lanky member of the team. This Nnachi always reminded Ginika of the Nnachi he knew in his primary school days, the protector of the Universe as they termed him, since his size meant protection from adversaries for his group of friends then. This latest Nnachi always asked Ginika how he came up with those phrases. Ginika would say, "They were given"! "By whom?" Nnachi would ask. Ginika would never divulge the source as he smiled each time the conversation repeated itself as it always did.

Ginika, as always, right from primary school, liked the presence of the beautiful ladies who were part of the Loveworld ministry. Working with the pretty ladies instilled discipline in him knowing that he could work with pretty women in close proximity and enjoy the communion as they were his sisters without thoughts of going to bed or having an affair with them. To Ginika, this was a whole new experience, and he cherished and enjoyed it so much that he prayed it would remain the same forever. It was even more fun having the senior pastor of the main church come around in the youth meetings to encourage the team, advising them on areas as were requested of him, and making sure they carried on in the vision of the church, encouraging the good upbringing of the youth.

It was in Loveworld that Ginika would learn to give substantially from his meagre resources. Prior to getting involved, Ginika would always strive with great effort to put into any offering basket the least and possibly dirtiest denomination in his pocket. It was a struggle as he wondered what the reverend father or pastor would do with the money since, to him, they were already very rich and did not need his additional contribution. That was one of the things that interested him about religion. First it was the Catholic Church, which would bar anybody who was not in a state of grace from receiving Holy Communion while encouraging everybody, even those not in grace, to contribute in the collection. This made Ginika worry. Why did the church not discriminate when it came to offertory and work time, but "chopping" (eating) and enjoyment time was only for those in a state of grace? If the Lord did not want the sinners eating His body, would He want them giving Him money? Ginika would always refuse to give during the second collection since those who gave during the first collection were denied access to the body of Christ. He recalled one church service he attended in the village where the reverend father advised the congregants to be generous to reverend fathers and even reverend sisters. The father narrated a story of how he offered a lift to a young man, and when he dropped the man off, the young man begged him for money. The father said that what made him angry was that the young man noted that reverend fathers do not have any needs since they were fully taken care of by the church. That was the reason the man "demanded" something from the reverend father in addition to the lift he just had given him. The angry father simply told him to quickly get down from his car *osiso* (quickly). He highlighted the incident so the people in the church would understand that reverend fathers were not people without need; rather, most of them were dying in penury and want.

For the Pentecostal churches, the new wave in town, the issue for Ginika remained the one about tithing and the apparent blackmail of worshippers to force them to give. At one point, special prayers were offered for those who came to church with their tithes separately to the chagrin of Ginika's spirit. Not only was tithing preached, but those who did not tithe were likened to thieves. This instilled fear and anxiety in the minds of worshippers who quickly went out in their numbers to give their tithe lest something bad befall them. And as if the tithing was not enough, the church went further to preach about first fruits, encouraging all to give their first month's salary in the year as first fruit with no mention of how these families were to pay school fees and other expenses that came due in January. And, of course, so many worshippers fell for the preaching and gave all they had and went cap in hand begging afterwards. The question remained as to the origin of the ceremonies and the relevance in the present day. But all the same, Ginika would find peace in attending to his church obligations and studying the word for himself and making sure he kept his eyes on the ball and was not swayed by the preachings of anyone who may not be aligned to reality. He would always remember the advice of Uncle Chuky: "*Nwa okuko na akpa nni, anya ufie akokwanaya.*" (A hen will always use the corner of its eyes to check out its surroundings for threats as it feeds.)

After months of searching and applying for jobs every Tuesday, Ginika started getting letters of invitation for interviews. At some point, he had to get brown or white stamped envelopes and template application letters ready. The only missing item would normally be the address of the company, which would come by noon every Tuesday. Getting a letter of invitation was a positive step that gave Ginika a foot in the door. It was then left to him to prove himself to whatever panel he was to meet, or if there was a written part of the interview, an opportunity to reaffirm his performance in school. At this time, it was interesting that most often, he and his friends applied for positions they knew they were not qualified to fill. That did not deter them as they also observed that most companies were also calling for candidates who had not studied a course directly related to their particular industry. The banking industry was at the forefront of this. They called for applications from almost all graduates. This kept Ginika and his friends wondering whether it was banking they were going to do or some form of engineering. In fact, the engineers were in the highest demand because they could easily solve the mathematics components of the written part of the interviews.

Ginika was fortunate to have made a second-class upper division from the university, a result that guaranteed he got invited to most aptitude interview tests for jobs for which he was qualified. Normally the engineers and most graduates who had finished their national youth service or those who were about to finish were reluctant to apply to industries that did not involve their primary university disciplines. The engineering folks initially restricted applications to industrial-related firms and banking and finance, and accounts graduates limited theirs to the banks and other financial institutions. With few new opportunities, and given that most of the establishments retrained the new hires, everyone realized it did not matter what one had studied anymore at the graduate level. With this leverage, the engineers started applying to the banks to the envy of the graduates of accounting and other more relevant subjects to the banking industry. Unfortunately, there was no guiding government or industry policy, and all it took was for the new hires to undergo make-up courses and probably go for higher degrees in their new chosen career paths. The very smart ones did this, enrolling in any available course that would bring them to a par with their colleagues who had studied the relevant subjects at the undergraduate level. This resulted in the increase in the intake of engineers into master of business administration (MBA) courses. Some others were, however, reluctant to retool and move on in the new profession. This was because of the passion and emotional attachment they had to their university courses of study. Some made a little money from the banks and resigned to pursue their personal dream of working in the industry they had studied for in school. The reality was that the Nigerian graduate, like any other graduate around the world, was basically a fresher who was just suited for no particular industry immediately after university graduation. Unfortunately, with the lower quality of education, and no hands-on experience during the years of study, most professionals rightly believed that the Nigerian graduates, even though intelligent, were not employable and could not compete with their peers in other parts of the world. Hence, there arose the need to retrain and certify them when they got hired in the industry. Even the industrial training fund set up by the government to help bridge the gap did not help matters as there were no guarantees that students would get a place in the industry to undergo industrial attachments. With the large number of students enrolling in the universities, there was no way the limited amount of industry could absorb them even if they were not expected to pay them any stipend. At one point, even getting a placement for an industrial training position required the traditional "*ima mmadu*" (who do you know) or as Ginika's professor in the university would say "*ima mmadu maruo ya ulo*" (not just who do you know, but who do you know personally to the extent of family ties). The likes of Ginika had been lucky to have gotten places to undergo the training relying not just on their own contacts but also on the contacts of friends who had wealthy and connected parents.

The interview that landed a job for Ginika took place all the way in Benin, Edo State, and was conducted by consultants for a new generation bank, which was the dream of every young graduate aspiring to work in a bank. The old generation ones were seen as banks for civil servants and old people, and no new graduates bothered applying to them until things started getting so tough that a lot of them understood that the Nigerian saying "half bread is better than *chinchin*" had been coined for a purpose.

Though Ginika's uncle lived in Benin, he had never visited the city and only claimed to have transited the city on the way to Lagos. But at times like these, it was easy to figure out who lived where and what help was available. Fortunately, a classmate had a guesthouse in Benin. He was available during the period, to the excitement of Ginika, as he knew it would be a sort of reunion after the first year out of school without seeing most of his classmates because they had scattered all over the world. He was not sure he would ever meet them again in life, just as he probably would not meet those he left behind in primary and secondary schools. Sometimes he would wonder what happened to all those people who had come into his life in school. There were times people ran into each other, and few still stayed connected by the weeks-long mail delivery systems or the recently developed email, which used the internet. It was interesting that, once the phase in life was completed, the old friends could virtually be assumed dead since there was no guarantee of meeting again. This was most true with regard to primary school and secondary schoolmates except for the mates who lived in the same area of town such as Aladinma or the federal housing estate for Ginika. For some others it was Gbodija in Ibadan. For yet some others it was the GRA in Umuahia or Enugu. A song that reminded Ginika of the phenomenon was a song they sang at Government College at the close of every school term. It started with the opening line "God be with you till we meet again". Meeting again back then would take place in three weeks after a normal vacation or two months in the case of the long vacation periods. Later in life, that song would be used at funeral services. "Meeting again" would take on a new meaning to Ginika as he reminisced on the life of his youth.

The Nigerian Postal Service (Nipost) was everybody's friend, delivering the good messages that lighted people's hearts as they read messages from loved ones and friends from distant places including abroad. Writing letters remained very popular even with the advent of email, and job applicants continued to rely on the system. It took a maximum of two weeks for their applications to reach the designated offices. Using Nipost for these applications could be risky because applicants could not be sure their applications would get there in time. That was why Ginika and his friends had stamped envelopes handy so that they could respond to any advert in the Tuesday edition of *The Guardian* that same day so that the chances of the application getting to its destination in the stipulated two weeks would be high.

Linking up with Fadi brought back nice memories for Ginika over a year after graduation. It was an excited Ginika who jumped up at the sight of Fadi as he came to pick him up at the park. Shouts of "Nna men! Nna men!" rent the air to the surprise of other occupants of the bus that travelled all the way from Port Harcourt. "Old boy, you done add weight, oh," Ginika told Fadi as he checked him out, wondering how he managed to be doing so well in Benin, a city they termed not to be as wealthy as Port Harcourt. "Leave that matter," was all Fadi said to Ginika as he smiled in excitement at the sight of his classmate. It was a Sunday afternoon, and they both went straight to Fadi's house in his car. Ginika admired the progress his very own classmate had made in such a little time after school.

They talked at length about which of their classmates they both had seen since leaving school. Who had secured a job and who had not? Which of the girls had gotten married and which were still on the market? To Nigerians then, once a lady was out of school, the next thing on the agenda was marriage. It was worse for Ginika's state of Anambra with the less educated males running a race to outdo others by making sure they married educated ladies whom they sometimes would not let do anything but make babies at home. Even the ones who were magnanimous enough to let their wives come to their business shops would make sure they kept eyes on them lest they be enticed by other men.

After the friends chatted and had lunch, Ginika took his shower and rested well that evening while he also took out time to revise some of the aptitude test sample question papers he had with him. Fadi dropped him off at the venue of the interview the next morning. Fadi was surprised at the number of people gathered at the venue for the interview. No one knew the number of people the bank was looking for, but whatever that number, the crowd Fadi saw frightened him, and he worried about his friend's chances of securing this job he had been so enthusiastic about. Fadi had been managing his family's pineapple farm in Akwa Ibom with regular visits to Benin where the family kept a home. He happened to be one of the few of Ginika's classmates who did not have to go through the rigors of looking for a job, opting to thread the family line even though he spent six years reading engineering. This was supposed to take five years but had to be extended because of incessant lecturers strikes. Fadi brought his engineering knowledge to bear in the development of the family farm, deploying his skills in making sure the farm machinery worked at optimal capacity while making sure the other infrastructure such as water distribution and waste disposal systems were carried out professionally including an attempt to extract bio gas from the droppings of livestock, which he also introduced in the farm.

Ginika was not frightened by the large crowd he saw at the venue since it had turned out to be the routine. Some candidates where known to turn up at every interview location whether invited or not, and sometimes this constituted problems for the consultants handling the interview sessions. After a couple of hours, it was time for the consultants to start the initial screening for the candidates who would sit the written examination. It was an excited and smiling Ginika who majestically walked into the hall as shouts of "You made it!" rent the air. They shouted same slogan for everyone who got called as they started making jokes about the ones left behind after the doors were closed, referring to them as "gate crashers".

The next thing after the last person on the list was called was a return shout from the inside the examination hall: "Gate crashers go home!" This referred to everyone who had not made the list of those invited into the hall and even some who had issues with the sorting out of their interview invitation letters. Unfortunately, some who had genuine invitation letters did not find their names on the list for interviews with the consultants, but there was nothing that could be done for them, and they had to go home even after travelling from very far distances to honour the invitation with no form of compensation. This infuriated some of them to the extent that they called the consultants unprintable names. Some of the candidates who made it into the hall felt pity for them, having made friends already in the short time they all sat around and waited for the consultants, exchanging experiences and strategies for improving their chances at getting a job.

After two solid hours of sweating it out in the examination hall, the stipulated time was up. One Collins who sat beside Ginika was bitter that Ginika had not responded to him when he asked him a question as if they were still in secondary school or university.

Ginika was surprised at the whispering sound coming from his side as the examination was going on. He turned around only to find this guy gesticulating at him for an answer to a question. In anger as to the reason a full-grown man would come to a job interview to ask questions, Ginika simply turned his head and did not look in the guy's direction again as the guy continued to whisper from one person to the other to the annoyance of everyone around. When they came out of the hall, Collins went to a crowd and asked no one in particular what the answers were to some questions as if it still mattered. They didn't have to wait as long as anticipated for results, and some people had even strolled out to find something to eat thinking it would take forever for the consultants to come back with the list of those who were now eligible for the oral part of the interview. Once the consultants started calling the list of those who made it to the oral interview stage, Ginika continued making jokes about how he was one of those who made it. He had earlier predicted to anyone who cared to listen that he was going to make it to the oral stage whether anyone liked it or not. He said this to the admiration and laughter of other candidates. Some of them shouted *"Okwu Nkasi obi"* (words of encouragement) to the jokes Ginika made as they tried to relax their minds and relieve the anxiety that accompany such occasions. Even as Ginika was making the jokes, he was aware of what awaited him if his joke did not materialize given that he had been marked as talkative even though others were smiling at his jokes as they tried to comport themselves seriously. Some others concocted a rumour that Ginika may have had some connections that would ensure he made it to the next round. That assurance could easily have caused him to display such a "big-mouth" attitude.

As soon as his name was called, to the surprise, admiration, and joy of everyone around, it was an elated and proud Ginika who shouted *"Omele eme, omele eme?"* (Did it happen? It did happen!) and *"Agwaram gi agwa? Agwaram gi agwa!"* (Did I tell you? I did tell you!). Some of the guys around him as he walked past touched his head and some others tapped his shirt in the belief that his luck would be bestowed on them. At the end, only about twenty of them made it to the oral interview, and the rest were dismissed and encouraged to seek opportunities elsewhere. That Ginika made it to the next round also confirmed the suspicion of some conspiracy theorists that Ginika was connected and already had things fixed for him.

The interview panel consisted of a young lady who wore a very short skirt with red underwear that directly stared in Ginika's face as he attempted to bend and take his seat in front of the panel. That distracted the young Ginika and almost cost him the job interview as he kept thinking about the role of the lady in such a setting. He had heard that ladies were mainly employed by the banks to go into marketing, targeting the wealthy in the society, using any available means for success including seduction. He never knew that the same seduction could also happen even during interview sessions. With his initial thoughts out of the way and having regained full composure, he faced the panel, answering all their questions including why he had chosen to pursue a career in banking when he had studied engineering at university. His discipline gave him the possibility of employment in the engineering industry including the lucrative oil and gas industry, a position every engineer longed for. When he was answering the panel's question, Ginika pointed out that the basic bachelor's degree education obtained from the Nigerian university mainly prepares a candidate for a career role in any field of choice, not necessarily the very discipline read in undergraduate school. He pointed out that, in some advanced countries, students could not even be admitted into some programs such as medicine or law without first undergoing some basic undergraduate programs. It was an impressed panel, one of whom asked what had kept him from getting a job prior to that moment given what they had seen of him at the session. A humorous Ginika smiled and said, "*Ima mmadu* has been the problem." The panellist just smiled back at him and promised him that, this time, he did not need to know anybody as they must ensure that the best candidate got the job irrespective of whether he or she had connections. Ginika thanked the panel and walked out of the room feeling very strong about the possibility of landing the job having impressed them to the best of his ability.

Exactly three weeks after the interview, Ginika got a letter informing him of his appointment. They required him to report at the Lagos headquarters branch of the bank for medicals. Ginika's excitement was so overwhelming that he burst out in tears in appreciation of God's blessings since it marked the end of his job search and waiting every Tuesday for *The Guardian*! He quickly went to Nitel in town to call Fadi and inform him that he had been successful in the interview, and he thanked his friend for his hospitality, encouragement, and wishes of good luck.

Even though Ginika had been confident he would land a job, he had been, nevertheless, apprehensive due to the fact that there were so many graduates roaming the streets who had even better qualifications. The universities turned out thousands of graduates every year, but there was no commensurate development of industry to absorb them. In fact, the few existing industries were closing shop due to the decay in infrastructure, especially power, which led to a high cost of doing business. Ginika wondered what was wrong with the black man. How come things like power eluded the country when every secondary school student who studied physics knew about the principles of dynamo and the generation of electricity from it? Even bicycles driven all over the place including the villages had small dynamos that generated light in the night. So why could a big country like Nigeria, with all its engineers and professors, not generate enough power for the country? Neither could he understand the inability of the country to refine enough petroleum products for its use rather relying on the importation of the products when every secondary school student who studied organic chemistry knew about hydrocarbons and the refining principles. Even the Biafrans refined enough products to sustain themselves during the country's inter-ethnic war. There were just too many things wrong with the country, and the politicians seemed to be the architects of the issues with their greed and lust for material things.

With the way things went, all Nigerians were left on their own with the responsibility to generate their own power through the use of generators that produced carbon monoxide fumes that killed Nigerians slowly. Water was obtained via boreholes, and there were no quality control considerations. Roads were left in un-motorable condition since the average individual citizen could not afford to invest in a road anyway. On some occasions, the government intervened to improve the quality of the roads, but usually only if there was a "big" man in the neighbourhood who could attract the government legacy. There was no marshal plan to ensure all the neighbourhood roads in residential areas were tarred.

Ginika soon heard a story that further emphasized his own gratitude for getting this job. His cousin, who was also searching for a job, approached a friend of her father. She thought his relationship with her father would guarantee his willingness to assist the poor girl in getting a job with one of the companies around, but she was in for a rude shock when the uncle asked the girl if she was available so they could go to a hotel and have some "quality time". The girl did not know what to make of that and was really embarrassed at the request coming from someone she had held in very high esteem. How could she stoop so low to have sex with a man as old as her father? Also, she knew his wife! She was so irritated, but she had to continue to see the guy. She gave all sorts of excuses as to why she did not need any "quality time" with him until she realized he was not ready to help unless she went with him. She discontinued her plea for assistance.

Women had always had terrible experiences when looking for jobs because so many men were ready to take advantage of the vulnerable girls. In some instances, even when the women got the jobs, their bosses made work unpleasant for them as they insisted on dates and disrespected the ladies when they turned them down. The situation was worse for companies that had not established any ethics and compliance policies, leaving the young women at the mercy of the rampaging men. Sex for marks in the university and now sex for jobs in the bigger world—who would bail the Nigerian girls? This was all Ginika could think of as he feared for his own sister and female cousins who would eventually confront this same world.

With all the troubles involved in getting and sustaining a job in the country, the excitement exhibited by Ginika was not surprising. He made immediate arrangements to travel to Lagos for his medicals.

Ginika arrived Lagos late on a Sunday evening after a luxurious bus ride of over eight hours from Port Harcourt. He had taken a *"Young Shall Grow"* bus. This was a company owned by an Igbo man from Anambra State. The joke then was that, if one was going to start a new life in Lagos, it would be better to take a luxury *"Young Shall Grow"* bus. On his way back to the eastern part of the country, he might take another bus depending on the outcome of his sojourn in Lagos. *"Ekene dili Chukwu"* (Thanks be to God) would be used by those who survived on their sojourn while *"Oso ndu"* (run for life) would be used by those who met with unfavourable situations in Lagos. The Igbo businessmen were fond of giving their businesses names that connoted ideas they could relate to; hence, the interesting names of the transport companies.

Ginika's brother Emeka was right there at the Mazamaza bus stop to pick him up and take him to his two-bedroom apartment in a block of about twenty flats in the popular Festac Town federal housing estate. Festac Town was developed in the late seventies as accommodation for athletes who participated in the festival of arts ceremony hosted by Nigeria in 1977 during the oil boom. Then, Nigeria was so rich that General Gowon, the head of state, was quoted as saying that Nigeria had so much money it did not know what to do with it. Unfortunately, this was not the case in the year 2000 when Ginika stepped foot in Lagos to start his career as a banker in the bustling city of Lagos. This opportunity was the dream of every Nigerian graduate. Visiting his friend's apartment reminded him of his visit to Benin on the eve of his job interview. He remembered how Fadi had treated him so specially. It was surprising that he was intimidated by the crowd of people at the bus stop late that night, since he already had knowledge of Lagos and what to expect, having visited a number of times while he was at university.

CHAPTER 12

Welcome to Lagos

Emeka dropped Ginika at the Mazamaza bus stop at six o'clock the following morning so he could catch a bus to Marina at the Lagos Island head office location of his new employer. Ginika kept waiting for a bus that would stop completely in front of him to allow him enter like a gentleman he termed himself to be without success. He could not imagine himself rushing and jumping into a moving bus after putting on his most expensive suit and clean shoes to match the image of the new banker he was. Not until he spent about thirty minutes at the bus stop watching other suit-wearing Lagos gentlemen from the same Festac area jump into the moving buses did he realize he was then in Rome and needed to behave like the Romans. Without wasting more time, he jumped into a *molue* as it passed through the Festac first gate that still had some empty seats. A molue was a rickety bus made from a big Mercedes Benz 911 truck. By the time the bus got to the next bus stop called Mile 2 it was so full with passengers that some were hanging out of the door to the amazement of the new young banker. Looking out the window of the bus without any glass, Ginika reminisced on the scene of the giant statue of three standing men with their fists knocked on each other, which he had seen on the entrance to Lagos. The slogan on the statue read "Welcome to Lagos".

He smiled quietly at the madness of a town known as the commercial nerve centre of Nigeria.

It was a mixed bag for Ginika working in Lagos. Transportation was one of the miseries he faced in the first few months before he bought his *tokunbo* (used car), which helped increase the frustration of every other Lagosian who did not have one and had to rely on the rickety yellow buses. Having gone successfully through the medicals and officially received his appointment, Ginika started work at the Marina head office. His first assignment was to work as a cashier attending to customers in the banking hall. Banking was fun for him as he interacted with his colleagues in a cordial and respectful way. A lot of them admired his gentleness and carriage even in the face of difficult times such as when his accounts would not balance, which led to deductions from his salary to make up for the loss. Losses occurred once in a while but not often, and the culprits who caused them were found on some rare occasions while it was also suspected that some missing funds were stolen by colleagues who pretended to be helping out during some pressure periods to the bewilderment of others when the news filtered around. There was nothing like closed-circuit cameras at the time to help with monitoring what was going on at the cashier cubicles.

At the time Ginika joined the bank, banking in Nigeria was on the fast lane. So much competition among the different banks led sometimes to falsification of records to make a bank's year-end results look excellent to the investing public. Banks borrowed from each other to shore up their balance sheets so they could quote huge returns to their shareholders. They traded on foreign exchange, most times round tripping the foreign currencies they bought from the central bank at lower official rates. They sent out women wearing miniskirts to woo men and encourage them to make deposits at the bank. When they were successful, the women were given promotions. The men employees sometimes engaged in same-sex relationships to acquire patronage for the banks. It was filth to the highest degree and an open secret nobody dared talk about. A case in point was that of Ada, a tall black lady who had joined the bank two years before Ginika. Ginika was shocked to learn that she had been confirmed as branch senior supervisor just after two years. His colleagues made fun of him and were surprised at his naiveté. Ada had been recruited, having been recommended by one of the bank's directors, and she was given preferential treatment in everything and a good appraisal by her branch manager, who was also looking for ways to please the director to advance his own career.

The majority of the young bankers were single, and they got together over most weekends after the early Saturday banking hours and had fun talking and gossiping about their bosses and clients. But Ada would never be found among them. Few of the colleagues had the guts to go beyond admiring Ada to venture into toasting her and getting themselves burnt. They would either be quickly transferred if such gossip made the rounds, or in the worst-case scenario, they would receive a very low appraisal and would be sacked at the end of the business year.

Ginika knew where he came from, and he knew the expectations from home and especially from Urem, his girlfriend, whom he had earlier met at PPMC. He knew better than to venture into Ada's realm and kept to himself. However, his friends and colleagues termed him a *mugu* because he shied away from the advances of the so-called powerful Ada. Not knowing the intentions of the friends, Ginika continued to keep to himself. How could these guys, having seen what had become of every dude who made a move towards Ada, encourage him to be next in line of fire? He kept brooding on this and questioned the loyalty of his so-called friends. A thought came to him: maybe, in fact, they were plotting his downfall because they had seen how successful he had become in just a short time since joining the bank. Because of his outstanding performance, management had gone beyond the norm to confirm his employment at six months. Not only was Ginika good, he had passion for his job.

As an engineering student at university, he had developed skills in computer programming as part of his efforts to solve the many numerical questions he and his fellow students came across. It had started when Ogadimma had given him a computer he had been given as gift during one of the courses he attended in Montreal, Canada, which had been sponsored by his office, the Federal Ministry of Works. During the conference, a white guy called Kevin had lectured them on the use of computers in engineering design. This had got Ogadimma engrossed in the wonders of the computer. Not knowledgeable, but with great passion to learn, it was a humbled Ogadimma who accosted Kevin after the class to engage in more interaction on the use of the computer. Admiring the passion exhibited by Ogadimma, Kevin extended an invitation to Ogadimma to his home for dinner. Afterwards, Kevin offered him his old computer as a gift. Ogadimma was delighted and promised to make very good use of the tool to provide better engineering design for the development of his home country when he got home. The lecturer was amazed and happy at Ogadimma's choice of words and aspiration but wondered what an analogue computer could do for Ogadimma or his country. He wondered how Ogadimma could place the hope of a better country on a small machine with very limited memory capacity.

By the time Ogadimma came back from the overseas course he had forgotten even how to start the computer, having spent the remaining part of the course period shopping in Canada and enjoying himself with the estacode that came along with such foreign trips. It was a frustrated Ogadimma who abandoned the computer, thereby dashing the "hope" of the Nigerian state on the use of the new tool to develop engineering design in the country. Ginika was lucky that his dad's busy schedule at the time and the frustration over the unavailability of a proper tutor persuaded him to give the old computer to him. Ginika was a delighted young engineer. Only the old Fortran programming language was installed on the computer, but that was good enough for Ginika. He began to practice coding and developed a feel and liking for the skill.

Ginika brought his computing skills to bear in his banking job, developing algorithms that enhanced the efficiency of his branch services. His work was subsequently adopted in all the branches of the bank across the nation, to the admiration of the management of the bank. To Ginika, being a banker meant retooling his engineering background and creating from it a new passion for his new career, and he was ready to give it his best shot.

But behind Ginika's passion and dedication to duty, trouble lurked. Word had it along the corridors that Ada was dying for Ginika! What had begun as a joke started to take a life of its own. Ada became frustrated when Ginika intentionally avoided her and pretended not to take notice of her. She moved the advances a notch higher by making attempt to ensure their paths crossed. Being the head of marketing at the branch at the time, she would insist Ginika accompany her to meet the branch clients. She would delay such appointments sometimes till very late, using the excuse that the big-ticket clients preferred meeting in the cool of the evening. But her intention was always to find ways of being around Ginika after office hours. During such visits, she wore miniskirts that almost showed her panties; this reminded Ginika of the lady at his job interview in Benin. She would sit facing Ginika in the back of the chauffeur-driven car as they travelled to the client's house or to a party as the case may be. In some funny instances, the clients would get the wrong message thinking her choice of dress was for him, and the client would end up flirting with Ada. She would wonder why Ginika was pretending to be a saint despite her advances. At a point she got so angry at Ginika's behaviour and even developed a complex, wondering if there was something wrong with her that made her not good enough to charm Ginika.

On one desperate weekend, Ada gave a weird excuse that they had to go to a marketing meeting in her private car instead of using the official car. She diverted to her house on their way back in the late evening to the hidden delight of Ginika. Ada had initiated some flirting conversations, but Ginika was calm, kept a straight face, and only responded absentmindedly. He thought that they were still at work. When they got into the house, Ginika grabbed her once they were behind the door. He kissed her and caressed her before unzipping her skirt slowly as his tongue was locked to her lips. He put his hands behind her back and drew her panties down with a stroke of his hands. He pinned her back against the wall with one hand and smoothly took off his trousers and boxers with the other hand. His penis was already as hard as Olumo Rock, an outcrop in western Nigeria. He moved quickly like a thirsty lion, sticking his penis into her as she screamed and called out his name in such a loving and passionate way. Ginika kept thrusting in and out of her wet pussy. When they were exhausted, they both lay on the carpet naked. They kissed intermittently for several minutes before getting up to clean up. Ada prepared dinner afterwards. Ginika's eyes and smiles expressed joy as he caressed Ada, holding her passionately and then following her all around the kitchen as she prepared their love meal. Ginika's colleagues would not have believed their eyes if they had seen both of them right then. To their eyes, Ginika had always acted like a saint, a gentleman. He had never seemed to care much about Ada, but now he was running around like a kid whose parents had just bought him candy.

Ginika was the world's best pretender, to the admiration and surprise of Ada. For some reason, Ada had known that Ginika liked her, but she had not been perfectly sure what went on in his mind, even on that fateful evening when she made the bold move to take him to her house. "So why have you been pretending that you didn't give a damn about me all along?" she questioned Ginika as he made his way to the fridge to grab a bottle of Coke. Ginika answered that he was sure Ada wanted the best for him, and that best would not be the loss of his job a couple of months after joining the bank. "How do you mean?" Ada asked. He answered, "Are you saying you have not noticed what fate was suffered by all those who have made any attempts at hanging out with you in the bank? Chyke, Edu, and Nkem all got thrown out under questionable circumstances, and the only tenable explanation and common denominator was that they were seen hanging around you." Ginika mentioned that he was even scared of Ada at that moment because he could be the next guy on the line. But he believed that God would forbid such a bad thing. Ginika then demanded that Ada must act as if nothing had ever happened if she truly wanted him as much as he wanted her. Ginika said this in a soft lovely tone, grabbing her again at the waist as he kissed her softly while dropping the glass of Coke in his right hand on the table behind him. "We can make things work out, but it has to be at the right time. For now, you have the answer you want—I love you," Ginika said as he promised to do anything to be with her. Ginika continued in even a lower tone, "But in saying that, baby, I have to be careful to protect myself. As my uncle would say, *"Okuko na akpa ni anya ufie akokwa na ya."* We need to use our heads so we won't risk losing our jobs. Your job might be secure because your boss would not harm you, but would protect you," he said. Ginika reminded her that he could be thrown out at any time if word filtered down to the director that he was hanging out with his "love bird" just like the other guys before him. At the back of Ginika's mind was also the fact that both of them could not even go far in the bank because colleagues were not allowed to marry each other. This was one of the rules meant to protect the bank against fraud. Hence, if they were to have any future of any kind, one of them would have to leave the bank.

In all of this, Ginika was still wondering about his feelings for Urem. Having come so far with Urem, he felt a betrayal would not appeal to his God, but all the same, he had to keep his options open because people never know what life's plans are. After all, he could not vouch for Urem, who might also have been dating someone else while pretending to be a saint in just the same way he had when he pretended he had no clue Ada was after him.

Ginika took a taxi to the office on Saturday morning to pick up his car because he had declined Ada's offer to drive him back to the office. He would have none of that as he did not want the gossip to start that soon. How would he explain leaving with Ada the previous evening on a marketing appointment with a high-profile client only to come back the next morning with the same Ada? It was obvious their colleagues would not be around that early for the Saturday morning banking, but the rumour mill was even more active among the gatemen, drivers, and cleaners than it was even among his banker colleagues. To the shouts of "Morning, sir. Morning, sir." Ginika waved his hands in greeting as he walked straight into the office without the usual protocol. Coming from a humble background, he realized the need to fraternize with everyone including the low cadre of workers. They always looked after him in anticipation of a handout. It was amazing to everyone how Ginika was loved by most people in the office. To the professionals, it was obvious that his intelligence and excellent performance at work earned him the rapid job appointment confirmation and good yearly appraisals, but what baffled many was the equally attractive connection he had with the tea ladies, cleaners, and gatemen. A jolly good fellow, Ginika would have a handout for everyone in the office as he drove through the busy Lagos traffic to work or as he walked back to the office from lunch at a restaurant known as First Bank down on Marina Road. First Bank had become the place of choice when it came to having a good meal for lunch. It was known as First Bank because the *buka* (local restaurant) was situated directly opposite the national headquarters of First Bank, Nigeria's premier commercial bank.

Prior to discovering First Bank, eating had not been a problem for Ginika as he could make do with rice in any restaurant in Lagos. As he would tell anyone who cared to listen, he could not choose any other food such as yams or beans in the presence of rice, which was a delicacy easily prepared by most Nigerian corporate restaurants and side bukas. Rice was it for him. On one free weekend he did not go to work, and Ada was not available, he spent time meditating and wrote something about rice in an email, which he sent to Ada. Interestingly, he sent the same email to Urem, but with a different ending depicting them living together as husband and wife. This duplication of actions had been his practice as he tried to balance his emotions and feelings between the two women who had come to define his existence, with one ever present and the other virtual, which required more effort to keep the channels of communication open.

His letter to Ada read thus:

I ate rice this afternoon at a restaurant, and it was nothing to write home about. I am complaining because I take my rice very seriously not just because I know the pain and suffering that goes into its production but because it has come to be my choice in the ever-increasing variety of food in restaurants. For me it is always difficult to choose another food in the presence of rice, and Sunday is another blessed day that must not go without my afternoon being anointed with a plate of rice. I can count the times that I have missed out on that tradition, and for the particular ones that had to do with my being at a friend's family's house where people do not honour that tradition, it would normally mark the end of such visits. I was mad at the rice this afternoon because it disappointed me even after I noticed the crispy appearance that suggested it was my type. And for a good measure, I combined the *jollof* rice with fried just not to miss out, but to my surprise both were tasteless. For God's sake, what is there in the preparation of a good meal of rice, be it jollof, coconut, fried, *ofada*, Chinese, Japanese, or whatever. I was particularly interested in the jollof because it is my favourite. With a good measure of crayfish and *mmiri anu* (stuck), you are sure to come up with something nice. So was it that the restaurant did not have good cooks or that they have not gotten feedback on their product, or that the cost of crayfish is so high that they cannot afford it? I hear a paint bucket now costs so much, so cost may be one of the reasons, but if they think of the economics, they should know that retaining customers means spending the extra that is required to ensure they return, not dishing out tasteless meals in the hope that the people who have no choice will keep them in business.

There are days I really long for jollof rice, sometimes for those specific ones they serve at weddings or other ceremonies. Maybe someday I will open up jollof rice restaurant where people can come and have a good taste of jollof rice and be sure to come back. One such restaurant was called Unini back in my university days. The restaurant spared nothing in making sure their rice came out tops with enough crayfish that sometimes you would see them swimming in the dish, not just making it smell good like poor Zebrudaya of the *New Masquerade* TV series in the early eighties because he wanted to cut down on the cost of domestic allowance. On one of such occasion when Ovularia, the wife, insisted that the meagre money he brought home meant that crayfish would not appear in the soup, Zeebee, as Zebrudaya was fondly called by his wife, insisted he did not want to see the crayfish but only to taste it.

And talking about sprinkling crayfish in the rice, I also have experimented with sprinkling ground coconut chaff in the coconut rice, and it came out tops. The tradition has been to grind the coconut and squeeze the coconut oil from it and then use it in the preparation of the rice, but if you dare to step further and add some of that chaff that is normally thrown away into the rice, you enjoy a sensation similar to that you enjoy with a crunchy snack. Coconut rice can be fun, and you can also include lots of crayfish and dry fish as well depending on the depth of your pocket.

I have not been a fan of fried rice, maybe because I do not know how to prepare it, but Chinese rice has always come to the rescue for me. I remember one Chinese rice I ate somewhere around Victoria Island that made me love Chinese and always want to go back. There was enough *orishirishi* on the plate, from prawns to fried egg to so many other sea foods. The truth is that "*Ofe di uto owu ego gburu ya*" (better soup na money kill am!"). But that is not always the truth; a lot of people may have all the money but may not know how to combine the required necessary ingredients to make a good pot of rice.

And if you want the traditional stew, whether tomato red, groundnut brown, or my lovely *Ofe Akwu*, you can go for it as they are all part of the package that comes with that wonderful short-or long-grain rice that gets my Sunday started. You have to be careful with me when it comes to Ofe Akwu because, if you don't get it right, it becomes *oto naka nne ya* (rejected in Mama's hand! (God help my interpretation!) But again, Ofe Akwu needs a lot of crayfish and dried fish with vegetables but can be tailored to suit the pocket of whoever is making it. Goat meat also brings out the best in Ofe Akwu, and I love it steaming hot just as those vendors open their coolers in the markets. Ofe Akwu rings a bell in the ears of any Igbo man in Alaba or Balogun market in Lagos, Ochanja, or the main market in Onitsha or any other major market for that matter and can hold its own when it comes to competition with Ofe Onugbu (bitter leaf soup).

Once it is about eleven o'clock in any of these markets you will see *umu* boys (apprentices), especially the very long-throated ones like me, wandering around with their very deep plates ready to deal a blow to the women's pots. That's one variety of rice I also don't know how to make, but I like it so much. *Ofada* is another delicacy that may actually win the day as the federal government tackles the depreciation of the naira with a ban on importation of foreign rice. Nigerians will not have any choice except to seek out our own ofada, which interestingly has even become more expensive and tastier than the foreign ones. Ofada stew is another dish that is not rampant in the South South and South East, but is very much well and alive here in the South West, which was where I encountered it for the first time. The wrapping leaves gave it some uniqueness unparalleled with the other rice dishes.

Enough said, I have to get ready for my Sunday. I am looking forward to my praise, worship, word, and a wonderful reward with my afternoon Sunday rice. Just wondering which variety, it will be. I don't want to guess. Just *Iyawo* me—surprise me.

The use of *Iyawo*, a Yoruba word for "woman" inspired trust in Ada that the relationship was on track and might be heading to a desired outcome.

The last paragraphs of the version Ginika sent to Urem (who had not been to Lagos at that time) read;

Enough said, I have to get ready for my Sunday. I am looking forward to my praise, worship, word, and a wonderful reward with my afternoon Sunday rice.

Very soon it would no longer be just me doing the cooking but *Iyawo me*.

And by the way, *Iyawo me* means "my woman" according to the Yorubas. Just wondering which variety it would be. I don't want to guess, but will very soon let *Iyawo me* surprise me.

With time, Ginika longed for a change in diet; he especially longed for *onugbu* soup, which he would normally get in the traditional Igbo women's bukas in Idumota, Alaba International Market, or the later trade fair complex market to which the Igbos moved from Idumota. There was a large Igbo population in the markets, and they offered the same foods that were available in the villages, especially those from Anambra. Onugbu soup made with bitter leaf vegetable, goat meat, and thickened with cocoyam was the best delicacy for businessmen who were into the marketing of motor parts and known as the largest market in Sub-Saharan Africa. Ginika was introduced to First bank restaurant by one of his colleagues who, incidentally, was a Yoruba and loved *Amala*, a starchy food made of yam flour and eaten with *Ewedu* soup, which is made of green vegetables and *okro*. It was always combined with stew and tasted very nice from the look on the faces of those eating it. Ginika had never tasted it.

On arriving at First Bank with Adebayo one day, it was a surprised Ginika who felt the place was filthy and wondered why Adebayo would bring him to such a place, leaving all the fine restaurants in Marina including Mr Biggs, a food chain owned by UAC, a multinational conglomerate. "No be you say you wan chop better home-made food?" Adebayo had asked Ginika as he joined the long queue waiting to be served while he surveyed the many pots lined up containing stew and meat bubbling up as the customers were salivating. It appeared that the open pots were meant to serve more than one purpose, not just to make the statement that the cooking was done in the open for everyone to see how clean and transparent the food preparation was done, but to also get everyone who came around so eager to eat that they would not leave. Such sights would be expected to linger in the memory of the customers so that they would think about coming down every afternoon. This was similar to what Ginika had described in his essay on rice and the umu boy who looked forward to eleven o'clock so they could go get some rice.

With the queue going slowly, Ginika excused himself to stretch his legs a bit and possibly find a place to urinate a little further inside the food park. That was the journey that took him to the place of no return, as to his surprise, he saw something that looked like *ofe onugbu* in a distant pot in another smaller but equally open-potted kitchen just behind the one at which they had queued up. On hearing the language spoken by the ladies and the boys pounding yam in the corner, Ginika knew he had found "the place" and had no need for Adebayo's frustrating queue as he quickly asked the woman dishing out the food the cost per plate for pounded yam and ofe onugbu with goat meat. When he discovered the second side of First Bank, Ginika's days in the office became brighter as he was able to buy his favourite dishes for lunch. And the thing that made the second side of First Bank even more wonderful was that they also offered jollof rice, prepared even in a better and in a more traditional way than the dish served at Mr Biggs, which he was used to. In fact, this restaurant almost matched the Unini restaurant Ginika had written about in his famous rice email to his two love birds.

With time, the romance between Ginika and Ada continued to grow while it remained so discreet that no one in the office ever imagined they were an item. The weekend rendezvous became more frequent, with sleepovers at either Ada's place when she was sure she would not have any unwanted visitors or at Ginika's. He had now moved out of his brother Emeka's place to an apartment of his own in the same Festac Town.

Emeka had since gotten married and had three kids while Ginika continued enjoying the Lagos banker's life. Their mum, Ngozi, visited once in a while and would stay more often at Emeka's house where she would have little children to play with or for the traditional *Omugwo* when Emeka's wife gave birth . On few occasions she would stay over at Ginika's place, especially on weekends when Ginika would be expected to be home. On such occasions, every appointment with Ada was cancelled until "mumsi" went home to Owerri or moved over to Emeka's house prior to moving back to Owerri. Ogadimma, on the other hand, rarely visited. During Mumsi's visits to Ginika, they conversed mostly on the qualities of a good and homely housewife. Mumsi expected some kind of introduction to the possible prospects even though she didn't want to be seen as pushing the subject.

On one Monday after a rendezvous weekend with Ada, Ginika smiled to himself as he read the two text messages that just dropped into his phone at almost the same time. The phone had been on vibrate while he was in the office and had remained so while he went to lunch with his colleagues. With one hand busy with his Oha soup, which was on the menu for that day, and the other stretched into his pocket, he felt the vibration. He removed the phone from his pocket and pressed the message display button. His was a Nokia 3310 phone, one of the latest and strongest phones on the market.

The first message was from Ada, who wrote, "Baby, I can't live wo (without) u, u a d luv of ma life!" And Urem, in the second text, wrote "Obi m, all I want is to be with u, can't wait for NYSC to come!"

This was a recipe for trouble! Ginika had seen it coming. His deep involvement with Ada had given her hope of a sustainable relationship. It was going to be a difficult task to manage the two women when Urem eventually made it to Lagos for her National Youth Service.

"Ginika, you have been smiling to yourself since we came here," said Akin, one of Ginika's colleagues. "Let us into your world now. Let us enjoy the fun with you!" He looked at Ginika's smiling face, which suggested he was really feeling good about himself. "My brother, you would not understand," was all he could muster in response. With the secret affair with Ada still under tight wraps, he dared not reveal it to anyone, even the closest of his pals in the office for obvious reasons.

Urem, having finished her final-year exams, was looking forward to her National Youth Service, which she hoped would be in Lagos so she could be close to Ginika and make up for lost time. One of her uncles had promised her dad he would help out if things remained the way they were with the director general being as lenient as he had been. Preferred posting to locations of choice was operated by a racketeering gang in the NYSC then just as it had during Ginika's time. All it took was some money to get a candidate posted to his or her state of choice. The business thrived because the director general was known to be nonchalant about happenings in the office under his watch. With this nonchalant attitude, corruption thrived to the highest degree. It appeared it was only the director general who did not perceive the smell of the corruption under him. Or could it be that he was neck deep in it too and that he did not have the moral standing to challenge his staff to desist from it. Ginika, knowing it was a matter of cash, knew that there was no problem getting Urem to Lagos but was still contemplating whether it was the right thing to do given the brewing trouble that awaited him if she made it to Lagos. There was no doubt he had fallen for Ada, but at the same time, he still remained loyal in his commitment to Urem.

As Ginika, Akin, and Adebayo arrived at the office compound, another text arrived from Urem confirming that her uncle had contacted his friend in Abuja who promised he would help work Urem's posting to Lagos. Ginika sent his reply—"That's great"—with mixed feelings.

As things happened for the good (or bad) for the young Ginika, a couple of months down the line, an excited Urem called announcing her luck. She had landed the Lagos posting as she had desired. She gave the news to the equally excited and troubled Ginika over the phone. At this point, he could feel the cloud of rain and thunderstorms taking shape; it was only a matter of time before he got wet! Not knowing how to handle such a situation and still keeping the affair with Ada secret from friends and colleagues in the office, Ginika was confused. He needed advice from "Aunty Kemi" in the "Relationship

Counselling" column in *The Punch* newspaper. He wrote Aunty Kemi and signed it "anonymous" in order not to be discovered by his friends:

Aunty Kemi,

I met a beautiful girl in my office, and we have gotten so used to each other that I have developed feelings for her while keeping my old relationship with a girl I met during my NYSC period. The thing is, I love them both and do not want to lose either of them. But I also realize that, sooner or later, I must get married, and I will have to make a choice. Both are beautiful, respectful, and good Christians with all the qualities I desire in a woman. For some time now, dating both women has not been a problem because my first girlfriend lives in Port Harcourt, and my work girlfriend lives in Lagos. But all that is going to change shortly as my first girlfriend is due in Lagos any moment now to start her NYSC. How do I manage this dilemma? Is it possible to maintain love relationships with two ladies at the same time? Please help me.

Yours Truly,

Anonymous

To truly remain anonymous, Ginika had to open a separate email account and use it to send the email to Aunty Kemi as he was afraid that, if by any chance, the letter was published, his friends might find out it was his. He had been a fan of *The Punch* newspaper, one of the best newspapers in town, and had always bought a copy for himself over the weekends, and he would scan through the office copies when he had time. Without the need to look for job openings, it was easy for him to shift allegiance from *The Guardian* to *The Punch*. *The Punch* carried job adverts, but not as many as *The Guardian*, the ever-ready companion of job seekers. After sending his mail to Aunty Kemi, it became an obsession for him to read *The Punch* newspaper every day looking out for Aunty Kemi's column in anticipation of her reply to his question. Though Aunty Kemi's columns were printed in the Sunday edition, Ginika would make sure he looked at *The Punch* daily hoping that the column might be printed on a weekday by chance. He didn't want to miss his sought-after advice, which he could not get from anyone else. About three weeks after he sent his letter, his response finally was printed:

Dear Anonymous,

It is not out of the ordinary to fall in love with people around you most times; hence, your falling for your friend in the office. However, you may have to ask yourself whether it was a matter of convenience or a case of true love; that is, if there is any such thing as true love in the first place. The fact that you maintain the love of your old relationship may mean that there is some other part of that relationship that has kept you tied to her even in her absence. The question to ask is whether such can be said of your office flame. You may have to use other indices to untie the two loves in your life before you are able to move forward; otherwise, you may be stuck in between for a long time. I do not have all your details, but I believe you are not a Muslim, in which case you could have offered to marry both ladies. Be bold and strong enough to come up with additional criteria so you can start the process of disengaging one party as soon as possible so she can also move on and find another person who can also love her as much as if she were to be a preferred choice in such a competition.

Good luck,

Aunty Kemi

Taking mental stock and including the additional information that he had not shared with Aunty Kemi, Ginika took a stab at making a choice between the two women in his life.

Ada, a pretty, tall, dark lady with a "figure eight" shape, including hips that would get any man taking a second look, was from Bonny Island in Rivers State. It had surprised Ngozi, Ginika's mum, that she had taken on an Igbo name being from Rivers State. She was reminded that most of the people from the island were actually from the hinterland and were in transit to Europe and America as a result of slave trade and had come from possibly Igbo land before their families settled in the island after the slave trade was abolished. Ada grew up in Rivers State and was from a rich family with everything going on well for her. Even with the relatively comfortable background, she would be unsatisfied with the provisions from the family, and at a point after receiving her university degree, she had decided to date older men she thought could progress her career and give her the other pleasures of the world she could not get from her own family. She believed she was destined for the top and was determined to get there by hook or crook even though she realized that there was much more to life after getting to the top. Her continued dating of one of the directors in the bank was a threat to Ginika, which meant that the relationship remained in the background for a long time to the eventual advantage of Ginika when this hard decision had to be made.

Ada had advanced in her career to become a full branch manager at the Apapa branch of the bank, so the secrecy for Ginika's colleagues in the office and the pretensions between the love birds was no longer a burden. However, the fact that both worked in the same bank was a stumbling block for the future of the relationship. Banking rules then required that one of them would have to resign if they were to get married. Given Ada's status as a manager, it was going to be a very tough decision for her to resign. Ginika, on the other hand, was not sure he would be ready to resign and look for another job in order to get married to Ada. What would happen if he did not get another job? What if Ada changed her mind at the last moment? What if she bossed him around when they got married because she earned more money than he did? All these were questions that kept flooding his mind. Was he suffering with an inferiority complex or what? And what on earth would happen to him if Ada resigned and married him only for the director friend to find out he was the one who took his supposed girlfriend away from him. Would both of them end up without jobs? "Men, men, men!" he kept shouting out loud as he bounced around in his room as he thought over his future. And even in these thoughts, he had not added what the *Umunna* (the extended family) would say to his choice to marry a Rivers girl when it came to that. Ogadimma, being a learned man, would have no issue with his son marrying anybody from anywhere in the world so far as the person was of the opposite sex and a human being and that the wedding was conducted in a Roman Catholic church. However, to the Umunna and other less-learned relatives, the choice of a Rivers girl would be seen as risky as they would not have the full information required to make a good judgment on her family background. Moreover, they already had the notion that girls from *Mba mmiri* (as those from River Rine areas were referred to) were always wild or rather too civilized and did not have the same cultural values and respect for the marriage institution as the Igbos. "*Ima na ndi be ha ana awaka anya*" (you know the people from their place are always stubborn) would be the default advice from most of the relatives in the village. But the relatives' view was not Ginika's problem. As long as he cared, they could keep their opinions to themselves as he was the one who would eventually go to bed in the night with the woman.

Most young men in Ginika's place had come to realize that such stereotyping of people no longer mattered when it came to choosing a marriage partner. All that mattered was that both partners loved each other. However, there were still a few that hid under such stereotypes to make their choices, but in most cases it was really to support other reasons they might not be bold enough to confront. Sometimes the distance also mattered to these guys with the realization that marriage links two families that are supposed to share a lot of things in common, especially the need for the children to visit both families often to bond with distant relatives. Again, they forgot to take into account that most of the family members live their lives outside the villages and the few times they come home can never make up for such bonding. There was a case of Ginika's cousin whose father refused to let him marry a lady from Uzuakoli in Abia State simply because the place was seen by him as being too far away. He banned the wedding and said his son would get married to the lady only over his dead body. But he got very old, and his son still didn't bow to his blackmail, so he eventually gave his consent for the son to go ahead with the marriage.

Urem, on the other hand, was from Imo State and from a humble background. There were no odds against her other than the typical Anambra people's stereotyping of people from Imo State. While the average Anambra man thought Imo State girls were stubborn, the average Imo man thought the Anambra ladies liked money too much. Both sides always looked for flaws even as they continued to intermarry. Urem was a delight to behold any day, a reserved, fair-complexioned lady whom any man would want to have as a wife any day.

The surface value odds appeared to favour Urem in the scheme of things as Ginika saw her as more of a sister who would make a better wife than Ada because she had a full understanding of the requirements of his culture.

The only challenge was that Ada was good at her game. Ada had, in fact, mastered how to cook all the Igbo delicacies she knew Ginika loved. She knew he took his food seriously and went the extra mile to ensure she understood how to prepare each dish the way he liked it.

And she made sure to serve the food on time without prompting. That was one of the things that drew Ginika ever closer to Ada.

There had been talks about the fact that girls from Akwa Ibom were trained how to take care of men from their youth with rumours of how they were able to hoodwink Igbo men in Port Harcourt. Ginika realized this was nothing but the good and warm service that these ladies offered to their men. With a welcoming arm, these ladies received their lovers, dishing out food immediately without prompting and ensuring hot water was made available for bathing. With the massaging and pampering, what man would want to stay where he would have to beg for food to be served or be asked what he wanted to eat because the lady was not prepared in the first place?

In 2003, four years after Ginika started work as a banker, things had gotten better for him. His was a rapid rise for a young man, almost equalling the steep rise of people other colleagues would term connected such as Ada. He had left the two-bedroom apartment he had moved into after leaving Emeka's place and now lived in a duplex in a gated community, which reflected the achievement of his Lagos dream, only yet to be completed with a matching wife. As Akin would chide his Igbo friends, an average Igbo man, when making a New Year's wish, which would definitely be repeated the next year, would say, "*Chineke God, biko nyem B-Voot* and yellow babe to match" (God, please give me a Mercedes-Benz V-Boot model and a fair girl to match). He moved into the new apartment with a heavy sigh of relief as the two-bedroom apartment he initially occupied was not really a two-bedroom as the area of the whole apartment was almost equal to the sitting room and dining area in his new duplex along 7th Avenue. The toilet in the two-bedroom apartment had no doors, and the shower, which was supposed to be the original design due to its small space, did not work. This meant using a bucket to carry and pour water. It was quite difficult to get the two items (himself and the bucket) into the tiny place. Water would normally splash on the floor pretty close to the kitchen area. The worst was that he had to rely on errand boys to fetch the water up to his second-floor apartment in the mornings before work.

With his success as a banker and subsequent promotions, it was no surprise he could afford the luxury that came his way even though it was a far cry from where his babe, Ada, lived in upscale Apapa close to her office.

Meanwhile, Urem had arrived Lagos and started her NYSC with the Nigerian Ports Authority along Marina Lagos, coincidentally the same street Ginika worked on. Urem was lucky to have been in the group to serve in companies before Lagos State adopted a similar practice to the practice across the country in which NYSC members were drafted into teaching services by the state governments. NPA was one of the most lucrative places to work then as a Corp member. Not that they were paid much, but the dirty deals that went on in the government parastatal meant the "big men" were ever willing to "drop" for the junior staff including the temporary hires like Urem. The NPA was under the supervision of the Federal Ministry of Transportation. Ginika was at liberty to discuss his relationship with Urem with Akin and Adebayo since there was no threat. He still couldn't tell them about Ada. The first week saw Urem joining their company-provided bus service to work. This meant waking up very early in the morning, walking a little distance, and taking a motor bike to the lonely Agboju junction where she waited until the arrival of the company bus.

The first day she rode on the bus was like a baptism of fire as she witnessed a bag snatching scene by hoodlums early that morning. As she got off her motor bike, the cries of "Ole! Ole!" caught her attention as she saw a wailing woman pointing in the direction of a disappearing motor bike occupied by two persons, one driving, the other adjusting himself on the back seat and holding the bag he had just snatched from the lady. The sobbing woman got some consolation from the small gathered crowd who praised her for putting up a fight but warned her from doing such a thing in the future as she might have been shot by the hoodlums. On several occasions, people had been shot in the early morning raids by thieves all over Festac Town they reminded her. Anything in her bag could be replaced, but her life could not. Urem took all this in as she climbed onto the bus, and the discussion continued on the subject of insecurity in the small Festac Town.

With the absence of streetlights and security operatives, Nigerians were left at the mercy of hoodlums. These people would normally target people leaving very early in the morning in an attempt to beat the traffic nightmare in Lagos. On some occasions, the thieves met their Waterloo as they were caught and given jungle justice there and then. Any such thief caught was quickly set on fire. A used tire would be hung over his neck, petrol poured on him, and a match struck to the admiration of a bewildered audience who would quickly disappear as the ever-missing police patrol vans approached the scene.

After experiencing danger during her early-morning trips to the bus stop, Urem explored an idea a neighbour on the bus gave her. She found a bike man who would come over to her place at an appointed time and drive her to the bus stop. When she arrived at the bus stop, she made sure she stayed close to a house that had proper lighting until just about a minute before the arrival of their bus. Only then would she step out onto the road, all the while looking all around to ensure there was no strange motor bike with two people approaching from any direction. With time, Urem started joining Ginika in his car to Marina since her office was a distance away. Ginika would wait for her or sometimes would drive over to her place to pick her up and drop her at her office before going on to his. There was no inconvenience as Ginika enjoyed the company of his second girlfriend, at least until the bubble burst between Urem and Ada.

Driving to Lagos Island was always fraught with dangers not only for pedestrians like Urem who walked to bus stops, but also for lone drivers, so the option of additional passengers was a way of warding off potential attacks by thieves. Driving through Liverpool Road at Apapa was one of Ginika's nightmares as he had encountered thieves on that road one early morning. Just as he made the approach to the flyover landing, he noticed that two men on a motor bike, who had been following him all the way from Mile 2 Road close to Festac, had suddenly stopped a white Toyota coaster bus similar to the one Urem took to work. One of the men, waving a gun, quickly ordered everyone out of the bus while collecting all that they had one after the other as they got down from the bus. As this was happening, the nervous criminal was busy looking around to see if any police vehicle was approaching. Ginika looked directly at the thief holding the gun as he continued to follow the traffic going down the bridge landing to the right while the bus was stopped right at the left of the landing as it was ready to make its way to take the flyover to the left.

The queue of cars lined up to the right continued going down the landing in full view of the robbery, which had closed the road leading up the bridge. As the traffic snarled along the landing, a frightened Ginika could not even contemplate stopping as the driver behind him had just hit his vehicle in the chaos that attended the scene. Of course, those way back in the queue all started turning back and headed back towards the Mile 2 area again while waiting for the police team to arrive. Not until Ginika got to the office that day did he get out of his car to check the damage; he was lucky it was not too bad. He then realized he was shaken from witnessing a robbery. The trauma lasted a long time, and he vowed not to go along that route again until such time as he would be sure that adequate security had been put in place.

Although there was a company canteen at NPA where food was subsidized for the company staff members and contractors, Ginika would always invite Urem over to the second side of First Bank to have a good "homemade" meal. The first day Urem joined Ginika and his friends for lunch, it was an excited Ginika who showed off his damsel to Akin and Adebayo who had been lecturing him on the need to get married like the rest of his colleagues. Ginika would always maintain the position that he was working on it each time the discussion came up. When he did not want to use the "working on it" line, he would say that things were in the pipeline! Akin would always suggest that Ginika should do everything possible to get the pipeline delivering or burst it in case it was blocked. On this particular day, upon seeing Urem and Ginika, an excited Akin noted that it looked like the pipeline had eventually burst. He received a suggestive affirmative smile from Ginika.

At this time, technology had improved a great deal. The internet was the source of almost any information anyone could think of in this world. Ihemba, Ginika's classmate and friend who had opened Ginika's first email account, had gone on to establish a Yahoo group account for all the members of their class who had Yahoo email accounts. This meant that, with a click of a button, a single mail was sent to all the classmates, and they could all reply to the email thread. This meant they could have full virtual discussions years after leaving school. It was one of the wonders of our times. Ginika wrote in one of his contributions, "Who has seen Onyema? Please let anybody that know the whereabouts of Nkiru drop her address for me. We have an opening for an engineer in my firm. Anyone with a master's degree who is interested please send me your CV immediately." "Chai! How time flies," Ginika would reminisce. When he first began to look for a job, it took two weeks for hard-copy applications to reach the hands of prospective employers. Now email applications were immediate. The second connotation the song "God Be With You Till We Meet Again" had for Ginika was no longer necessary. In the "new world" there was no longer a parting of old friends till the beginning of the next school term or the indefinite loss of friends after primary, secondary, or university education. The world was now one in both space and time!

With time, the discussions on the Yahoo group moved from "experienced job search" to "marriages" and then moved on rapidly to "baby dedications". Quite a lot of the marriage invitations were sent out in the group email account, and those who were near the location would attend and reconnect with their classmates. All that added to the pressure Ginika was under to get married, and the pressure did not come only from the discussions with Akin and Adebayo during lunch times.

For all the wedding invitations then, the group members would make contributions via the bank account number of one of the trusted members, especially Ihemba, who was the group account moderator. On some other occasions, the money was paid into the account of the person closest to the town where the wedding would be held and who would be sure to attend, with the house making a choice of the item to be bought as present. On rare occasions, physical cash was given to the celebrant if he or she so wished, but it was always the last option since the members preferred a souvenir for which they could be remembered in future; cash could be used for anything.

Urem loved the meals at First Bank and would opt to join Ginika for lunch most times; after all, she was not paying for the food that was similar to what she could obtain at NPA with the subsidized meals. Their lunches for a very few early weeks were not a problem until word started making the rounds in the office about a babe down the road who had caught Ginika's fancy. Before Ginika knew it, everyone in the office wanted to go to First Bank to have a chance of running into Ginika's babe! The worry for Ginika was that word travelled very fast in his office, and not just his local branch but nationally! A little gossip in a local branch could easily travel around to the other branches of the bank in Lagos, as most employees were moved around from branch to branch and thus always knew someone who knew someone who knew someone, and so on. Sooner or later, he knew, Ada would hear, given that the hottest topic around the office every morning before work began was who got married and who was next in line. He did not want to be in a position of having to explain things to Ada in the event she heard he had another girlfriend. At this time, Urem and Ada each believed she was the sole candidate for the affection of the admirable Lagos bachelor. By a stroke of luck, Ginika had managed the dual affair for a few weeks, but he knew it was a bubble waiting to burst. He kept on strategizing, meditating, consulting, and enjoying the adrenalin that came with the double dating game.

In a typical "close call", he had just come in from the second mass service of the afternoon and was relaxing in his sitting room with Ada when Urem knocked at the gate. This was unlike Urem, who would always call or send a text that she was coming, which would give Ginika enough time to arrange a story or discharge Ada in the smartest way he could think of. Earlier he had told Urem he would not be around on Saturday since he had to take care of some weekend banking tasks at the office, and he would then drive directly to Unilag for his evening Saturday lectures. Urem was staying with a friend of her family and was not disposed to night visits or outing most times. This was very convenient for Ginika as Ada had the nights all to herself, and she stayed in her own house and alone. On the nights Ada stayed with Ginika, he maintained contact with Urem through several intermittent text messages. Sending the text messages depended on when he was able to slide away from the presence of Ada while using the toilet or some other excuse that saw him run into his room.

On the Sunday night, a sweating Ginika was lucky enough to hear the knock and was, in fact, wishing it was not Urem as he looked out his room window and saw a figure that matched that of Urem. As the figure approached the gate, he was still hoping it would not be her but was already with his hand pressed on the dial button on his new phone when she knocked. Her knock coincided with his pressing the dial button, and seconds later it was an apologetic Ginika who announced that he had just gone out with Adebayo and two other colleagues to a colleague's house at Satellite Town for a baby dedication. Thinking ahead of the implication of his absence with his car parked right in front of the house, he mentioned they literally dragged him to join them in their own vehicle if the fuel scarcity was going to be his excuse for not wanting to join them. The narrow escape did not last long as he had to provide another lie to cover that of the Sunday baby dedication the next day at lunch. Ginika was taken aback when Urem asked Akin about the baby dedication the previous day to the surprise of Akin. "Oh, that's true, you were not there yesterday," said Ginika quickly. "No wonder I kept on thinking that someone was missing but could not figure out who. You know Somebi at Apapa branch, right? She was in Marina branch a few years back." Akin nodded in the negative. "OK. No wonder you were not invited. She just had a baby, and Adebayo and the rest of the crew came to drag me out of the house yesterday, so I missed my damsel's visit." *What a narrow one*, Ginika thought to himself.

On a second occasion, he was not so lucky and had to face the two ladies head on. This time a similar event happened, but before Ginika realized what was amiss, Ada, who had just arrived on a Sunday afternoon, went out to open the gate for Urem. Suddenly, the two ladies were walking into the living room as Ginika was descending the stairs. Ada had asked Urem who she was looking for without any suspicion but coldly all the same. Urem answered while she went through the gate Ada had just unbolted. Ada stepped into the living room as Ginika asked who had called, but he stopped midway down the stairs when he realized the trouble he was just about to step into. Wishing he could run back upstairs to allow himself some time to think, or better still, wishing that the ground would open up so he could jump in and hide, he knew the game was up. He made a bold face and introduced the two ladies in a cracked voice that revealed the discomfort he felt. "Ada, this is Urem. Urem, this is Ada." This was all he could muster as he quietly made his way to the three-seater sofa with his face focused directly on the television. "So how was service today, Urem?" Ginika finally asked in a bid to strike up a conversation that all parties knew was going nowhere until the full details of their relationships were ironed out. "Are you feeling hungry, Ada?" He asked. She was surprised at the sudden change in his tone. The excitement they just shared a couple of minutes before the arrival of this stranger was gone. "Didn't we just finish breakfast? Or do I look like a glutton?" she replied in a bid to make the statement she was the lady of the house for anyone who cared to listen. Ada joined Ginika on the sofa while Urem sat on the single chair next to the television with her beautiful legs stretched out on the rug.

After a couple of minutes, a profusely sweating and confused Ginika looked at both ladies and asked if they were feeling the heat. "Heat kwa! In this air-conditioned room? Are you sure you are OK?" Ada asked. Mumbling something incoherent, Ginika gradually stood up, buttoned his shirt, and excused himself outside on the pretext that he had forgotten that his elder brother had asked him to come around after second mass service that afternoon. When he was outside the living room, he looked back and quickly made a dash for the gate and disappeared into thin air leaving the two ladies alone.

"*Bros, yawa don gas*" was all he could mutter to Emeka as he stepped into his house. He confessed his ordeal and requested counsel on what to do next. He quietly sat on the sofa in Emeka's living room as he took time to think of how to get out of the situation. "I think you simply have to make up your mind at this point on who you want to move forward in life with. After all you are old enough to get married. Most of your mates have," Emeka advised him. "The ladies also need to know where they stand so the 'loser' can cut her losses and move on. They are not getting younger, and you know they are time-bound where we men are not."

Urem, after waiting for some time, tried Ginika's number, but Ginika did not pick up the call. She tried several times and only became annoyed with the response. She finally got up, picked up her bag, and left the house. Ada waited longer. Because she knew her way around the house, she made herself lunch, ate, and watched a little television before locking up and driving home. Ginika sneaked into the house later in the evening praying that both his visitors would be gone. He did not have the guts to face any more embarrassment.

Urem cried like hell that night knowing the meaning of the neglect and feeling betrayed by her Ginika, whom she had trusted so much. It had never occurred to her that she might actually be in any kind of competition for her boyfriend's affection. He had sent her so many love notes and gifts. She never knew they were all duplicates to the ones he sent to Ada. She made up her mind that she was not going to see Ginika again. She would stop commuting to work with him. "Life can be so cruel," she told her friend in the office with whom she had been chatting on several occasions about men and their cheating skills. They had noted how the cheating had been made so much easier by the introduction of mobile phones. She quickly woke up the next Monday morning and called her bike man to ask him to drop her off earlier than usual so she would not run the risk of meeting that stupid cheat at her home. A frustrated Ginika arrived at her gate, waited for some minutes, called her phone without a response, and eventually drove off to work encountering some heavy traffic because he had left later than usual because he had been trying to contact her.

It was a distrusting young man who entered the office that morning with so many thoughts on his mind. How was he going to get out of his mess in a convenient way? For one, he knew he was going to move on with Urem. But he had to think of how to peacefully call off the affair with Ada. He sent a text to her but got no reply. He sent an email through his office account, but he got no reply from that either. Lunch was not for him that day as he tried to avoid his friends who would want to find out how his weekend went. He drove straight to Ada's house on his way home after work to explain things to her. Entering the house after Ada reluctantly opened it and let him in, he sat on the sofa, gazing at the ceiling. Then he stood up and walked to the other seat where Ada sat. He knelt down and tried to take Ada's face into his hands, but she quietly removed his hands and asked him not to touch her. "Sweetheart, let me explain," he said. "It's not as it seems."

"Explain what, Ginika! After all I did for you, you stooped so low as to involve yourself with that filthy rat. What do you want to explain? It was so obvious that you slept with that girl; you could not even look at me once she came into the house. What is wrong with you men? When a woman gives you her heart, you take it for granted. Do you know the number of men that chase after me every day? I had to give them all up for you! I loved you from the very first day I met you!" She burst into tears. "And I thought you were the ideal one for me irrespective of our class difference. I made all necessary sacrifices for our relationship to work, but see what you have done?" She sobbed. "See what you have done? See what you have done?" She burst into another bout of crying like a baby with tears rolling down her cheeks.

"I'm so sorry about this, sweetheart," said Ginika as he made another attempt to hold her. But she cried even harder as Ginika continued to console her. Meanwhile the name "Ginika" sounded strange to him. He heard distance in the name as she pronounced it in the most unromantic way he had ever experienced since they got together. Through all her sobbing, Ginika thought it was a different Ada he was consoling. The tone of her voice scared him. He had never heard her speak in such a strict tone, and he wondered where it came from. Was this a taste of the pudding? He wondered about this even with the guilt he felt for letting her down. All along, their relationship had been rosy with no major quarrels to bring out the bad side of either of them, especially Ada, until this point. There had been petty quarrels but nothing near the magnitude of this one.

After what Ginika saw, he called Emeka up late that night and narrated the events of the day to him. They both had agreed that, with time, the best candidate would emerge from the two ladies naturally. Emeka, from the start, preferred Urem simply because she was from Imo State, a sister Igbo-speaking state, even though he would have preferred someone from their village just as he did. To him, Bonny was too far, and he would not want to drown in the waters in an attempt to go see his in-laws for any reason. Time would tell, they both agreed.

The cat-and-mouse game between Urem and Ginika continued. Ginika's frustration was getting out of control. Sleeping at night became a problem, and texting was not going to solve the problem. So, he drove straight to Urem's house one evening in defiance of Urem's warning that she would not entertain any male visitors in her uncle's house. A little boy came to answer the door after Ginika knocked and ran back inside the house shouting, "Urem! Urem! One man is looking for you!" This surprised Urem, who came out of the room only to meet Ginika as he walked into the living room smiling and saying hello to her uncle. With the august visitor already inside the house, Urem had no choice but to make introductions. Her uncle smiled and welcomed Ginika warmly as if he was his in-law to be. A few minutes later, Ginika excused himself to leave, and Urem walked him out. "Urem, why have you not been picking up my calls or responding to my text messages?" he asked as they got close to his car. "Look, I am truly sorry for what happened the other day, OK? I swear it will never happen again. You know you are the love of my life. I cannot live without you." To Ginika's surprise, he was using almost exactly the words he had once used when talking to Ada! "I will surely make it up to you. OK?" Urem, after some reluctance, embraced him. She did not utter any word as she sobbed in his arms.

With time, Ginika minimized and eventually stopped communication with Ada and concentrated his energy on his relationship with Urem. He used as an excuse the existence of Ada's parallel love affair with the director. Though it had not been a problem at the beginning, it had started to be an issue when he began exploring ways of severing the relationship. Then there had been a gentleman's agreement between them on Ada's days off. On those days, she was free to indulge in activities like satisfying those that had helped her come up to the level she was in her career. Though Ginika condoned this arrangement, it was one of the reasons he had kept his relationship with her secret, most times feeling humiliated by the fact that his woman could boldly be with another man and he could not do anything about it. He had hoped that, with time, and when they firmed up any future arrangements, he would be able to stamp his feet and instruct her to stop all such communication. In a way, he also saw her relationship with the director as justification for his parallel relationship with Urem. Now it was added grounds for ending their relationship while they remained friends.

Ginika and Urem's relationship took a turn for the better with Ginika's relief at the severance of the Ada angle. A delighted Urem was now always in Ginika's house. She would even sometimes lie to her uncle and stay at Ginika's, saying she was staying over at her girlfriend's. They would both go to work from Ginka's in the morning. When Urem's NYSC year was over, she was offered a contract appointment with the same NPA and thus remained in Ginika's company as they commuted to work every day.

It was Christmas season, and Ginika and Urem were looking forward to travelling together to the eastern part of the country. For

Urem, it was going to be easy because her office gave every person holiday time during the period so they could be with family members and friends. Ginika's situation was a little bit tricky as the bank's busy schedule during the period meant that even more hands needed to be on deck. Both of them, however, travelled during the New Year celebration. Urem stayed over at Ogadimma's house and continued her journey to her village in Imo State the next day. It was unusual for Ogadimma's children to bring girls home except for a few times when Ginika was attending university. To bring girls home and sleep over in the house was a different level. In fact, it had been a taboo to bring any girl to the house in whatever form. However, times had changed, and Ogadimma, in his old age, had relaxed a lot of his strict attitudes to the surprise of many who had known him when he was much younger. Of course, with the children also grown up, he realized he needed to give them the respect they deserved as adults and not lord things over them. Who knew? The lady who slept in his house the night before might be his daughter-in-law soon. Ngozi's case was worse. Chinedu remembered the episode that led to the famous *"Ina achoro ya gini, nwoke na nwanyi ana akwu?"* episode. (Why are you looking for him? Do boys and girls hang out together?) Ogadimma and Ngozi had been looking forward to the day Ginika would take his "final investment decision" (make up his mind) on a lady to marry. Unlike Emeka, Ginika's elder brother who had not wasted time making a choice, Ginika had kept everybody guessing. So bringing Urem home, even for a sleepover during transit, was a good sign.

"*Nnem, kedu afa gi kwanu?*" Ngozi asked Urem. (Sweetheart what is your name?)

"*Mma echem ma agwaram gi aha ya yesterday,*" Ginika replied. (Mum, I thought I told you her name yesterday.)

"Leave me. Let me talk with my daughter. Did I tell you I did not hear when you told me? How will I bond with my daughter-in-law without hearing her name from her own mouth and learn where she comes from? Now that you brought her home to me, let me do the rest."

It was a surprised Ginika who looked at his mother in bewilderment. He could not explain where that one had come from. Was she trying to blackmail him into committing to a relationship without his consent? "OK, Mum. I have not told you anything about getting married. Urem is my friend. Please stop embarrassing the poor girl. She is only on her way home."

"On her way home? Is the way to her home via your bedroom in this distant village? Or is there a tunnel through your room to her village? If she is good enough to be your friend and sleep in your house in Lagos, visit other family members, and hang out with you to ceremonies and parties, please be sure her final destination is this house in no distance time! And for your information, I remember her very well, and I liked her the first time I saw her. I think I even prefer her to that other tall dark one I saw you with the day you came to Emeka's house to say goodbye to me when I went for Omugwo for his last child."

As the three of them were chatting, Ogadimma quietly walked into the living room to join in the interrogation of their supposed yet-to-be-announced daughter-in-law. Ginika thought that bringing Urem home might have been a mistake after all even though he would not deny the fact that he did not mind sampling her semi-officially to his parents before he made any formal announcements.

Their trip from Lagos had been a tortuous one, with the large number of bad spots on the road leading to so many accidents. At one point, a female federal minister was said to have broken down and cried profusely on her official inspection of the road to the delight of everyone who hoped that soon something would be done, but it was all to no avail. The bad road meant slow traffic. A journey of an hour could end up taking up to four hours or more. Some smart guys would drive off as early as five o'clock in the morning to be sure to cross all the bad spots before the rest of Lagos and their co-travellers on the road woke up. Ginika woke up quite early that morning but got delayed when he went to pick up Urem. He lost all the advantage he had planned for with his early start. The result was a late arrival to the village the previous night. Because they were tired from the long trip, their greetings were brief and more conversation had to wait until the morning.

Had Ginika known about the ambush by his mum, he thought to himself, he would have quickly made a dash for it pretty early to take Urem down to Imo State, but as things had turned out, he was already caught in the web and could not wriggle out of it. A smiling Ogadimma joined in the interrogation, and as would be expected, the first thing he asked was where the poor girl came from—where in Imo State? "Mbaise," she replied.

"Where in Mbaise? Onitsha? Ah, is that not where Mpa Chiamaka (Chiamaka's dad) is from?" He was obviously very knowledgeable, and as he had lived in Owerri for several years, it was not a coincidence that Ogadimma knew Urem's exact village and even had a friend who was from the same place.

Ogadimma made a mental note that it would be easy to investigate the girl's background given the contact he had already made. It was normal for parents to investigate the backgrounds of any aspiring in-laws. Such investigations were done both ways and often entailed sending an undercover agent to ask people in the surrounding neighbourhood about the family. They would also ask for any contacts who might know about the family. The parties would be interested in knowing whether there were any diseases that ran in the family, especially any cases of mental disease which might signify the presence of bigger omens such as generational curses by their ancestors! They would want to know if the family had any history of theft of any kind, whether there had been any divorces in the family, and whether the women from the home were humble enough to make good wives. Perhaps the most important information to establish was whether the family was an *Osu* (outcast). This refers to descendants of servants or priests that presided over the shrines for gods that were practiced in the olden days before the white man came and replaced the African man's religion with his own. They were known to be sacred, and for that reason were avoided by the rest of the population.

Thus, while the white man's "chi" priests are revered today and celebrated with the children sought after as candidates for marriage, the African man's "chi" servants were relegated to an outcast system. The irony was that those from such families were known to be very wealthy and their girls so pretty that even the so called free-born lusted for them, and only the bold ventured to go against the odds and marry them. Realizing the foolishness in tagging a fellow human beings as outcasts, the Christian church, which is the most powerful institution for people like Ogadimma from Anambra, abolished the tradition and warned that anyone caught describing or gossiping against anyone else with respect to the Osu cast system would face serious consequences. However, as it was in several other areas where there was a clash between tradition and white man's civilization, it was easier said than done. Part of the ceremony involved in the abolishment of the system was a big party where food and drinks were served. Everyone in the whole village ate together signifying that people should not avoid each other again. However, when the chips were down, it was not uncommon to see family members giving one flimsy excuse or another as to why their child would not go ahead with a wedding. A typical excuse was *"Ona agu akwukwo"* (she is still in school) as if Anambra people loved school too much that they would choose school over marriage. For the men, once the bride was known to have come from such a family, they would get an ultimatum from immediate family members who would not give any reason for declining the union since they could not risk going foul of the church orders for voicing such a reason.

With the interrogation over, Ginika took Urem to her hometown, spent a short time there with her, and made his way back to his own village to continue the other part of the discussions that did not require Urem's presence. That evening, some of Ginika's mates came to the house to see him. The village was always fun, especially for friends who could hang out together. The age grade system—social organization based on age—helped quite a lot to get mates together in a club. They would see each other at least once every year during the

179

yuletide season. The age grades normally had an executive committee that piloted the affairs of the meeting, and they had branches all over the country. One of the activities of the age grades was to carry out a town development project of any kind they deemed fit. Such groups and the determination of the Igbos led to the development of the towns that did not receive much government assistance. In some cases, the town unions pioneered the initiation of major developmental projects such as electricity or water projects before engaging the government to help. Kpajie was the chairman of Ginika's age grade and a personal friend as well. He always came around first thing in the morning once he knew Ginika was around in the village. "Old boy, *nekwa ka irazi!*" Kpajie shouted as he walked into Ginika's room. (See how big you have become.) A known face in the house, he did not need anybody's directions to Ginika's room. He greeted Ogadimma and Ngozi in the sitting room before he walked in the direction of his friend's room. Ginika heard his voice and made his way out at the same time. They both shared some shots of whisky before delving into matters, especially the agenda for the age grade meeting. "Meanwhile, my cousin is opening his house tomorrow evening, so be sure to be there," Kpajie said. "*Inwete Igba* the boy *tiri!*" he continued. (If you see the mighty house the boy built!)

Building large family houses remained a thing of pride in the village. Some people lived in rented apartments in towns, and then they would build mighty buildings they would live in for a maximum of two weeks during the festival seasons. In several cases, the argument was that the land for the building already existed in the village because of inheritance. This meant that no money was spent to acquire the land compared to the high cost of purchasing such land in the towns. They would rather use the money to purchase the land in town to build in the village first. Villagers gave owners of such houses great respect. The circumstance obviously was not the same for everyone. In some cases, the parents already owned big houses, so the children were not under the pressure to build theirs. In other families, houses were non-existent, and the children were forced to construct their own. For polygamous families, new dwellings also became necessary as the children of the later wives were expected to move out of the main house as soon as practicable.

Ginika did not know for how long his mouth was open, but it sure was a long time as he guessed at the beauty of this extravagance! Even as he admired the house and enjoyed the company and merriment that went on that day, he kept asking himself if it was necessary that such an edifice should be built in a low-activity village. As they were drinking in one of the rooms upstairs, Kpajie's cousin walked into the room. They all rose and greeted him, congratulating him for his achievement. They suggested to him that, next on the agenda, he should take up a chieftaincy title from the village to complement the house. "I hope you guys are well taken care of," he said. "Not yet, oh. But we are OK, and somebody is at it already," Kpajie told him. As he walked out, Nkiru walked in with two small coolers of food, including meat. Nkiru was also Kpajie's cousin and some years younger than the cousin who had built the big house. Like magnets, Ginika's eyes continued to follow her as she walked in, dropped the coolers, and walked out to get their drinks. "*Naa onye bu ifea?*" (Please, who is this?). "*Ibiakwa ozo!*" (You have come again). "That is Nzube's younger sister. I thought you knew her. When I tell you guys that there are damsels in this town, you would not believe me. *Onwebedighi ihe ifuru.*" (You have not seen anything yet.) "If you want, I can give you her number, but you have to promise me one thing—you will not mess around with her. I even heard she is a virgin but cannot guarantee that one. All I know is that she is a very homely girl, and there is nothing like marrying from our village so that if anything happens things can always be resolved immediately," Kpajie continued. "That is why I like marriages from our town better than *ndi mba*" (distance marriages).

Ginika tracked down Nkiru later that day, having been introduced. Thanking her for all her services in the room was the excuse he used to engage her for a few minutes. Then he digressed to other topics as he recalled his days in primary school when he would fall in love once every week and run back home to narrate the experience to

Okechukwu. A smiling Nkiru showed some interest that sent some butterflies to Ginika's stomach as they agreed to meet the following day. The following day was the village church's thanksgiving harvest, and a bazaar was to be held. It was an opportunity for the village church to get all the "abroad" people (those living in towns and cities) to contribute to the development of the village church. It was a very busy event with lots of sales, and it was the perfect time for Ginika to hang out with Nkiru with intermittent interference from Nkiru's friends and immediate family members. Luckily for Ginika, no one laid claim to a higher stake on the girl. Such girls were always popular in the village as every ready bachelor looked around for the available marriageable girls to hook up with. Mothers encouraged their daughters to go out to church to as many services possible in a day including the early morning service and church bazaar sales in this case. They would advise that their daughters might never know where they will find Mr Right or where they would be noticed.

Carried away by the presence of Nkiru and the noise around them, Ginika did not notice his phone ringing. He had to apologise to Urem later that evening and explain why he had not heard it. He did not mention that he had been with another lady. Ginika struggled to get Nkiru off his mind that evening to no avail. He did not want to be put in another difficult situation like the one he had just come out of between Ada and Urem. Eventually, he let things be and forgot about Nkiru after the short Christmas romance as he faced the bustling and hustling of Lagos. At this time, he had set his mind on moving on with his plans to get married to Urem. He settled on a December target date for tying the knot, and he needed to progress with his plans. But first he had to pop the question to her. However, it then occurred to him that they had not even had a blood test, which was then a requirement from the church to ensure couples had compatible blood groups before going into marriage.

The result of the blood test was unfavourable to the devastation of Ginika and Urem. It was difficult to judge who was hit the worst of the two. Ginika's mother, after all, had extracted a family introduction from all the suggestive questions she had asked Urem during the Christmas visit. And Urem had had hopes that their marriage would happen soon after she conquered the initial competition between herself and Ada. Ginika could not believe he had been so careless as to carry on the relationship for so long without bothering to check out the compatibility of their blood in case marriage was to be considered. What if she had gotten pregnant from one of their several sexual escapades? It took serious counselling from friends and family members before the two love birds could come to terms with the reality and move on with their lives while remaining the best of friends.

Several months later, Nkiru called Ginika on the phone. She wanted to know how he was faring having not heard from him after their short, hot, but cordial village romance. Luckily, the call came just as Ginika was coming out of the depression that had devastated him over the issue with Urem.

"So why have you not called me since January you travelled back to Lagos?" she asked. "That is no fair, oh. I was actually looking forward to your call but shied away from calling you thinking you would remember, but obviously you have not."

Ginika pleaded that he was so sorry. "You know how it is with this town," he told her. "Once you get sucked into your work, you cannot do anything else."

"OK, I get it," she said, "but are you saying you don't have time for your friends or are you saying you don't even have time for your girlfriends too?" Ginika asked her who had told her he had a girlfriend. "I am sure you do," Nkiru insisted.

"How do you know?" Ginika responded.

"I know because there is no handsome dude like you who would go unnoticed, especially in that you peoples Lagos where I hear the girls are so wild they are not even afraid of asking a man out!"

"Hmm, that is for the men they see on the street," Ginika responded. "With work one hardly has time not to talk of being wooed by a lady. Think about it. Where would a guy even run into the girl.

Monday through Friday there is work. On Saturday there is work and school. On Sunday there is church and a little time to rest unless there is one function or another to attend," he continued.

"Well, what about the ladies in your office? What about those NYSC ladies in your office? I'm not even talking about the ladies in the church. And are you saying you go to church with your eyes closed?" Nkiru insisted. As the flirting continued, Nkiru got the message she'd been searching for—this guy was single though maybe he was not searching. All the while, Ginika enjoyed the attention and thanked her for checking on him. He promised he wouldn't be a bad boy again. He would return her interest. "And if you think of visiting Jos for your holidays," she said, "please feel free to come down to Pankshin and see me. I have loads of stuff to show you, I promise. I know you bankers like travelling abroad for your annual vacations forgetting that there are really nice places around this country that can compete on equal terms with some other locations around the world. You go and waste our dollars!" she noted.

"Waoh, Lord, I really like this girl!" Ginika exclaimed as they hung up. "Such humour and a nice voice! She's down to earth and so practical." This was the type of woman who would make a home. It was also good that she was from the same village. An elated Ginika simply stood up, put his hands on his waist, and nodded his head saying, "Truly, when one door closes, another is sure to open." He was already resigning himself to fate and thinking of how he had lost two promising relationships within a couple of months, and then Nkiru had walked into his life without any struggles. It was a grateful Ginika who raised his voice in a praise song he had come to like and enjoy:

Great is thy faithfulness, Oh God, my father.

There is no shadow of turning with thee.

Thou changeth not, thy compassion fails not.

As thou hast been, thou forever will be.

Great is thy faithfulness. Great is thy faithfulness.

Morning by morning, new mercies I see.

All I have needed thy hands have provided.

Great is thy faithfulness, Lord unto me.

Not minding the implications and suggestions the question would bring, Ginika asked Nkiru to tell him her blood group the next time they had a chat over the phone. She told him in exchange for his. A week from confirmation of their blood groups, Ginika flew into Jos for a visit to Nkiru and spent the weekend in the beautiful city enjoying the cool breezes and cold mornings. Nkiru took him through the town that would soon cease to be her home as she made her way to Lagos to join her husband. She would visit home only on holidays as they alternated their holiday vacations between Nigeria and overseas.

CHAPTER 13

Made in Heaven

Since Ginika's childhood days in the east, the wish of every child born in that part of the country was to visit Lagos. And not just visit, but also visit Bar Beach, the very famous beach in Victoria Island that was home to all sorts of people including tourists and spiritualists. You see, families, horses, and prayer groups set up at different corners of the white beach, which stretched for about two to three kilometres. The next site for visitors from the east was the National Theatre in Ignamu on mainland Lagos. The National Theatre was one of the monumental buildings used during the Second World Black and African Festival of Arts and Culture, otherwise known as Festac. The festival was held in 1977 and was hosted by Nigeria at a time the country was awash with so much money the rulers did not know what to do with it.

Prior their wedding, Ginika and Nkiru had attended friends' weddings, had been to celebrity weddings, and had watched weddings in movies, but nothing prepared them for their own wedding at the National Theatre in Lagos. With their busy schedules, they had engaged event planners to do the legwork for them while they concentrated on the key personal items like rings and dresses. The planners were such professionals that Ginika did not check on them regularly to be sure everything was going as expected. The setting blew their mind so much that they kept talking about it for a long time after the event. Ginika's colleagues were also surprised at the setting but were even more surprised that Ginika and his bride were surprised at their own preparations! The setting was so impressive that, when Ginika got home, he had to check his photographs to remember everything that had happened.

The first part of the surprise started with the venue, an open garden full of colourful roses exactly like the ones in the movies. With the bouncer instructing it was not yet time to visit the site of the wedding, some of Ginika's friends who had arrived early to the wedding indulged themselves by strolling around the garden. One of the friends said he was looking for the large-petal red roses he always longed for. At the last count, a friend was supposed to deliver the seeds from India he said out loud to confirm his seriousness. And that was part of the surprises for the guests. Most weddings in the National Theatre were conducted inside the building, especially during the rainy season. No one contemplated having an event in the open garden. The concept was new and was really worth it, adding the real feeling of a movie-type wedding to the excitement of Ginika and Nkiru as they kept giggling at each other all through the ceremony.

The place was so colourful that Ginika's brother Emeka could not wait for wedding guests to arrive before he started taking personal pictures. Thank God he had just bought a new phone, as if he had known what was ahead. With the open sky, Emeka looked around for "plan B" in case the heavens opened, given that Lagos is not a respecter of persons when it comes to rain. There were no rainclouds in sight, and that confirmed the couple's faith in God to withhold the rain, or in the rainmakers to test their powers. The wedding quickly got underway, and while the reverend father was at it, an old lady behind Emeka started complaining about the dressing of "some" sisters. To the lady, even if they must come to church to look for husband, did they think the guys were up for ladies with skimpy dresses? Emeka quietly turned around looking for the "culprit ladies". When he did not see anything that bad, he looked at Mama as such were referred to and asked her if any of the ladies' panties were showing. She said "No!" Emeka then asked her what her worry was about. She kept on insisting that at least the lady should go outside, almost threatening she would throw her out herself.

The real spectacle of the day came at the reception. But even before then, Emeka's wife, whom he had agreed would leave after the church service, changed her mind. Emeka never figured out why; maybe she sensed what was going to happen. In fact, it was because of that agreement that Emeka insisted they take pictures of the new couple in front of the beautiful altar decorated with thousands of roses. The planners had arranged for photographs at the reception, but Emeka insisted on taking some himself, knowing his wife might not make it to the reception. And his argument was simple—the church wedding was the main thing. Reception is for food and drinks, and those who came to the church must have the right of first refusal when it came to pictures or privileges. Ginika agreed, confirming that Emeka was the first to arrive at the church—*sef.*

The reception, staged in one of the halls in the National Theatre, was magnificent, and the couple had their first photo shoot on stage before anyone came into the hall. It was an amazing experience with specially selected background music. The lightning was different from anything Ginika had seen before. Emeka took his time to join in the photoshoot with his new phone. The stage where the shooting was done was laced with a rose picture on the floor that felt like epoxy. Of late, Emeka had a fancy for epoxy flooring and recognized the picture immediately he saw it. He imagined it was made of similar materials used for epoxy 3D floor finishing.

The zenith of the event was when the latest couple in town were called upon for the cake cutting. Ginika smiled like someone who had just won a lottery. He held his wife, Nkiru, confidently and protectively to the admiration, laughter, and clapping of everyone in the hall. The cake literally flew in gently from the roof in an amazing spectacular display. And the guests were surprised and impressed when a drone flew in the knife for the cutting of the cake. Each time

Emeka went to take his seat, the bride and groom pulled off another stunt that got him running back on stage to catch a video of the action.

When he got to his office, Emeka showed his colleagues everything he had seen and photographed. The guys all shouted that he should not show their wives so that they would not demand a similar thing, albeit a repeat of their weddings. When Emeka teased the ladies about the need to double-check with the latest standards whether they had a wedding in comparison, some argued that theirs would probably be similar or better if it were recent. In fact, they insisted that their cake would come out from water, to which he said it would be "mermaid cake"! Emeka told all of them politely, "If your wedding was not in a garden open to the sky with lots of sunshine and thousands of roses, and your cake did not fall from heaven like my brother's own, my sister, you did not have a proper wedding, and you will need a repeat event.

Ginika's marriage was the talk of the town. *Ovation Magazine* was given the exclusive right to cover the wedding of the most eligible bachelor in Lagos. Ada and Urem were, surprisingly, in attendance and were happy for Ginika. Even though they had not gotten married at the time, they both had found other serious relationships that were equally on their way to the altar. And the social media sites and blogs were not left out from the frenzy. "Linda Ikeji" blog, the most famous of Nigerian blogs, carried the news and pictures while Ginika tweeted and posted the pictures from the wedding venue on Facebook.

A grateful Ginika would thank all who attended. He sent out greetings on Facebook and his Yahoo group and humorously asked the rest of his mates to follow his footsteps not minding that he was among the last of his classmates to get married.

— CHAPTER 14 ——————————————

American Wonder

Four years later, Nkiru and Ginika took an overseas holiday that turned out to be a nightmare. Their first baby had come exactly nine months after marriage. This theoretically confirmed to Ginika's parents that the young couple had not gone against church rules by indulging before the marriage in practices meant only for married couples. It was assumed that, since nine months passed before Nkiru gave birth, the couple had not met sexually prior to marriage. Only God knew what the hypocrisy was all about as virtually everybody slept together before marriage. There were stories of some brothers who did not "taste" their wives before marriage only to regret it afterwards. Regret could be that the beautiful bride the guy thought was a virgin, turned out to have been a free highway! In some instances, the woman might be so naive about sex that it would have been better to start early to teach her. In some cases, the guys would want the woman to get pregnant as assurance that she could bear children. Such smartness, however, had caused some couples to run into roadblocks in some cases in which, for example, the pregnancy was lost after the wedding and the woman in question found it difficult to get pregnant again. And if for any reason the couple decided to defer having children, the family brought pressure on them to rescind their decision.

Getting visas to the United States was not a problem for Ginika and Nkiru since they had good jobs and were not going to be any liability to the US government. Ginika's worst experience traveling to America was about that country's health system. Their baby had just turned four when they travelled to the US for a vacation. The child took ill a couple of days after their arrival in Fort Worth, Texas, and they took her to the Cook Children's Medical Center. That was when the drama started.

As Ginika sat at the back of the car looking at the serene fields that lined the route from the medical centre to their vacation apartment home in Dallas, he felt like a man on a major battle field. What came to his mind was that, if David could walk through the valley of the shadow of death, then, he, Ginika, could also walk through the valley of the shadow of this American fraudulent and criminal health system. Ginika was highly persuaded, though, that this was not the health care system dreamed of by the many notable founding fathers of America including the likes of George Washington, Abraham Lincoln, and Sam Houston, whose imposing statue on the Interstate-45 highway to Dallas wowed him. Almost immediately, Fela's paraphrased "double *wahala*" rhythm came to his mind: "if you *waka* go America, come get malaria when Ebola outbreak *de, na tripple wahalaaa*, you de find". The other thing on his mind was the land he would probably have to sell in Nigeria to pay his kid's medical bills. He tried to think of any other way out of the mess.

It happened that, when the child took ill, he and Nkiru started a malaria treatment from a malaria pack they had brought with them from Nigeria. Four days after treating the child for fever, it did not abate. Ginika then insisted on taking her to the hospital against the advice of some friends, who resided in the United States and knew the system. They suggested allowing another twelve to twenty-four hours for the malaria drug to kick in. Ginika's childhood friend, Ogbonna, then a surgeon, and another friend, Akachi, who happened to live near the apartment where Ginika and Ngozi were staying during their vacation, came around that evening. Scared at the possibility of the worst outcome, Ginika insisted they should err on the side of caution rather than be sorry. That was how Ginika, Ngozi, and Akachi went to CareNow Urgent Care clinic in Denton. Once they told the doctor they had come from Nigeria, he advised them to take necessary precautions since they had arrived from an area where there had been an Ebola virus incident, even though their itinerary and the fact that they were not healthcare providers suggested they were low-risk candidates. There were no known cases of Ebola at their Lagos departure location at the time of the incident. Schools had also been closed for about a month, and the kids had been at home throughout the holiday until their flight to the United States. They pretty much understood the situation and acknowledged that the suggested precautions were correct. The doctor subsequently redirected them to the Texas Health Presbyterian Hospital in Denton about three miles away.

As Ginika, Ngozi, and Akachi arrived at the hospital and Ginika carried his child towards the emergency room, suddenly the full circumstances dawned on him about the stories he heard every day about family members' antics in trying to protect their loved ones in the areas where it was known that the Ebola virus had broken out widely in East Africa. At that point, he knew that, even as informed as he was, nothing could separate him from his little one, and he appreciated the vulnerabilities people faced when family members were in circumstances like theirs.

On their arrival, the emergency team was already suited up and waiting, having been alerted of a possible Ebola case. They went to work immediately with necessary tests while isolating the family. Dr Xing and Sister Ying, the nurse, were the staff members on call that evening when Ginika arrived between ten and eleven o'clock. They were as efficient and professional as they could be. Dr Xing discussed his summary four-point plan with Ginika and Ngozi. Fluids would ensure the child remained hydrated while they conducted a malaria test and contacted the Center for Disease Control (CDC). They then took the child off for a chest X-ray and gave the couple a final warning to prepare for a long night! The isolation suites were so interesting,

Ginika asked Dr Xing if he could take his picture, and he agreed. Ginika took a snapshot of him and Sister Ying in their isolation gear.

Dr Xing informed Ginika and Nkiru why he had to contact the CDC. One reason was that they had only ever been able to read about Ebola; they were required to get directives from CDC on the necessary steps to take.

As panicky as the isolation was, Ginika and Akachi laughed off the fact that they might be featured on FOX television any minute as the first suspected Ebola case to hit Texas. They even jokingly discussed TV rights of the story when it eventually hit the news. Akachi left for home shortly after that.

Not long after the samples were taken for test and Akachi had gone home, the result of the tests came back, a 99 per cent confirmation for malaria. At that point, Dr Xing suggested that the child be transferred to a special children's clinic, Cook Children's Medical Center in Fort Worth, where he hoped they would be able to take better care of her. He confirmed to Ginika that he had already been in touch with the hospital and worked out the necessary details so that they could bypass the emergency room protocols and could be transferred straight to a room to save them the stress. Ginika contacted Akachi, who had gone to bed. He also contacted Ogbonna and another friend in Houston and told them the "good news" that malaria had been confirmed that early morning.

When he told them about plans to take the child to another hospital, the friends warned that, on no occasion, should Ginika allow the child to be taken in any ambulance to any other hospital with the confirmation of malaria. Ginika quickly called Sister Ying and asked her to cancel the ambulance, which they had arranged with the receiving hospital. Sister Ying called Dr Xing, and he coerced Ginika to accept the ambulance transport to the children's hospital. This was because of Ginika's "err on the side of caution" stance and been without his "guards"—his friends who were US residents and knowledgeable about the dynamics of the American system. The ambulance arrived, the child was put in the ambulance, and they drove for about forty-five minutes to Cook Center, arriving at about four or five in the morning. The child was transferred straight to an intensive care unit (ICU). No one gave Ginika and Ngozi any indication of the cost of the ambulance service.

Ginika called Akachi and informed him where they were. Akachi shouted and asked why they had to put a child who was stable and whose disease had been confirmed as malaria into an ICU. Akachi knew the financial implications, and that was why he was worried. When Akachi arrived in the morning, Ginika asked him the likely charges of the services. Akachi said an ICU could cost anything between five to seven thousand dollars per night, and a normal observation room between three and five thousand. At that point, Ginika went into panic mode.

Earlier, Ginika had been playing a mind game, fascinated by the near perfection of the system. He and his family were experiencing things a poor African kid like him saw only on television—like the quick response of ambulances and rescue helicopters. Ginika actually started looking for any lapses in such an excellent system as part of his mind game. The first lapse was the malfunctioning of the door in the ambulance between the patient and the driver; it refused to close. The second lapse in the system was one of communication. The doctor on duty at Cook Center told Ginika they had not been informed of the 99% confirmation of malaria. This warranted their conducting another round of malaria tests and full isolation of the child in the ICU.

It took the intervention of Akachi and Ogbonna to get the doctor to concede to the fact that the child did not need to be put in the ICU. They warned that the payment was going to be out of pocket since Ginika and Nkiru were visitors to the US and had no medical insurance. Meanwhile, the doctor argued that she preferred the ICU to enable her monitor the child properly because her choice of medication for the malaria (which had been confirmed a second time) was quinine based and one of the side effects was heart attack. Ginika's "team" considered this "blackmail" from the system! Ginika's "guard", Akachi, Googled the drug and found that the chances of heart attack from the suggested drug was only 3 per cent! Again, he challenged the duty doctor, who in this case, was a so-called infectious disease (ID) doctor. Dr Zing conceded and confirmed that she and her hospital team had discussed and offered to let the child stay in the ICU for the rate of a normal observation room.

Ginka called another friend in Houston, who was also a medical practitioner. The friend practically ordered Ginika to get them to discharge the child from that hospital immediately knowing the fraud in the system. Ginika was helpless at that point because the friend in Houston was an older relative. The friend emphasized that he was ready to make the four-hour journey from Houston to Fort Worth that night to get the child discharged. At that point, Ginika informed Dr Zing that he wanted his child discharged and that he had made the call as the father insisting he was ready to sign the AMA (against medical advice) paper to relieve them of any liability, since there was now a dilemma between their so called "professional calling", prudence of their proposed options (the insurance companies, Ginika was informed, insisted on this to make payments for residents who had such insurance coverage), and non-relevant cost implications of the treatment.

At this time, Ginika had informed Dr Zing that he and Nkiru had given the child a first course of malaria treatment they'd brought from Nigeria before taking her to the first hospital. Dr Zing confirmed she knew about the drug Ginika talked about. In fact, it was what she was going to treat the child with initially before she changed her mind and decided on the quinine treatment. Ginika wondered whether the deviation was deliberate to justify keeping the child in the hospital.

Having projected an estimated cost of over twenty thousand dollars for treatment that would cost less than ten dollars back home in Lagos, Nigeria, Ginika continued appealing to Dr Zing to discharge his child. He asked her to consider the monster staring him in the face and the fact that they had no medical insurance. At that point, he started feeling for the thousands of aliens without health insurance who were the people the Obamacare had been fighting for with fierce resistance from the cartel running the US health system.

After Ginika won the battle on the non-necessity of the ICU and demanded discharge of his child, Dr Zing again coerced him into letting his child remain in the hospital, this time informing him of the threat of the low platelets count, which she said were at dangerous levels. Ginika wondered if this was another case of blackmail. She also said that the malaria parasite was at 20 per cent, which was considered a severe malaria; a minor case was about 5 per cent. Again, Ginika's guards countered the argument on platelets having seen cases of worse platelet counts in other situations. They insisted it was not enough of a threat to warrant having the child stay overnight at the hospital. Akachi Googled the CDC website and confirmed that malaria is not airborne and confirmed the child's case was not as severe as Dr Zing, who was reading from books sent by CDC, claimed. Meanwhile, the CDC document Dr Zing showed Ginika listed ten reasons for considering malaria severe. Only one—parasites at more that 20 per cent—was relevant in this case.

After exhaustive argument, Akachi planned to go home and leave Ginika at the mercy of the hospital that evening. But before Akachi left, they extracted a commitment from Dr Zing to conduct another malaria test immediately. They agreed it should be done at around six in the evening, with the intention of making sure the child did not stay overnight and incur any overnight charges if the results could be gotten within three hours. The malaria test at Presbyterian Hospital and the first test at Cook Center had taken about an hour or two.

Later that evening, the duty nurse confirmed that some test results were back, but results from the malaria test were not going to be ready until morning for reasons best known to them. More blackmail? Ginika wondered. Ginika again called Akachi, who again insisted that the child be discharged. The friend in Houston had a "difficult" conversation with the duty nurse that night, all in a bid to get the child out of the hospital, but all to no avail. Ginika and Nkiru slept at the hospital that night, and in the morning, a different duty nurse informed them the lab opened at around 8.30 and that the malaria test result would be ready then. Within the suggested time, Dr Zing came around and informed them the malaria parasite had gone down to 0.2 per cent but that she also needed to do a complete blood count (CBC). Akachi was not happy when Ginika informed him, noting his arguments the previous days evening.

Even before the confirmation that Ginika's child was OK to go home, they had gone into negotiation over the price of the treatment. A lady named Ging had come to meet Ginika at his daughter's bedside the previous Wednesday evening. She had brought a preliminary bill that amounted to over $7,000. She coerced Ginika by asking if he could immediately make a down payment of $5,000. Ginika insisted he could not do anything about the cost until he had his guards with him for proper advice. Ging went ahead to inform and bait Ginika with a 25 per cent discount if he was willing to pay immediately. *More blackmail!* Ginika thought. Ginika quickly scanned the crazy preliminary bill for the large-ticket items. Behold, there was an ambulance charge of over $4,600 for a fifty-mile journey from Presbyterian to Cook Center. At that point, Ginika knew he would need a full team to argue the charges for the treatment of malaria at Cook Center. Ginika then asked Ging the reason for the high cost of the ambulance ride, and she said she did not know. She would need to ask her superiors to find out. She noted she would not be at work the next day but would give the information they discussed to her stand-in.

Following the results of the CBC, Dr Zing issued instructions for the discharge of the child while arranging with Ginika for an appointment in a week's time. She recommended that Ginika take the child back to their vacation home and continue giving her the remaining dose of the Nigerian malaria medication Ginika had earlier shown her! This again made his friend Akachi unhappy when he arrived, and they went to discuss the financial situation and take the child home.

Ginika's financial team comprised Akachi, Nkiru, Ogbonna, and another friend who understood the US system and was, at that time, dialling in from Ghana. Also on Ginika's team was a social worker from Cook Center, who, Ginika learned from the nurses, could help him drive down the costs. However, the social worker had no real powers because, when Ginika demanded to see the impact of the social worker's influence on the bill, he was told her involvement was already part of the 25 per cent discount earlier suggested by the financial counsellor he had met. The hospital's team comprised the hospital's patient representative, a lady called Hing; the patient registration director, another lady called Ling and her bosses; and members of the hospital's board who occasionally issued directives as the engagement progressed.

At the start of the discussions, Ling, the patient registration director, presented the same initial estimate her colleague had earlier presented, which she claimed was the estimate of the bill as of midnight with the posting already received thus far. When she was prodded as to why the observation room charge was not already reflected on the bill, she claimed it was an hourly rate, so it had not yet been possible to determine or estimate because the child had not been discharged! When Ginika's team insisted and argued it was not rocket science, demanding that she pull the time records so they could do a quick calculation, she then agreed to crunch the numbers. She came out with about $3,200. This brought the preliminary hospital bill alone to well over $10,000! Ginika's team noted the deviation from the original observation room rate the ID doctor had informed them of. Now there was a so-called "hourly rate", which they noted was part of the grand fraudulent scheme. The bargaining on the over-$10,000 bill then started. Meanwhile, at the time, the discussions centred only on the hospital bill since other medical professional bills and those of the two hospitals they had visited previously that first night had not come in. Ginika was made to understand that they would all be sent within about a month, which was another strategy in the overall scheme of the fraudulent system.

Ginika's team forged ahead with the discussion. The hospital team offered a 25 per cent discount. Ginika's team first offered to pay $2,000 within a week as final settlement for the whole cost of the treatment from Cook Center. Ginika's team threatened that the hospital had a chance to extract the little money he had left for his vacation and noted that they might lose entirely if he chose to go back to Nigeria without paying anything. The threat did not make the hospital team budge. Ginika also emphasized to the patient representative that he had spent so much in the American economy shopping in the past days in Houston that his money was exhausted. He had come to Dallas only to relax and do some personal writing, which he shared with his little audience on his personal blog. He noted he would share the experience back home so that people would be aware of how things worked in the US and would not make the same mistake. He threatened to advise people to consider making Europe their preferred choice of holiday vacation. He believed Europe had a better health care system, and he noted how long it had taken him to save for this vacation, which had turned out to be an albatross.

Ginika's team worked their way up to an offer of $5,000 dollars, but no agreement was reached. The director insisted that her superiors would not let her agree to even $6,500. At that point, the discussion became deadlocked. Ginika and his team took the child home and agreed to continue the discussion over the course of the next week. The director gave Ginika her card so he could call her and continue with the negotiation.

As all this was going on, Ginika kept asking himself whether it was happening because he was a foreigner or because he was black. He wished he could get an honest response from the administrators of the Presbyterian Hospital and Cook Center if they would be willing to pay as much as $4,600 out of pocket for a fifty-mile ambulance ride.

It was a nightmare of a vacation for Ginika and Nkiru. He later poured out all his spirit and emotions in a long diary entry about this unfortunate experience in the United States. Nkiru would later read what he'd written and marvel at the time Ginika had spent and the attention to detail he had displayed in writing down the details of what transpired during the memorable vacation. Her instincts would tell her that it would be better to restrict their future vacations to Jos and other lovely places in Nigeria instead of wasting their money traveling to foreign countries in search of pleasure that they could find right there under their noses.

Nkiru later jokingly told Ginika that the volume of writing and the research he conducted those two nights following the hospital incident were enough to earn him a real "pull him down" (PhD) in a subject of his choice given that the Americans could not "pull him down"! To Ginika, it was another time to leverage the wonders of the "new world" of the internet, which put an enormous amount of information at ones finger tips at the touch of a button. This was something that had been unthinkable when they were at university and had to conduct research using textbooks and other books in the school libraries. With the internet, he could find information quickly on any subject, such as medicine. This had helped them greatly to challenge the doctors during their daughter's treatment.

CHAPTER 15
Banker Blogger

A wounded Ginika came back from the vacation full of distrust and regretting his decision to step foot into the United States. He had liked the scenery and the nice parks, which confirmed the stories he had heard about America from colleagues, members of his extended family, and relatives, but nothing had prepared him for the worst aspects of American life! He kept wondering how long was it going to take him to pay off the medical bill. Unless serious discounts were offered, the bill amounted to more than his basic annual salary. With the experience came the humbling of the Lagos banker who thought he had arrived only to be shaken by the realization that he had no reason to get puffed up over his achievements.

But something good came out of the whole frustration because Ginika became more active in his blogging. He explored all channels available to him—his Yahoo group and several other groups he had joined, Facebook, and he even developed a dedicated website for blogging. Initially the discussions centered on the broken American health care system as he wanted to educate his audience of the dangers he had gone through. He later digressed to other social topics that generated interest among his audience.

The whole blogging thing was new to Ginika, and he did not consider himself a blogger in the real sense. He basically thought of issues of general concern in society and put them into words in his spare time. He was amazed at how people reacted to the articles with wide views beyond what he could ever imagine. He would normally add some humour to his writing, and surprisingly sometimes people misunderstood his sense of humour. He could tell because their commentary gave away their misunderstanding to the amusement of Ginika and Nkiru. Take, for instance, commentaries on an article he published when their domestic help left the house meaning Ginika had to take on some of the chores in the house. The title of the essay was "I Am Happy She Left".

> Things are no longer the same since she left, but I am happy about that. It is no longer business as usual after work. All those times I practised my brother's hints from Warren Buffet are long gone. Then, he told me that Warren Buffet said he relaxes after work and enjoys his evening with a bowl of popcorn. Aspiring to be like the guy, I would come home and lazy about and enjoy some popcorn on the few days I managed to find some. I'd watch TV and subsequently go to bed. But that is all history now as I take my rightful place in the Ministry of Home Affairs.

> This was going to be titled "The Day I Ironed My Iyawo's Dress". I was going to describe the pleasure and excitement I felt while ironing my "Iyawo's" dress, something I cannot honestly remember ever doing before now. It was a silk dress designed to perfection and handmade to ensure that all her curves would be displayed at the right places. Ironing it, therefore, required an equally dedicated and patient hand. I was careful to handle such delicate materials made to clothe one of the few perfect women on earth, a person a mere mortal like me would ever remain

grateful to have. It felt kind of romantic and reminded me of "serving her breakfast in bed"—something few romantic men around do to spice things up and blow their ladies' minds.

It started with ironing my kid's clothes as we prepared for the next school week over the weekend. This earned me an embarrassing exclamation from my daughter that she did not know I could iron. I was dumbfounded, but then I smiled, taking note of the indictment underlying the honest confession of a kid. Of course, she must have seen me iron, but I guess not with the passion and dedication that followed this particular period when everyone was contributing his or her quota to make up for "her" absence.

And then came the juggling of other duties, a little time spent here boiling water, putting the laundry in the machine, rinsing and spreading the clothes together while chatting and catching up on those jokes the social media sometimes deny us. You would be surprised how many couples are coping with their phones "pinging". At least two friends have confessed that they sneak into the toilet to "ping" in order not to be scolded by their mates.

Now, I know my way around the kitchen. Gone are all those times I used to starve when staying at home alone when on leave or for other reasons because I hardly had the appetite to go into the kitchen and help myself, having gotten used to support from "wify". Now it's a happy me who rejoices when they say. "Let us go to the kitchen". At least my culinary skills are back in full force. Thank God I did not deteriorate like a friend that used ground *ogbono* to cook beans the day he was holding the fort for his wife. The poor guy thought every ground brown thing in a container was crayfish and, without smelling one of them to confirm, he used the first brown thing he saw. He ended up making draw- beans for lunch. Now his wife takes pains to tag all containers in the kitchen cabinet to avoid a repeat performance.

My little contributions around the house now make me feel proud of myself. I carry that lunch box proudly to work knowing that at least I contributed to some chores in the house to justify the gift, unlike before. And given the sedentary nature of my work, it is really a very useful and beneficial thing to get moving around the house and not just sit around because I am "*di nwe uno*" (husband).

No wonder women with step counters easily rake up thousands of steps in a typical day while going through their daily routine while the men struggle to make a few thousands and have to do extra walking or other exercises to get their numbers up.

But it is not going to be like this for a long time as her replacement is on the way. My hope is that I will not lose my rightful place again in the scheme of chores around the house irrespective of any additional personal assistance in the house.

Ginika Ogadimma wrote from www. ginikaogadimma.com

One would think that, after reading this essay, people would appreciate the position of the writer and probably guess correctly why he wrote what he wrote. Bizarrely, one commentator replied to Ginika's group mail offering his sympathy. He had wrongly assumed that Ginika's wife had just left him! It was a surprised and shocked Ginika who wrote back immediately confirming that his wife was with him in the house and had not left. Luckily for Ginika, one other member of the group email came to his rescue correcting the guy and saying that the essay suggested it was the house help that had left and not the lovely wife they all knew. But how the guy understood the essay to mean that his wife had left was what baffled Ginika. It opened his eyes to the wider perspective and implication of social media that had come to dominate every space in the lives of people. With so much information thrown at people, most simply scan through headlines, make up the rest of the story, and more importantly, form an opinion based on incomplete facts both from the actual data and the fact that they read it in a hurry upside down! The worst thing was that even subsequent commentators took a cue from what others had said about the issue and continued with the misunderstanding.

For Ginika, weekends were sacred days. He spent them with his audience, whom he respected so much. He avoided making any subsequent clarification on any essay he published because he did not have the manpower and time to delve into such extensive exercises. He did not think himself as a blogger even though some people referred to him as one. His blogs normally would start when he picked up thoughts around anything he observed in his environment. Interestingly, as he brooded on the subject at hand, it was always possible to come across closely related phenomena, and he would continue to brood on the subject for days or even weeks before he made a final decision to write about the subject. By the time he sat down to write, the story would usually have already been completed in his head so that it took about an hour or two to pour out the story in its final format.

When he started, he would be so excited about the subject that he would rush off to publish immediately after writing, sometimes without even proofreading the essay to the disappointment of his audience. They would come after him for typographical mistakes, and he would end up apologizing only to commit the same errors the next time. Several times people called him up and advised him how important it was that he proofread the material before publication because a lot of people were tuning into his channel and were put off when they saw small grammatical mistakes. If it was really bad, they would sometimes leave the subject of the essay and start looking out for mistakes and eventually lose the essence of the writing, which was to educate and entertain. With time, Ginika got an editor to help out, and his relationship with his audience improved as they continued to enjoy his writing.

Ginika's posts were intermittent in the beginning because he wrote only after his so-called brooding and took his time to ensure he dished out well-thought-out and articulated blogs. With time, the number of blogs improved and he published weekly issues like a regular magazine. Some of the publications made it to the national newspapers, to the excitement of Ginika. It also did not take much deep thinking anymore to generate essays that kept his audience yearning for more. When there were breaks in publication, friends and relatives would call and ask what was wrong. It was easy to see why his audience yearned for more; he wrote to their hearts because he used their own language and thought like them. He wrote about everyday experiences in a manner that suggested he was conversing with his readers in a close family-like setting. In one blog, Ginika wrote about how his mum struggled with her business and the fact that she kept working at it. A young woman called him up immediately after the publication to tell him how much she had connected with the subject because her very own sister was also in that same space, struggling in a similar start-up business. She informed Ginika that she encouraged her sister after reading his blog. Ginika thus became a household name and a councillor of sorts for some of his readers, and this brought him tremendous satisfaction and courage to write more.

While Ginika derived joy from the counselling, he derived even more joy when he saw one of his essays in a national publication. He would scout for the email addresses of several newspapers and send them copies of his essay, begging them to publish them as they deemed fit. The poor boy was neglected by most of the newspaper houses. That neglect eventually led to the debut of his private website where he subsequently published all his work in addition to publishing on the now "old school" Yahoo email groups and Facebook pages. As social media was changing so fast, to catch up, one needed to change as frequently as the different apps changed. Ginika's excitement over his publications on Facebook did not come from the number of "likes" as was the measure for normal users. For Ginika, it was about the number of views of his Facebook page that was connected to his website. It started with trickles and then began to pour like the rain with some highly placed individuals in society "liking" his page. In the first instance, it was the governor of Lagos State who "liked" his page. He was so mad with excitement that he went to the rooftop to announce that the Lagos state governor had just "liked" his page! After a couple of minutes, some friend called to ask him to confirm it was indeed the governor who had "liked" the page and not some hacker or impostor . As it turned out, it appeared it was an impostor, and that dampened poor Ginika's spirit, but he felt better when his brother Emeka asked him to claim it whether it was the governor or not. That lifted his spirit up again, and at least he could still claim ignorance of the actual validity of the Facebook account so far as it meant some increased traffic to his page and website.

At this time, blogging had become a common phenomenon as most Nigerians had taken to the subject especially having seen the big mansion Linda Ikeji bought with proceeds of the business coming especially from advertisements on her blog. Her blog had become a household name in blogging in Nigeria with news, entertainment, and gossip being the high points. Nudity, of course, sold big, and Linda would not be left out of that as she gave the gullible audience what they all wanted.

The contents of most of the blogs were reports from different sources with no clarification or well-thought-out analysis of issues leaving a huge gap which the few available "honest" blogs like Ginika's aimed to fill. Issues Ginika discussed were everyday issues, and he provided crisp analysis and humour in the mix that meant his writing was not for everyone, and those who mattered in society paid attention to what Ginika had to say every week. From all indications and the calibre of people who visited Ginika's blog, it was evident that his opinions counted with regard to serious national issues.

To remain in the business, Ginika knew he had to up his game; otherwise, he would soon lose his audience to more dynamic blogging sites that offered all kinds of entertainment. Then he began a short story series, a new program on his blog. He wrote a full book and divided it into short stories, which he published each week in parallel to his normal essays. Thus, like the followers of any television or radio series, Ginika's audience were now able to follow a written play online as part of his or her blogging experience.

In *The Converted*, Ginika displayed his master stroke as a gifted story teller as he described the life of a conman of God who duped his gullible audience out of so much money while playing on their ignorance and fears, which he had instilled in them in the first place.

Episode one depicted Reverend Fineboy as this particular guy was called. Reverend Fineboy advised the wife of the church's neighbour to beware of her mother-in-law! Reverend Fineboy was the pastor in charge of a branch of Mountain Christian Ministries, a small church in Benin, Edo State. The church was bizarre even in the type of songs they sang. Every Sunday morning this is what was heard: "*Ma ijigi kobo iji agba nkwa, chukwu ga gi nchufu!*" (If you do not have *kobo*—money—to dance with, God would send you out!). What kind of church is this? The neighbours asked each other, but no one had any answers. But the bells would ring again, and the song would be repeated the next Sunday.

Mama David sold soft drinks in front of the church where they lived and owned the property. Married to the son of the landlady, she lived in a flat in the same compound while the landlady and her other children lived in another flat. Mama David was busy cleaning and opening her shop on one particular Monday morning when Reverend Fineboy walked in. Mama David thought he had come to buy some red candles and matches as usual only for the man to call her to his side and speak in a hushed tone. He told her to beware of her mother-in-law because she was up to something! "Up to what, Reverend Fineboy?" she asked.

"I don't know," he said, "but I received a vision about her!"

"A vision from whom?" she enquired. "What were you thinking about me that I came to your vision?"

"A word is enough for the wise," he said. "If you want some prayers or deliverance or protection, meet me in the church later for spiritual fortification!

"*Tufiakwa, spirit gbukwaa onwe gi ebe ahu!*" she shouted to the reverend as he left for his church. (God forbid you and your spirit!)

Though Mama David called the fake Pastor's bluff, she was, all the same, worried about the so-called revelation from the pastor, so much so that she narrated the incident to her husband and her mother-in-law. Her mother-in-law told the other children, and they too did not know what to make of the revelation, but they quietly decided to see what would become of the relationship between Mama David and their mother. Funnily, nothing happened, and the relationship remained cordial. Within weeks, Reverend Fineboy moved out of his church and opened his own church in a nearby village. This was after falling out with the main pastor of the church because they disagreed over the sharing of the proceeds from the Sunday offering. Reverend Fineboy sighted the fact that the church membership had grown in number since he joined; he insisted that the growth must be attributed to his joining, and hence he demanded a heavier share of the Sunday offerings.

In Episode two of *The Converted*, Reverend Fineboy was at it again. This time Ginika wrote about the experience of a pretty girl his friend, Fadi, had told him about after he went for his job interview at

Benin. Fadi had been longing after the girl for a while but decided to take things easy as he expected to have a sustainable relationship with the girl. The girl was from a respectable home from Fadi's hometown and was living with a family friend in the same street as Fadi. On several occasions, Fadi had run into the girl while driving out or coming in, but he'd never had the chance or reason to talk to her until one day when he saw her in a street adjacent to theirs when he was on his way back home. Fortunately for Fadi, it was raining, and the girl was about to take shelter in one of the shops along the street when Fadi saw her and another of her friends. Both girls were dressed in blue skirts and white tops with purple scarves around their necks. As their eyes locked, Fadi quickly put on his brakes as he blessed God that he finally had his chance to talk to this girl who had intrigued him for so long. "Hi! Are you going home? Please get in so I can drop you," Fadi told her.

She responded with a smile that suggested this was a won battle. "Meet Chichi, my friend. She lives by the corner. Could you drop her off just before you turn right into our own street?" the girl asked.

"OK," said Fadi. "And what is your name?" Fadi asked.

"I am Padi," she said. "How similar our names sound—Fadi and Padi!" Fadi said, and they both burst out in laughter. That broke the ice, and they started chatting as if they had known each other for a while. And it really felt that way because, though they had not spoken, both of them had made all the gestures expected of neighbours who were checking each other out and waiting for the right time to hook up or for the one person to make the necessary move. With time, they got so close that Padi would tell Fadi all about her daily routine including her attendance at a new church that had just opened a little distance from their neighbourhood. Padi had just visited it, liked it, and planned to stay in the new church. The owner of the church was one Reverend Fineboy, she told Fadi the first day they talked about the new church in town.

"Owner *kwa*!" Fadi exclaimed.

"Not really, she replied. "I meant the overseeing pastor in charge."

"OK," he said. "What does he look like?"

"You can use your imagination from his name now. Common," she said.

"OK, I get it. So you are already checking out the pastor of the church you just visited, is that right?"

"You are not serious, you spoiled brat!" she retorted. "How can you say that? Don't you know he is a man of God and married for that matter? Anyway, the thing is that there are so many nice people there. I got a feeling of prosperity in the air. I am already thinking of joining the workers in the church to be sure I fully participate in the activities. However, they said I must be interviewed by the pastor before I can be admitted into the workers' club."

Fadi was impressed at Padi's disposition, especially her participating in the church activities, even though they would go make love after the workers' meetings, and he did not feel it was right. But the happy Padi would take him on as if nothing happened, and they kept their lives as separate as possible.

"So tell me how the interview with your pastor went," Fadi asked on the day of her scheduled interview with Reverend Fineboy for admittance into the workers' club.

"Not so well," a dejected Padi told Fadi. "The pastor asked if I had had sex in the past year. I said yes, and he said I could not be admitted into the workers' club for that singular reason. He wants his workers to be as pure as possible, and because I've had sex outside marriage in the past year, I failed to qualify."

"So how would he know if you lied and told him you had not?" Fadi asked.

"I do not know. I just told him the truth," she said. "I guess he expects people to tell him the truth, but I am sure some may tell lies, and there would be no way for him to find out. Some people probably have to grapple with their conscience for the rest of their stay in the church."

"This is really getting interesting," was all Fadi could mutter then.

Soon after the interview, which Padi actually thought had been awkward, she was called for another interview by the same pastor. To her wonder, Reverend Fineboy offered to lower the bar for her since she was pretty and could serve as a main usher in the church because they wanted pretty ladies to lead the men to God. Since men who were not that attracted to God were attracted to women who were attracted to God, Pastor Fineboy's new church hoped to eventually get men attracted to God in the process, which he called linking or leading souls to God! "And do you have a boyfriend?" he asked during this interview. She answered in the positive to the disappointment of the pastor who was worried that the boyfriend could lead her to sin. "Does he touch you?"

"Yes, pastor!"

"Where?"

"Everywhere!"

"So sad. That means you are defiled and may need cleansing to be pure again. Even if I am to waive the one-year no-sex criterion, I may need to dig further to be sure of who you are and to know you inside and out before we can have you join our workers." As Reverend Fineboy spoke, he moved closer to Padi and lay his hands on her shoulders and tried to run his fingers over her dress. Just then, Fadi came into the meeting room unannounced. This shocked the pastor, who moved quickly from running his fingers on Padi's body to shouting in unknown tongues as he pretended to be praying for her.

The Converted became an immediate success boosting online hits to Ginika's website and attracting commentary on other social media channels. Religion remained a topical issue around the country with fake pastors doing all they could to woo unsuspecting, ignorant, and gullible people into their congregations. Ginika knew this and made up his mind to exploit the situation to drive more traffic to his blog. Nudity was even the greatest opium for bloggers who wanted high traffic, but this was a no-go area for Ginika, who thought his blog should remain ethical and draw lessons only for the better good of society.

In the third episode, Reverend Fineboy's church had grown, and he had even opened branches in some parts of the country including Lagos where so many of his earlier congregants had relocated. To ensure a constant filling of their spirit, he made monthly visits to the outside parishes from his world headquarters in Benin City.

Interestingly, most of Reverend Fineboy's converts were ladies who were mainly looking for husbands or looking for children. Revered Fineboy travelled to Lagos every two weeks to minister to his flock, which included Njideka. Njideka lived with her cousin and always talked about her daddy in the Lord, Reverend Fineboy. She was so possessive of this pastor that her cousin feared that she might have been hypnotized. One day Njideka's cousin came home, and his wife told him what Njideka had been up to lately. She informed him Njideka had broken coconuts in front of their house at midnight as instructed by her pastor. "And what is the significance of the coconut breaking?" Njideka's cousin asked her. Njideka responded that he would not understand the things of the spirit. "What things of the spirit are you talking about? Better be sure and open your eyes before they start taking you to a *Babalawo*," he retorted. "You will be the object of their laughter."

"Taa, there is nothing like that! You don't understand that some things need to be broken both in the spirit and in the physical. Hence the breaking of the coconuts," she explained.

Her cousin sighed as he looked at Njideka. "Njideka, let me tell you something. I do not trust either you or your Reverend Fineboy. The way I see it, you would be ready to undress for your reverend so he could check you out if he asked you, given that he has so much control over you and your thinking. I am indeed surprised that a graduate like you would be so deceived. You are not able to pick up the Bible and read for yourself. You can only be deceived by your so-called Daddy in the Lord whom you would always go to see in the hotel in the guise of ministration. By the way, do you meet him alone or in the company of his wife or other ministers?"

Njideka kept quiet and did not answer his question, confirming his fears about the actual happenings at the so-called outreach meetings she attended. A couple of months later, Njideka started vomiting and showing symptoms of pregnancy. Her cousin's wife noticed and suggested to her husband that they advise Njideka to go for a pregnancy test. After much reluctance, Njideka succumbed to the pressure and went for a test, confirming their suspicion and finally letting the cat out of the bag. She had been sleeping with Reverend Fineboy for some time during every outreach visit to the shame of the cousin who had somehow suspected that something untoward was going on.

On a subsequent outreach visit, Njideka's cousin followed her undercover. He was armed with a video recorder to nail the fake pastor in the act. He burst into the room where the reverend had already removed his clothes and lay on the bed with Njideka by his side. She was still wearing her brassiere and panties, but her cousin got a clear picture of the naked Reverend Fineboy. Njideka's cousin confronted the "reverend" about his illicit affair with his cousin and the fact that he was responsible for her pregnancy. "I can explain this! I can explain this!" was all the reverend could mutter as Njideka's cousin asked him why he was taking advantage of poor ladies who had gone to him for help. After being threatened that Njideka's cousin would report him to both the police and his wife, the reverend signed an agreement to take care of expenses incurred at the birth of the baby and also to send upkeep allowance for the baby.

Meanwhile, as Ginika continued to excite his audience with his skilful writing, he started making arrangements for his work to be published in a book. The title was *The Converted*, and he planned to debut it a couple of months down the line. It was interesting when he wrote as part of his "Why" series an essay he titled "Why You Need to Buy My Book". He flipped between his essays and the script, keeping his audience tuned in!

> So, I thought of writing a book, but I need to make
> sure that I will be able to sell it first, hence my attempt
> at first conducting a market survey here. If you have

heard that D'Banj's song (why should apostrophe be in somebody's name *bikonu?*) in which he sings about how people are telling him "*na* your papa and your mama, na only them you go sell your song to", you will understand where I am coming from. But he made it at the end of the day, and I am sure all those who said those things to him then are friends with him by now, though it's definitely at a small fee knowing that success attracts brothers and sisters very fast. "I know him before", na like that oh. So, as I begin to sample opinions, I believe you will be better off being on my side and standing up to be counted among those to get their hands on the first printing with, of course, my autograph. *Choi!* That one sweet oh. And please don't ask me why I am already talking about sales for a book that has not been written. After all, have you not heard of two people fighting over money they anticipate they will pick up on the road?

But let us discuss why you should not buy my book first. First, you have read the damn book, so why pay for an old newspaper? And if you do not think that reading all my busybody small essays amounts to reading a book, wait until you read *The Thing around Your Neck* by Chimamanda Adichie. Believe me, the short essay is meant to address the reluctance of those who find it difficult to sit in one place and read a whole book! By putting it out in small pieces, via Zuckerberg's platform, I guarantee an easy read. OK, that's a small lie. You and I know that carpenter *kufie osisi osi na owu* style. (Carpenter's mistakes sometimes can be construed as a style in the design.) But the fact remains that these small pieces can be put together to make a book, and that would definitely make me an author! We'll see about that!

Coincidentally, it sounds as if the reason you should not buy my book is the same reason you *should* buy it. For heaven's sake! It would only be fair, you have read it already "*naa*"; otherwise, you may not have any basis for criticizing my pals at the newsstands who are even registered members of the Free Readers Association. I can only apologize—and I mean it—for not letting you know the price up front, and who can blame me for that? If I did, you probably would have gone to the competitor's site. You can ask *The Punch* newspaper what happened when they denied free access to their website. But at least they can generate money from adverts while my own site has not started seeing traffic until recently, probably because we don't have enough gossip and naked ladies to go round. But we remain steadfast that our due share will come to us; after all, the Lagos state governor liked our page the other day. As soon as that "like" dropped, I shouted and started dancing that I had arrived, but my brother was quick to point out that it might be a scam! But my sister, who was in the "spirit", fired back that she didn't care whether it was an impostor or not, and that emboldened me to claim my "Ambode like" by fire by force. I insisted to anyone who wished to listen that it was him, or his brother's brother! The truth is we just got noticed—period!

Again, when you buy my book, you will be among the chosen few destined to fulfil a prophesy. I know you remember about "That Money They Said They

Would Pay Us" in around twenty fifty something? If you don't, then contact me, and I will send you that essay. I know we are all religious people, so this one, if nothing else, should excite you naa, being part of a prophecy, and who knows? You might as well be part of those who will receive, as it surely will rub off on you.

But on a serious note, you will realize that such a book will be a record of Nigeria's history at a point in time wrapped in story form for the delight of the lucky ones who get a copy.

And if you think that is not enough, then brace up, as I am ready to give you more. You will be getting the background behind all those essays you have been reading, and you will get to know the circumstances and frustrations that gave birth to each one, including the internal bedroom stories that have been kept away from your prying ears these long years. Even my private conversation with Ambode after he liked my page will be laid bare for all to read.

But then we need to get this thing to a publisher first. It is still a long way from happening. Can you imagine? I surfed the internet, looking for someone to do some small compilation of my work and put it in book form only for one *Oyibo* in the UK to offer to do it for $10,000, and she said she liked the work anyway. And this was before the naira got floated oh, but after "Mr Common Sense" started singing the song "buy naija, to grow naija". For five million naira at the conversion rate at the time, I did not even need Mr C to think and seek out naija. But I do not seem to be getting traction in that regard, so I am also thinking of establishing my own printing and publishing firm. After all, that same Mr Common Sense started using his own channels to speak out on his positions on policy issues when they wouldn't give him the chance to talk on the floor of the national assembly. He demonstrated that by saying that "Only you can stop you!" So, Madam UK, if you won't come down from your high price, then watch out for my private publishing. It will take me only a little more time, but it will definitely happen before twenty fifty something!

Ginika Ogadimma wrote from www.ginikaogadimma.com

CHAPTER 16
Pull Him Down

Finding content for his audience made Ginika always on the lookout for opportunities to travel. Travelling was always an opportunity to meet people or witness events that turned out to be stories that he could share. Most of the travels were peaceful and enjoyable and not associated with the kind of trouble he encountered in the United States of America that made him wary of international travel. After the American hospital drama, Nkiru had said he had done enough research to earn a PhD to which Ginika agreed. The research they did those few days had unconsciously transformed him into an informal researcher. This happened to the extent that Ginika turned a doubting Thomas and would always ask anyone arguing with him to "Google it" first before he can agree to your position. Please Google it before you "pull him down", Nkiru would echo in the background whenever she was around the discussion

The experience left Ginika an inquisitive person and a voracious reader at the same time. From writing short essays to short stories, Ginika branched off into a new area of commentary on new book releases. Reading new books and commenting on them became as important to Ginika as writing essays. His favourite authors were Chimamanda Adichie and Chigozie Obioma. Chimamanda specifically became his idol, and he took note of Chinua Achebe's comment that "She came fully made", a phrase he would use to describe any new author who met his expectations.

One reason Ginika went into book reviews was to encourage his audience to also read and look out for new publications. In writing about the books, he created interest and did not give away the main exciting themes of the books. Sometimes he also created conflicts in the reviews with the expectation that it would generate discussions and hence more inspiration for people to go out and look for the books. With time, Ginika started receiving requests from authors to review their books and publish his opinions as part of his blog for a fee. This created an additional level of income for Ginika and even more inspiration to read and write more. Ginika read and wrote about the big names for free, and the upcoming folks paid him to feature their books, an irony he once laughed about with Nkiru.

As they hung out one Saturday evening, Ginika was shaking his head as he told Nkiru, "This writing business can be interesting oh. Do you know that one guy accused me of copying Chigozie Obioma's slang without his authorization in the last essay I posted? He was furious that I breached Chigozie's copyright!"

A surprised Nkiru shouted, "*Inukwa!* Please, is the person Chigozie's brother?

"Mba," Ginika answered.

"Is he the father or mother or Chigozie himself?"

"Mbakwa oh," Ginika answered.

"So what is his problem then?" Nkiru asked. "I hope the guy does not want to 'pull him down' this time 'himself' and not you," Nkiru said, laughing. "That reminds me. I have not even read your last post," Nkiru confessed.

"But you have 'liked' it already on Facebook! Chai! So you are one of those who will 'like' even when you have not read the material?" Ginika queried.

"Don't you know it is the weekend?" she asked. "With all the house chores to do, I have to 'like' now and read later," Nkiru said, smiling.

"I don't have a problem with that as long as you read it eventually," Ginika responded.

The comment on copyright had come from Ginika's publication of an essay on Chigozie Obioma's recent book, *An Orchestra of Minorities*:

> ### Chigozie Obioma's *Orchestra of Minorities* and the Nigerian Analogue
>
> "Ah, so you are now into politics!" My senior colleague said to me as he saw me with Chigozie Obioma's new release *An Orchestra of Minorities*. I smiled and told him that the book has nothing to do with politics. I had to explain further seeing the unconvinced nature in his facial expression. The reference to an orchestra of minorities in the book has to do with a scene that the writer observed—small chicks with their mother crying in frustration and helplessness as they watch a kite swoop in and carry off one of the chicks. Nonso, the lead character, and his girlfriend, Ndali, rush out when they hear the cry of the chickens, but they are too late to ward off the threat as the *Egbe* has already flown off, and even Nonso's catapult cannot catch up with the flight. It is a concerned Ndali who observes a rhythm in the cry as Nonso explains to her that the chickens feel pain and cry about their loss just as we human beings do.
>
> Having explained the title, we went on to other things and analogues of minorities in our national life. The term minorities can refer to tribes as is the case when it is used in politics, but its meaning can also be extended beyond tribes to include the poor and less privileged in society. We know that there is

nothing like tribes among the elite when they want to share the national cake among themselves. Take, for instance, the 5.5-billion-naira SUV vote of the national assembly. In that issue, they are all one. Tribal minorities are used when the elite want to have advantage against themselves while using the poor who are the real minority in sharing of national cake and not in numbers. So, in Nigeria's case, the orchestra of minorities refers to the sharing of the national cake by the elite minority. The poor would refer to this as an orchestra of majority—the majority that are helpless in the midst of plenty, the majority that cannot access decent wages, housing, medical treatment, or education because the minority think they do not matter. The majority is ever willing to collect the stipends dished out in the name of TraderMoni on the eve of election so they can learn the song in preparation for an orchestra of the minorities. The orchestra of minorities in this case turned from helplessness to "share-the-moniness". No, these minorities are not helpless or frustrated; they are the oppressors who have taken the common good of their countrymen and women and taken off like that kite! They have taken off to Dubai to buy properties. They have taken off to London to get some fever taken care off. They have taken off to London for the graduation of their children while leaving the schools in their country that are used by the majority in ruins.

But what is wrong with this Chigozie sef? Must it always be tragedy? Coming from the "fisherman", I thought and prayed he had repented but "for-where"! How can one use such a gift to dish out sorrow? I hope Obioma repents and gives us something with a happy ending next time. He has the power to change the narrative; that is what writers do. They are gods. They create and destroy. Nothing stops Obioma from ending the sorrow that Nonso goes through and making things happen so that Ndali comes back to him at last. He is a god and has the power to do that, but he will not; instead, he chooses to break my heart and make me angry at the character after spending my money to buy the book and spending my time reading it. I am sure going to think twice before I read his next novel.

But do not get me wrong. This guy is a master. I think I was just on the second chapter when I climbed Mark Zuckerberg's board to shout on the rooftop, "This guy is good!" Only a week after I wrote that, I read that the book had been nominated for the Booker Prize for Fiction. It was not a surprise to me because I had never read anything like that before. I had read very interesting novels, but never had a writer described his characters through the eyes of his "chi".

Gaganogwu, you would bear me witness that I am telling the truth because, in these days of blogging, we can never know what is true and what is false. Some people have died because of fake news. Some have become jealous over what they see on social media. And "I have seen it before".

Chigozie Obioma is a master of his subject, and I was not surprised to learn he is an assistant professor of literature. I would ascribe the same words of Chinua

Achebe to Chimamanda Adichie. Chigozie Obioma came "fully made".

Ginika Ogadimma wrote from www. ginikaogadimma.com

"So, because you mentioned Gaganogwu, this young man wants to hang himself!" Nkiru asked. "Chai, people can be busybodies in this life, oh. Did he not realize the whole essay was about Chigozie's work itself? You were even publicizing the work. How can that one word trigger a copyright issue. Anyway, talking about copyright, have you even thought about protecting yourself as well? Or do you think you do not need copyright for all your materials?"

"You can trust me on that one," answered Ginika. "I have Googled it already."

Ginika had read about stolen works and had researched the issue of copyright, though it never occurred to him that he could be involved in a copyright issue until the fan made that comment. He understood the specific elements that applied in Nigeria where he lived and had even taken steps to protect his own work. Ginika knew about the Berne Convention, the General Agreement on Trade and Tariff (GATT), fair use, and fixed and tangible form. These were key words that come to his mind whenever he thought about the subject. They were living in the eighties and nineties, and he knew that works published after the first of March in 1989 did not need to include a copyright notice to gain protection under the law, though it was still important to include one so an infringer could not claim ignorance. The fact that Ginika wrote his essays and published them on social media channels meant he had put his work in a fixed and tangible form. He knew this for a fact from the research he had conducted on the subject.

Like every one of Ginika's essays, he drew some lessons from the description of Chigozie's book in making an analogy to Nigerian society. Ginika was so passionate about his country that anything that affected Nigeria affected him emotionally, especially when he knew that there were so many hardworking citizens out there who, like himself, were from good homes. These were the kids of public servants. They had worked their way to the top and were still raising their shoulders high in competition with the children of big politicians—kids who had had everything going for them since the days of Azikiwe!

To Ginika, Nigeria remained the giant of Africa even though some of its citizens try hard to "pull her down" dragging her name to the mud like the so called "Yahoo Yahoo" boys.

It all started as a joke, with young boys at university touting fraud as the next big thing to happen to them. The desire to wear the best clothes and win the acknowledgement of girls in school prompted a lot of university students to practice internet fraud. This was now a raging issue in the society, and the country's world image was at stake. The internet was the main backbone of business, so criminals infiltrated it to cause sorrow to unsuspecting individuals. They gradually sent out very enticing soliciting emails. Then they sent them in droves as the menace took centre stage. In Nigeria, the Economic and Financial Crimes Commission (EFCC) was in charge of investigating internet fraud and had sent out notifications to social media platforms asking parents to monitor their children and be sure they were not involved in any illicit crimes.

Ginika had read about the "Yahoo Yahoo" boys but had never given them much thought other than realizing that society was really going downhill, and with society went his beloved country. He, however, took more interest in the reporting of the EFCC when he read a news thread that listed some names he thought he recognized. He was eating his popcorn as he listened to the political discussion on the seven o'clock news on TV. Suddenly he took note of the scrolling words at the bottom of the television screen and had to shift closer to read the information. At number ten on an EFCC's list of offenders was Uchewuba. *It cannot be him*, Ginika thought. He had recognized the name from Aladinma but was not sure it was his friend. In any case, the information from EFCC did not mention the exact crimes of those on their list; they simply asked that anyone with information on how to contact the people on the list should contact the commission.

"Who knows? They might even be offering him a job or just want to get information on some other issues from him," Nkiru suggested when Ginika brought her attention to the list on the television screen.

"Or they just want to 'pull him down'," Ginika said, laughing as he discarded the thought that the list had to do with any financial crimes for which the EFCC had been established to investigate.

— CHAPTER 17 —
The Copyright

"Old boy, I thought you said you had banned yourself from travelling to America after your American wonder experience!" Ogbonna said to Ginika. Ogbonna had been one of Ginika's childhood friends. They had gone to the same primary and secondary schools. They went to different universities, and afterwards, Ogbonna departed to the United States on a Shell scholarship and became a practicing surgeon in Dallas.

"Who can resist the temptation of this place, my big friend?" Ginika said. "It can only be for a while. As they say, *Iwe nwanne anaghi aba na okpukpu.*" (The differences between brothers are only skin deep.)

America had always been the place to be, especially given that Ginika had relatives there, so his accommodation was guaranteed. Moreover, the things he liked, especially clothes, were cheaper there than they were in Europe, and for Ginika, children's clothes were the focus. Ginika could wear anything and even depended more on the *adire* textile art and other Nigerian handmade clothes. This time, though, Ginika prepared well and made sure he got a travel insurance plan worked out to avoid any surprises.

Ginika told Ogbonna he had heard there was going to be a reunion of Umuahians in Dallas the next day, so he had brought Nkiru to attend. "We came in two weeks ago and have been in Houston with the kids, but we left them there with their cousins so we could have some exclusive fun time together without their crying!"

"I bet you it's for the best," said Ogbonna. "Sometimes it's nice to rekindle your love for one another as the stress of family life can take away the affection couples have."

"So tell me, Ogbonna, what is this movie premiere you talked about?" Ginika asked.

Oh, it's the premier of a movie Uchewuba recently wrote and directed. I hear it is an excellent movie, and many people around Dallas are already talking about how the storyline reminds them of their childhood days and how it resonates with them," Ogbonna said. Ogbonna knew Uchewuba from Aladinma days but from a distance. One of Ogbonna's patients, whom he happened to know through Uchewuba, had told him about the movie.

Uchewuba had read theatre arts in Nigeria before emigrating to the United States. He studied communications at postgraduate level and had taken up roles in several small African American news channels without much to show for his American dream expectations. A friend of his came to the United States and asked to stay in his apartment for a period with his wife, who was expecting a baby. He obliged the couple, who stayed for the duration of the pregnancy while avoiding seeking any medical care for the mother. A worried Uchewuba contacted Ogbonna for help so his friend's wife could get some cheap health care that would not involve high-cost facilities. The couple did not have any health insurance, and they wanted their baby born in the United States only so the baby could become a citizen. Ogbonna had given them a reference, and they had remained in contact ever since.

"Waoh, this is a small world you know! The Uchewuba you are talking about is my Owerri *kporakpo*," Ginika exclaimed. "He is Johnbosco's brother. Johnbosco was my 'paddy man' in primary school, and the boy had his way with girls like mad. They lived behind Ngwa Street in Aladinma. He was one 'lankish' tall boy."

"Yes," Ogbonna said.

"In fact the husband who came with his pregnant wife on holiday to Uchewuba's house is also a primary school classmate of ours, though I have forgotten his name now. But I heard some story about their visit," Ginika continued. "You know how news flies around among peers like that. We know who lives where and who has travelled to where and all that and I think it was Johnbosco who mentioned that story to me."

"So will you stay over for the premier since you know the guy?" Ogbonna asked.

"Of course," said Ginika. "And come to think of it, we are even friends on Facebook. But let me confirm with my Oga at the top!"

"And who is that?" Ogbonna asked.

"You mean you have not been following happenings in Nigeria or what? Are you that busy making your American dream sustainable?" Ginika asked, noting how he thought Ogbonna "had arrived" a long time ago given his medical practice.

"Well, you know the downside of all this social media. I try to follow news, but I'm not that addicted to everything that happens," Ogbonna replied.

"I get it. And you are right about having to be careful about social media. It can tie up people. They can unconsciously become addicted the same way they can become addicted to cocaine and other hard drugs, which make people lose focus. And they don't even realize it's happening," Ginika responded. "The key word should be *moderation*. Anyway 'Oga at the top' is slang for 'the boss'. A government official who was being interviewed on television used that term to describe the ones who called the shots, but the video of the interview went viral because he did not know the web address of his organization."

"Yes, so sad. But do you blame them when the politicians fritter away all the resources that are supposed to go into training. They do it in the name of allowances no one accounts for," Ogbonna retorted. "Think of the headings—security allowance, constituency allowance, wardrobe allowance! All sorts of rubbish leaving the civil service comatose because it serves their purpose to have ad hoc organizations that duplicate the work of the ministries and continue the culture of waste and corruption. OK, *abeg*, go consult your 'Oga at the top' so I can firm up plans if you guys are going."

Ginika said to Ogbonna "OK, it's all settled. The Umuahian event is tomorrow, and thereafter we attend the premier of Uchewuba's new movie and head back to Houston the next day. Umuahians are very active in the US, and I am guessing it has to do with the love they have for the school, given that the most important aspect of their formative lives was routed in the school," Ogbonna said.

"Well, I think it may also have to do with the fact that the people in United States want to have every excuse to gather with brethren at least to close some gaps of brotherly love they miss back home," Ginika replied. "I mean they seek out every opportunity to party—wakes, birthdays, and graduations. Just name it, and they'll celebrate all through the night, rocking till day breaks. This is in addition to the fact they have the money to spend too. Interestingly, people back home do not groove as much as those here."

"Baby, I am confused over what to wear for this movie oh," Nkiru said to Ginika.

"It is not a movie premiere in the real sense," he told her. "This is kind of a preliminary version, as a lot of work is still going on. The director just wanted to showcase the work to a select audience for criticism. They are expecting the full work to be completed in a couple of months from now, and that is when the actual premier for the final version will happen."

"I get it," she said. "That means I can be as casual as I want then, since the likes of Oprah are not expected at this stage!"

"Ya, right!" said Ginika.

"This is feeling romantic already. It blends in with our plans to have a lovely time alone for a change. At least once in a while married couples should indulge themselves," Nkiru kept fantasising aloud. "It mustn't be only about the children. How I wish the story would be about romance you know! Like a love story where prince charming comes in and sweeps his love off her feet as you did a few years ago! I want to be like her, but this time I want diamonds lavished on me and maids attending to me! I want to be like the queen I am and deserve!"

"OK! OK! Please come back to the real world. There will be no diamonds here and no maid servants today. We are only going to see the preliminary version of a movie. It will cost us nothing because it has not been released yet. Please!" Ginika retorted.

"The storyline has been kept under wraps because it has not been released," Ogbonna mentioned to them as they made their way to the seats at the middle row in the air-conditioned dark room. "You know how the industry is. In fact, the organizers initially thought of restricting the use of phones and cameras but changed their minds since it's just family members and close friends who are invited. Any sharp man could easily copy the lines, and before you know it, it would already be in the market before the real thing."

An hour into the show, Ginika said he wanted to leave.

"What is wrong, honey?" Nkiru asked. "Aren't we going to stay to see what happened to the reverend?"

"No. I am feeling sick to my stomach and need to get out of here as soon as possible."

"OK. Let's go if you don't feel comfortable staying, but I wish we could stay to the end. It looks like a good movie to me," Nkiru said.

"It sure is a good movie, and I know what happened to the reverend, so there is no need watching *my own* movie being presented by someone else!" Ginika said in a slightly raised and angry voice.

"Hold on! Hold on! What are you talking about here?" Ogbonna enquired as they exited the room and walked towards the car.

An obviously angry Ginika only mumbled, "*The Converted! The Converted! My Converted! My Converted!*

"What is 'my converted'?" Ogbonna asked.

"Chai! Chai! The internet *egbuom oh*! Internet egbuomu oh! Facebook *emee m alu* oh! Facebook eme m alu oh!" cried Ginika. (The internet has destroyed me oh! The internet has destroyed me, oh! Facebook has dealt with me oh).

"Ogbonna, I need a lawyer immediately," Ginika pleaded with his friend. "I need a lawyer—please—as soon as possible! Uchewuba must be stopped today!" He turned to his wife. "Nkiru, are you saying you do not have the imagination and retentive memory to recall the scenes in *My Converted*? The story Uchewuba showed tonight is mine! Every bit of it is mine! He did not even have the imagination to change or add anything. He retained even the names and locations! Oh my. This guy is a bastard! That is why he was always stocking me, asking for the date of the release of the next episode. He was the first person to 'like' each posting I published! Worse, still, he subscribed to my website and also had the posts delivered to his email! I cannot believe this!"

"Are you sure of what you are talking about, bro?" asked Ogbonna. "This is America, oh, and he can sue you for defamation of character along with pain and suffering and much more rubbish that people do here."

"America indeed!" said Ginika. "I am one hundred per cent sure he plagiarized my script. I can prove it in any court, but first I have to stop him from going ahead with the development of his movie to safeguard my intellectual property."

"OK, since we both know him, I suggest we both call him to a meeting. You can present your claim, see what he has to say, and take it up from there," said Ogbonna. "Let's treat this as a family affair. I am sure he is a responsible man and will do the right thing."

"Responsible man?" Ginika asked. "What responsible man would steal a friend's work and pass it off as his own? Family affair! I am not a PDP member who uses family affairs to cover the misdeeds of its members to the detriment of the country," Ginika continued.

The People's Democratic Party (PDP) had been ruling Nigeria since the country's return to democracy in 1999 with no tangible progress made to nation building or institutionalizing governance. Most infractions and corruption cases levelled against its members had been swept under the carpet and accepted as a "family affair". This was what Ginika referred to when he insisted his copyright case would not go the way of the PDP corruption. "Ogbonna, you must help me here, please. I know Uchewuba is your friend, but you must put yourself in my shoes." Ginika told him he needed his help especially given that he and Nkiru would be going back to Nigeria the following week. Ginika told his friend he would need support to oversee the case in the United States, and Ginika would file an immediate concurrent suit in Nigeria once they got home. "This idiot must not reap where he did not sow!" he blurted out. "He read theatre arts at university and should be able to write his own scripts or buy one and not steal someone else's!"

"No problem," said Ogbonna. "I will get you a contact immediately, but I will also have a chat with Uchewuba to let him know what is coming his way. Come to think about it, I told him you were here in the US, and he did not seem to care much. He only mentioned you were friends on Facebook. And on the night of the movie showing, when I told him I had come with you guys, he somehow excused himself and hurried backstage to attend to his crew, whom he said needed him. It was surprising that he left so abruptly, but I just did not make anything of it."

"Filing a suit in the US is most important for two reasons," Ginika said. "One, I hope to get good traction with the case here because of the more robust legal system. Two, the system is also more advanced so that more circumstantial evidence can be admitted in court. This is not the way it is in Nigeria, a country that is still struggling with judicial reforms. There, the impact of certain digital evidence is still a tall order given that some of the judges are not even computer literate at the moment. So, while I wait for Nigeria's legal system to sort itself out, I will have to use the US system to stop this guy, and I believe the US is even a bigger market where the most money will be made, even though the Nigerian market is the main market."

"Hello Doc, this one you are calling this early morning. *Odikwa mma*?" Ogbonna asked Uchewuba. (Is it OK?) "I have an issue I need to discuss with you right away. It is urgent. Please can you meet me at my office at, say, eleven o'clock?"

"Waoh, Doc, that will be too early for me!" said Uchewuba. "You know, we worked until very late last night with the select audience viewing. We had to stay behind to take in all the critique from the audience. By the way, I did not see you when we finished. Did you leave early?"

"Yes, I did, and that is partly why I want us to meet immediately."

"OK. Let's make it lunch, then, so I can get a bath and tidy up a few things."

Uchewuba lazily rolled out of his bed leaving behind the naked girl he had slept with over the night—one of girls at the viewing who had fallen head over heels for him because she thought he was cute, intelligent, and sexy. She had boldly walked up to him after the show, offered her praise and appreciation for the great work, and introduced herself as an upcoming artist looking for a mentor to bring her up in the industry. Uchewuba had been overwhelmed by her boldness. They had hit it off almost immediately, flirting at the after-viewing party. He had given her a ride home, but she had told him her family was out of town and she did not want to go home alone. This had surprised Uchewuba but also made him quite happy.

"OK," he'd told her, "you can stay in one of my two rooms. You are lucky my friends are not on vacation this time around; otherwise, you might have had to sleep on the couch!"

"Oh my, don't tell me you are not that romantic! How could you let a lady sleep on the couch while you sleep on the bed? The least I expected is that we sleep on the same bed, or at least you sleep on the couch and offer me your private room!" the "upcoming" actress said. "You look too gentle to suggest what you just did."

"Well, it depends on my mood," said a laughing Uchewuba. "After all you left your family home to come into my small crib. Maybe we would have been better off going to your own house since your folks are not around and you do not want to sleep in the house alone. Anyway, we are here now, and I have no guest, so you have an empty room all to yourself. On a lighter note, the couple that stayed in that

236

room last summer had a baby. I hope you do not get infected and have a baby after sleeping there tonight!"

"I did not know having babies was contagious," she'd said, "or is it only in your guest room that it happens? Why don't you come show me the side of the bed they laid on so I will be sure to avoid that area and not have a baby by the morning please?"

"What do you mean," he'd said. "I did not sleep with them! How would I know the side of the bed they slept on? I would assume the whole bed would be contagious in that case, so you might try sleeping on the rug if you do not want to get pregnant. On the other hand, if you do not want to contact pregnancy, then you may have to come over to my bed, but that one is not fool proof either, and I cannot guarantee you will be left alone all night. You know the weather is pretty cold this season in Dallas!"

Uchewuba had ended up sleeping in the arms of his newly found protégé until Ogbonna woke him up with the call early the next morning. "Honey, I have to get over to a friend's office for an urgent meeting at lunch, OK? The guy is a doctor friend of mine, and I hope he does not already have a diagnosis of your pregnancy at hand." He smiled on his way into the bath, knowing his guest was watching his naked butt.

"Doc, you requested this urgent meeting," said Uchewuba. "Tell me it is good news to wrap up my day please. I sure had a great time last night. The viewing was a success. Everyone praised the script and wondered where I got my inspiration because I had not mentioned the storyline to anyone before then."

"Well, that is exactly why I have called you here," Ogbonna said while looking straight into Uchewuba's eyes. "Because someone you may or may not know is claiming the script is his! And the problem is that the person is also a personal friend and school mate of mine!"

An obviously shaken Uchewuba laughed at Ogbonna briefly before getting his composure back and telling his friend, "You can't be serious! What are you talking about? Did you not know I studied theatre arts at university even before delving into communications and the recent surge of social media? What is the name of the fellow you are talking about here? Is it the guy you mentioned who came with you last night?"

"Yes! How did you know it was him?"

"Who else would it be if not him since he was there with you, and he left without seeing the entire film?"

"Anyway," continued Ogbonna, "as of now, he has hired an attorney to file a suit to stop your work. That is why I had to call you in. I need to hear your own side of the story before things get out of hand. You know the embarrassment this would cause, especially with the news media here in Dallas and the whole of the US, not to mention what will happen when the word filters to Naija which I am sure it will as soon as my friend gets back to Nigeria. He also plans to take you to a court in Nigeria at the same time since he knows your ultimate market is Nigeria."

"What did you say his name is?"

"Ginika Ogadimma!" Ogbonna said.

"Ginika … Ginika. I am not sure I have heard that name before. I don't think I have made his acquaintance," Uchewuba lied.

"Are you sure you do not know him?" asked Ogbonna. "Because he mentioned that you are friends on Facebook."

"And what does he do for a living?" Uchewuba asked.

"He is a banker," Ogbonna replied.

"A banker all the way from Naija claims my script is his? Just listen to yourself, Ogbonna. How can you believe him? Can you imagine the insult? How can he defend this claim? A banker! When would he even have the time to sit down and write a full-page essay, not to mention a hundred-page movie script? You know what?" he continued. "I do not care what his name is, what his profession is, or whatever he calls himself. You can let him know that I will see him in court. I won't spend my precious time over any discussion on the matter. I won't lose my sleep over him either!"

But you have not answered my question, brother," said Ogbonna. "Did you copy this work from anywhere? Did you copy even parts of it from anywhere? Can anyone claim ownership of any part of it for any remote reason?"

"You know what, Ogbonna? I will not stand here and answer your question because I know you have already made up your mind, and nothing I say will matter. You mentioned he is a classmate of yours, and I would not expect anything less from you than to side with your friend, so it would be pointless for me to tell you anything. Let's just leave it at that and let him go to the so-called courts. I will respond accordingly."

"OK. OK," said Ogbonna. "There is no need for us to quarrel over the issue. As I said earlier, both of you are my friends. I just wanted some transparency about the whole thing. I am not judging either of you at this time. For all I know, it may simply be a miscommunication or misunderstanding that can be sorted out easily." Ogbonna tried to cool his friend down.

An obviously worried Uchewuba left Ogbonna's office dejected. Ogbonna observed that even Uchewuba's pretence of raising his voice to cover his fear did not help him much. He had sweated profusely in the air-conditioned room and had left in a hurry, rejecting Ogbonna's offer that they go out for lunch together since it was already lunch time.

The reality of the allegation dawned on Uchewuba the next morning when he received a brown envelop at his door. He had not slept all through the night following the meeting with Ogbonna. He had kept telling himself he was the author of the work and nothing could happen if anyone challenged him and came forward with a law suit. *This is America!* he thought. *Let him come now! The idiot thinks he can come all the way from Nigeria to make noise? Little brat like him! Instead of sitting in his bank office attending to his clients, let him poke nose where he should not! Is his salary not enough for him? What is he talking about, sef?*

Uchewuba had seen it coming, but he had not expected it to come this sudden and early in the game. He had thought that the worst-case scenario would be a fight for the rights when the movie premiered in Nigeria, by which time he would have consolidated his claim to the script through the history of the work in the US. Nothing had prepared him for the mess he was about to enter so early in the scheme. His hands were almost shaking as he quietly opened the brown envelop fearing for the worst.

> From the office of the Chief Magistrate, District Court of Dallas County, Dallas, Texas
>
> Dear Mr Uchewuba,
>
> A case of plagiarism and stealing of personal works have been instituted against you in this court. You are requested to …

An obviously defeated Uchewuba sank into the sofa as he took a closer look at the words of the letter. He kept rereading the words as if they were going to make him sick. "Damn it! Damn it! This is serious. This is serious. I can't believe this! I can't believe this!" This was all he kept muttering. "This was not the plan. Damn!"

Meanwhile, Ginika and Nkiru had returned to Houston to reunite with their children. The first thing Ginika did was to call Johnbosco, who was Uchewuba's brother, to let him know what he had just learned. He wanted to give him a breakdown of his line of action so he would be aware.

"Hello, is that Johnbosco?"

"Yes. Who is speaking please?"

"This is Ginika. I am calling you from the US."

"Waoh, US kwa? I thought you mentioned your foot would never set in that country again after the mess the health system put you through?" he enquired.

"My brother, as if you know, this kind American na one trip, one trouble.

"*Hia*! What is it this time?" Johnbosco asked.

"This time it is not their health care, oh, but something that could also give me a heart attack. Guess who I ran into a few days ago? Your brother! I did not speak with him, actually, because things kind of happened so fast. My wife and I went with Ogbonna to watch the preliminary version of a movie that is supposedly coming out in a few months' time. But the script was a carbon copy of my work, which I have openly shared on Facebook! The worst thing is that the supposed owner of the work claimed it to be his, and he happened to be your brother, Uchewuba!"

"No, no, that cannot be true! The guy read theatre arts at university, and even though he has gone on to study other subjects it's still possible he has a flare for works like that. Remember he was even your drama director at Aladinma?" Johnbosco reminded his friend. "And by the way, how did you know it was your exact story that was played out?

"Come on, J. B.! How can you be saying something like that?" Ginika responded. "Are you saying that, if you see your own handwriting, you would not recognize it? Unless it is not yours! It is like chatting with someone over time. You would already be in a position to guess how the person would respond to any topic you raised. I mean even Osuofia recognizes his wife's abacha when he tasted it in someone's house. I am able to recognize my writing when I read or watch it acted out on film. Anyway, I am trying to prove that it is my work now. It will be my mission for some time to come because I know it is not going to be easy, and that is why I have called you," Ginika said. "Please tell me if he mentioned to you at any time about his emerging work and what the work was about?" Ginka asked.

"Not really," said Johnbosco. "I recall Uchewuba mentioning he had something big coming out, but he was not sure when it would be completed. He further mentioned he would keep the story under wraps for now since he did not want anyone hijacking the work midstream. Funnily enough, that had not been his style. He had always been quick to share any little thing he had going on. When he wrote short plays, he would send them across and ask for feedback, but he didn't do that this time. I assumed he had a number of colleagues who could do real critiques of his work so he didn't need any freelance family reviews. I wouldn't normally deliver my reviews in good time anyway because of my schedule. So even if you have proof that it is your work, what do you intend to do now?" Johnbosco asked.

"This is going to be very embarrassing, you know?" Ginika told his friend. "Indeed, that is why I called to find out what you know about the deal, and I wanted to let you know what is coming. As we speak, he has been served court papers to stop any further action on the script here in the US, and I intend to file a concurrent civil case in Nigeria once we get back. Nigeria is his final 'bus stop', so I must initiate processes to make sure he is stopped and that the audience knows the real owner of the work even if, for any reason, I am not able to stop the work before it hits the market."

On arrival in Nigeria the following week, Ginika mentioned the brewing storm to Akin and the rest of his banking crew, who came visiting on the Sunday following their return. "Choi! Igbo boys always trying to reap where they did not sow! How can someone not just use his own brains but would rather steal someone else's?" Akin queried. "Could he not have simply taken a cue from the trails of your publications and developed his own story rather than copying everything in toto?" he continued. "This reminds me of someone who copied his neighbour's paper in the exam hall but was so dumb at it that he even copied the person's university matriculation number. I trust you know what to do. At least from the Naija angle, it is a matter of highest bidder! I hope you know what is involved in the Nigerian judiciary. This one is not a matter of behaving like Ogadimma, your father, oh. That way, nothing would come out of the case; in fact, you would be going to Silverbird Cinema to watch your own movie with others while crying 'had I known', and your case would be pending in court till kingdom come! We will help you find a good lawyer who will take up this case, preferably a Senior Advocate of Nigeria—SAN—so that the case can be given the priority it deserves. I understand cases are actually lined up for mention in court by seniority of the lawyers.

Copyright cases can drag out for a long time, and this one is even more tricky, given that you have not officially published this work and thus, in a true sense, do not have any valid or approved instrument to claim this is your work. And you know what? Your case is even more complicated because the laws here are so old that digital evidence is not really relied on here for the resolving of cases, so this would indeed be a test case. It will take a sound lawyer to make a convincing argument, and even at that, a lot of novel and liberal open-mindedness will be required before any judge will buy into such argument, unless your lawyer sights cases around the world in which similar situations have been resolved, and the court is then boxed into a corner to do the right thing. Even at that, court cases are not about the right thing, but about what the law books say, so by and large, the case may be thrown out on technical grounds. In recent times, social media has helped to shape opinions even in court, but that is mainly in advanced countries where the system operates as intended and has a conscience, not in a place like Nigeria. In such a system it would be easy to start a social media thread on the issue and raise people's awareness. Your only hope may be traction in the American courts that may be disposed to giving a wide-reaching judgment that may go beyond America."

"You may not be entirely correct, oh, Akin," Ginika replied. Have you heard of the Berne Convention? Do you know Nigeria is a signatory to the convention? Do you know that, since March 1989, you do not have to include a copyright notice to claim ownership of your work? Do you know what it means for material to be in a fixed and tangible form? It is not true that the Nigerian judiciary may claim the inadmissibility of electronic evidence. There have been recent reforms, though more needs to be done. The guy thinks he is smart, but he will find out that he cannot fool everyone this time!" Ginika recalled the incident during their primary school when Uchewuba had passed off Ginika's script as his, and Ginika had been unable to prove it.

Barrister Shittu was a well-known legal presence in Lagos, and his chamber had been touted as one of the best in town, specializing in criminal and civil law. "So tell me," said Shittu. "What makes you think the script you watched is your work? Let me even play the devil's advocate here before we go into details," the lawyer said to Ginika.

"OK," said Ginika. "For a start, I can tell you he did not change anything from the essays and stories I published on my Facebook page. Well, he did change my name to his," Ginika responded. "The only thing he did, and for which he thought he was smart, was to go straight to producing the movie from the script. As part of my blog, I write short essays, which I publish on my website, www. ginikaogadimma.com. The themes of the essays range from everyday family issues to politics and a little romance here and there," Ginika continued. "However, in the recent times, in order to remain dynamic and in the spirit of continuous improvement, I elected to diversify. I introduced a separate series of short stories that combined into a longer dramatic story. My ultimate goal was that it would end up as a book. The audience, of course, would have read it all as they followed me both on Facebook and other social media platforms. I designed the series to encourage reading. It is supposed to be a new concept! People can read an entire book online gradually before they buy it, essentially making sure they get full value for their money. So, as part of my regular publications, I also wrote an essay titled 'Why You Must Buy My Book'. In this essay, I outlined for my followers the details of the concept. Of course, I mixed It up with humour, which is one of the main reasons they follow me. So the series was supposed to come out in book form first and eventually end up in the movie theatres until this issue came up."

Ginika took a deep breath and continued: "Now, going directly to the question you asked, sir, as I watched the drama that night, the exact lines from *The Converted* came to my mind, and before I knew it, I was already reciting the script along with the characters in my mind right there in the hall with my host and my wife oblivious to what was going on in my mind. At first, I thought it was a mere coincidence and that Uchewuba just used the first episode of my work as a starting point for what would be a different story. But I was so shocked as the script continued with my episode two that I had to literally burst out of the venue. What other proof is there than the fact that he used the exact lines I wrote? Moreover, we have now obtained the full movie manuscript from a guy in the US, and the damn thing is word for word. I know most of the stories were about our experiences during the eighties and nineties, and we both share a common childhood, having grown up in Aladinma, but for God's sake, there is no way we could both have written the same thing word for word! My Aladinma cannot be his Aladinma word for word, even if we were conjoined twins! I called his brother, who happened to be my classmate, and asked him about it," Ginika said. He said his brother had told him he was working on something big, but it was still under wraps! Why was it under wraps when he used to share his other scripts with his brother and other family members? I bet it was still under wraps simply because it was a stolen work! I ask you to please go through my posts of my story, *The Converted*, and then take a look at this. Ginika dropped a bound document on the table. "In fact, Uchewuba turned out to be one of the guys who 'liked' every post I made on the subject and would always be enquiring why I missed an episode if I did. At least the trail of his enquiries and comments are still there on my Facebook page. Thank God he cannot delete those! I never knew he was not just reading but also waiting in the wings to plagiarize and distribute material he had not authored." Ginika finished: "I will give you time to study the materials. I'll come back tomorrow so we can discuss the matter further, but meanwhile you may have to start preparing to institute the case in court immediately. We need to ask for stay of action, real or imaginary, that he may be planning to initiate in Nigeria with respect to this work."

Several days later, Ginika was again at Shittu's office to discuss progress. "Good morning, Mr Ginika. Please take a seat. I have gone through the material, and as you insisted, the words exactly match. The only problem is that there is no way of telling who owns the work! He can just as easily claim that you copied his work, you know? And the fact that you posted the work on your Facebook page and through other social media channels does not in any way confer copyright of the works on you. It is really going to be a novelty case here in Nigeria to be honest. We will give it our best shot, and if nothing else, take it to the court of public opinion for the final arbitration. And talking about copyright, are you sure that your friend has not gotten this work copyrighted in the US? If he has, the dynamics of the case will take another turn."

A worried Ginika got up from his seat and walked up and down the large office. "Barrister, there must be something you can do," he said. "For example, I signed my name at the end of each of those episodes. Does that not confer any right to me as the author even though there was no copyright declaration on each one?"

"I am afraid it may not since the copyright laws refer mainly to the copying of materials that contain a declaration of copyright. And even at that, digital copying does not count! And by that I mean copying by computers, for example. If you look at most copyright laws, for example, the key message is 'thou shall not copy', but then you ask yourself, when you drag and drop a music file from a server to your hard drive, what are you doing? There are millions of examples of copying going on all over the internet. You must have heard that Google Books copied and stored millions of books in their database. I know there have been so many twists to copyright law, but in all of that, the key message is that the intellectual substance must not be copied without authorization or outside the boundaries of fair use. Hence, in your case, if and only if the material was copyrighted, whether here in Nigeria or oversees, Uchewuba's use of it without authorization would definitely be against the copyright laws."

The lawyer continued, "An option would be to investigate the agreement clauses on the channels on which you posted the material the first time. We could see if there is anything there that confers any atom of right on the individual. I mean, at this time, we have to grab every straw we can find. Perhaps there we can find something that can help, if not here maybe in the courts in the US. All the same, we are filing the charges first thing tomorrow morning at the High

Court of Lagos State here on Lagos Island. I have contacts who can facilitate the case and give us a favourable position. We are suing him for criminal breach of trust and stealing intellectual property. We are asking that he stop all activities involving the material within Nigeria and anywhere else in the world pending the determination of the substantive suit. Since he does not live in Nigeria, you may have to effect service of court papers to him. This may be at his last known address in Nigeria. It may be at his family home, and it might be helpful if news about the suit is picked up by national newspapers and online media. This means you have to get ready for some real expenses."

"Yes, I know that," said Ginika. "And, as I mentioned, his brother is my classmate and friend, so it will be easy for me to take the papers to him and have him follow up with a phone call to his brother. I also have contacts at some of the online news channels, and I can influence them to broadcast news about the institution of the court case so he is forced to respond from wherever he is."

"OK," said the barrister. "That is fine for the news channels, but you also have to remember to shy away from blogging anything about the case yourself as anything you write may be seen as prejudiced and may, in fact damage, our position."

"OK. I understand that, although I wish I could start blasting him already, but that can wait till a later time."

After the filing of the court papers and facilitation by Barrister Shittu, the first hearing date was set for about a month later. A parallel action was undertaken by Ginika, who leaked news about the case to various online media. Akin, Ginika's colleague had contact with Ikeji's social media empire, and they made use of it to get the information across. They had it published for a small fee, and of course, they phrased the headline to reflect the fact that the original work was truly Ginika's. As expected, the gullible public feasted on the news. The headline attracted a large number of comments in which people called for the head of Uchewuba! Those who knew him realized he had never overcome the copying habit he had begun at university; in fact, he had carried it over to his professional life.

One person called Gregory wrote, "What do you expect of them, Nollywood! If their females are not sleeping around with the directors for roles, their guys are cheating in real life even after cheating at university!

Another person, Nkem, wrote, "One wonders why Nigerian society honours these guys only because they are TV celebrities leaving aside our doctors and engineers who make real contributions to the building of our nation. You can imagine the number of national awards they get each year, and maybe that is why this country remains the way it is today—backward!"

A more intuitive Chinelo wrote, "Who told you guys that this Ginika guy was the original owner of the damn work? We have not even seen it. Has it even been published? It is like arguing about who owns some money yet to be picked up by two friends. For God's sake, read the story very well. This was just something the guy claimed he posted on Facebook. How many such posts have you even copied and reposted today? All those jokes we post every day—you mean if I decide to now compile them into a big volume, one clown would come out and claim he posted it first, so he should have the title to my book? Think for yourselves, guys!"

The different perspectives outlined in the comment threads brought out a number of the points that Shittu had made in the earlier discussions he'd had with Ginika before he filed the court papers; it was not going to be an easy ride. With the hype of social media, it was no surprise when Ginika encountered a cluster of cameras swarming around the High Court of Lagos State the first morning of court proceedings.

Ginika took the morning off so he could attend the opening of the case. With him were two friends who were interested in following the case through. Surprisingly, after Shittu registered appearance for the prosecution, two lawyers from the chambers of another SAN stood up and registered appearance on behalf of the defence, as Uchewuba was not in the country. Johnbosco was also in court that morning; he had exchanged pleasantries with Ginika, who enquired why his brother was not in court. "I think he already has enough fire on his buttocks back in the US, so he could not make it down here," said Johnbosco. "I feel for you, brother, having to go through this mess. Let us see how this plays out. If Uchewuba did this and saw his game was up, I think he should simply have given up and settled this thing quietly like a family affair rather than letting it go this far. Now all eyes are on us, and I mean the eyes of all the one hundred and seventy million Nigerians and some extra eyes across the globe! And come to think of it, Ginika, has he made any gestures to you in terms of settling this thing?" Johnbosco asked. "Has he offered some soft landing like handing over to you the work he has done thus far or even offered to share proceeds from the work with you or something of that nature?"

"Not at all," said Ginika. "But even if he approached me, I doubt if I would oblige him because for me it is a matter of principle not even money. What he did is terrible. He has basically taken away the fun in my work and caused a lot of distractions for me. The time I would have used to write I now have had to use to prepare for this case and do research on copyright infringement laws and engaging with my lawyer. As you can see, two lawyers are representing him, which does not suggest someone who has not done anything wrong. I have made up my mind that I will pursue the case to the supreme court if need be until I get justice. He cannot reap where he did not sow, and especially not from my farm! *Mbanu*—no—it cannot happen," Ginika said while gesticulating for emphasis

Social media was awash with the details of the first day's proceedings. Captions depicted the tricky nature of the case and highlighted the limited capacity of the current Nigerian legal laws to do equitable justice to the case: "Friends at war over non copyrighted work on Facebook!" "Top Lagos banker and blogger in war of his life to save his non copyrighted intellectual work!" "Who owns this writing I saw on Facebook?"

This was a real test of the robustness of the Nigerian legal system.

A lot of reforms had been advocated in the past, but they were mainly focused on the need to eradicate bribery and corruption in the system; and most recently they had focused on the electoral laws, but there still existed a huge gap in what needed reform in Nigeria. The laws, for example, derived either directly from the colonial masters or from the military. Efforts at reforming them had been slow. This case along with the large coverage it was generating seemed to put the Nigerian judiciary on the spot, especially with the concurrent case going on in the US, which had also started getting some news coverage since the involvement of Facebook had been brought into the case. It was not the first time a parallel case concerning infractions would come up in Nigerian and foreign courts. Some corruption cases had been discharged in Nigeria only for the same politician to have been convicted and jailed in United Kingdom to the shame of the Nigerian system.

The Dallas judge handling the case had invited top management members of Facebook, Inc., to provide the details of their copyright guidelines for individuals who posted on their platform. These guidelines were to be considered during the court proceedings in what he termed a novelty case. The honouring of that invitation by no one else than the owner of platform, Mark Zucks was all it took to give the case the international dimension and attention that had in no way been intended, exposing Uchewuba to even more ridicule and disrepute, Ginika thought. However, Uchewuba stood his ground and vowed to protect what he called his own as he spoke in front of the cameras with a smile that exuded confidence even as some US media commentators who had followed the case within the US and Nigeria via Nigerian social media posited that the real author was Ginika. They expressed confidence that the US courts would do justice to the case and also hopefully set precedence and help tighten rules that applied to ownership rights to social media content.

"So what are your thoughts on the genuineness of the claims on both sides?" a reporter asked Zucks as he stepped out of the courtroom.

"And what specifically made you interested in this case out of all the other cases that Facebook has been involved in recently?"

"Well, as you know, we have user agreements attached to the use of our site, and like every other human endeavour, there is no way to know the dimensions things will take at the end of the day when put in use. We are watching the case closely and will adopt any measures to mitigate any property right infringements in the future. We will also adopt any recommendations that may arise from the case. I am interested in this case, and I felt I had to attend in person because, as you already know, one of my chief executives is from Nigeria, and we were actually there a couple of months back to visit with some of the young chaps who are already doing a lot to improve themselves. We were at the Yaba IT hub in Lagos and met with a lot of highly intelligent and energetic young Nigerians who are developing programs. The zeal they exhibited attracted me to them, and I had to make a second visit within a week to engage the country's president on the possible ways we could collaborate to ensure a good working and business environments to maximize the potential of those kids. There is no doubt that this case will revolutionize the user agreement codes attached to our platform, and our lawyers are following up on the case."

The headline was all over the news: "Mark Zucks, founder of Facebook, attends court case on ownership rights between two Nigerians!" CNN, CBS, and FOX news all covered the court case that was taking place somewhere in a small court room in Dallas where a historic judgment would turn around copyright laws the world over.

Ginika got a call from a correspondent who introduced himself as a CNN reporter, and before he knew what was happening, he was already on a live Skype call with Christian Pourman sharing his thoughts about the court case and having to fight the fight of his life to prove to the court that he, indeed, was the author of the script in question. "Thanks, Christian, for having me," Ginika began. "As you may know, a parallel case is also being pursued here in Nigeria, and I believe that no one in his or her right senses would go that far if he or she does not believe in the claims. The work is mine, and I know it like the back of my hand. My DNA is in the work, and I hope the lawyers I have engaged will prove it and that technology will also play its own part in proving my case."

"So tell me, what was a banker doing blogging?" asked Christian. "And when do you find the time to do that, because I understand you are a successful banker as well."

"I suppose it all has to do with passion." Ginika adjusted his position and faced a window as if he was facing a camera while talking on the phone. "I always believe that, if something is important to you, you will always find time to do it no matter how tight a schedule you may have. For me, especially, I stumbled into writing, and it became a way for me to relax. First the writing was intermittent, and then it developed into a habit. I no longer felt accomplished if I did not do any writing over the weekend. And come to think of it, there is so much to talk about given the state of affairs in the country. One thing you can observe in any business office in the country is people engaging for the first thirty minutes of the morning as they discuss the happenings in the country. It is a conversation that is burning in everybody's heart. So for me, that fire keeps burning past the office mornings and into the weekend, so much so that I have to write my thoughts down in the absence of my office colleagues. It's the only way I can let out my anger and frustration."

"It is indeed remarkable to see how social media is changing lives and habits in this new world. Thank you for joining me," Christian said as he signed off.

"Honey, this case is entering another phase, oh! Look at all the publicity this is generating," Nkiru said as soon as Ginika got off the Skype call with Christian.

"Well, the wider publication it gets, the better for me since it will put pressure on that thief and encourage him to confess. Unfortunately, it seems to have been working in the opposite direction now. It seems Uchewuba may now be feeling too ashamed to throw in the towel. He may want to hang on to the case on technical grounds," Ginika said.

"But the more he clings onto his claims, the worse it may be for him at the end because there is a remote chance of a criminal angle to this whole thing."

"How do you mean, criminal kwa?" Nkiru asked.

"We are talking about the US here, babe. It is not like here where sometimes anything goes and people who break the law can brazenly rub it in the faces of the public," Ginika lamented. "We live in a country where someone can steal the people's money and even file for enforcement of his or her human rights to be allowed to have back the stolen funds when the source is obviously fraudulent. It's a place where a person can work as a civil servant all her life, have millions of dollars in her account, and still take EFCC to court claiming the money is her hard-earned money. The US law looks at not just technicalities, but the intent. And public perception of issues is brought to bear to ensure that justice is not just done but is seen to be done, babe." Ginika continued: "I guess that the publicity is a good thing because, at the end of the day, the book may even become a best seller irrespective of what is inside."

"You can say that again! A book that is already causing so much controversy?" Nkiru responded. No one needs to tell you it is already a best seller even without publication, and it sure will now have much more coverage than you originally intended."

With the case advancing rapidly in the US courts, Ginika paid more attention to the proceedings and instituted a regular conference call with his US lawyers and Ogbonna to review every strategy and course of action. On one particular occasion, Ginika mentioned something that he had not told them before because it had just occurred to him. "Gentlemen, I forgot to mention that my Yahoo account was compromised a few months back. Is it possible that someone may have hacked my account in search of something? And the weirdest thing is that, when I looked at the manuscript Uchewuba had, the last episode in my book, *The Converted*, was also included, even though I had not published that episode at the time we visited Ogbonna in the US and discovered the fraud."

"This is a big one!" shouted Ogbonna. "How come you did not say anything before now? This may be the break we have been looking for, guys. We can get the timing of that breach and have the FBI investigate Uchewuba's email account and computer hard drive to trace any link to the hacking of your account. Given that he was almost stalking you for the next publications, it may well be that he was frustrated waiting for you to publish, and he sought to help himself! We will notify the judge and have him issue the necessary investigation warrants to allow the FBI to proceed. Damn! Your friend may well be on his way to jail without knowing it. OK, guys, we all need to be discreet about this information. Share it only with people who need to know and no one else. It will be absolutely necessary to ensure tight lips to prevent anyone playing smart and attempting to destroy evidence."

"Not really," interjected the lead lawyer on the case. "This copyright case is not a federal offence, so the possibility of the FBI entering into the case is remote at this point. You need to understand how the US law system works, guys."

"Hello? Who is there?" Uchewuba said. Someone had been banging on his door.

"This is the FBI. Please open the door. Open the door now!"

Uchewuba reluctantly unlocked the door to his now-famous two-bedroom apartment. With the news and headlines blowing the case of electronic plagiarism out of proportion, as he saw it, he was now daily bombarded by members of the press who knocked at his door or stopped him along the road to enquire about his own side of the story. When he heard the knock on the door, he thought it was another of the nuisance reporters, only to be confronted with a search warrant for his house on the orders of the Dallas judge. "Do you have a warrant?" he asked.

"Yes, we do. Please step aside, sir, so we can do our job."

The FBI team quickly moved into the house, bypassing Uchewuba as he looked on in bewilderment. His life was about to take a new turn in the America of his dreams. After a couple of minutes, the team came out to the sitting room.

"OK, sir, I guess you will have to accompany us to the office. We have questions for you, and we will have to do further forensic examination of your laptop and desktop computers," the leader of the team told Uchewuba.

"That is not a problem at all. I just have to put on my shirt, and I will meet you guys outside."

"No worries, sir. We will just wait right here in the sitting room for you to get dressed, and we will be on our way."

"I will be with you guys in a moment, and I can assure you, you guys are just wasting your time, as I do not have anything to hide."

Back at the FBI office, Uchewuba was allowed to declare ownership of the properties that had been confiscated at his house to help in the criminal investigation of wire fraud. He provided the passwords with which the investigating team unlocked his computers as well as his Yahoo password so they could get into his email account to review his messages. His phone was also checked for only God knew what!

"OK, sir. You may go for now, but we will have to retain your computers for now. However, we can release your mobile phone to you."

A worried Uchewuba put in a call straight to his lawyer. He told him of the latest events and asked him to come down to the FBI office immediately. "Did they arrest you?" the lawyer asked.

"No, but they made me come to the office after they searched my house, and after looking over my computers, they informed me they would keep them for further investigation. They released only my mobile to me. I want to know what is going on, and only you can extract that information from them. Please come down as soon as you can so these guys do not play any funny games with me."

"So what is the problem?" Uchewuba asked his lawyer after he had arrived at the FBI office and made some inquiries with the officers.

"Things are not looking good, my man," the lawyer said. "They seem to have traced a hacking attempt to an IP address matching your desktop's. And they have obtained a valid court warrant to investigate you. They have been doing that for quite a while from their own end."

"Is that not a breach of some sort of my privacy?" asked Uchewuba. "Is that not an offence on its own? They cannot just do that in this country!" Uchewuba shouted.

"Well, they can as long as they have a valid court warrant, and they did," the lawyer replied.

Uchewuba was confident they would not find anything on him since he had only signed into Ginika's account and copied what he wanted. Nothing could ever link him to Ginika's work directly; he was sure about that and was afraid only because of the pornographic films he had on his laptop. His sex tapes were his private life and were no one's business, so they were not going to be a problem. And if, for whatever reason, the contents reached the public, he swore he would take the authorities to court and claim the maximum damage.

"They are not interested in your sex tapes, my friend, so that should not worry you," his lawyer assured him. "Rather we have to come up with explanations for the coincidence that the author of the first Word document in which you saved your script was identified with the name Ginika Ogadimma instead of your computer's name. Also, the hacking attempt at Ginika's email account was made at exactly the time you first saved the document on your desktop. The time stamps match so well that the coincidence surely will raise suspicion. All that is not their concern, though, given that it is not a federal offence and that is not why they arrested you. They apparently took notice given the widely publicized news about the copyright case."

Over the past weeks, things had taken a turn for the worse for Uchewuba with respect to the criminal wire fraud case the FBI had been investigating. It was no longer only the press shadowing Uchewuba, but now also the police were on his tail, and the chances of his going to jail were high in addition to losing the case with Ginika. Commentaries shifted from who was going to win the rights to the work to how many years in jail Uchewuba could be serving if his hacking were proved. At this time, no longer would he raise his head in defence of his supposed work and vow to fight for his right to his material. Now he would bow his head and claim he did not want to talk to reporters who swooped down upon him after court sessions or squatted in front of his house.

"Mr Uchewuba, tell us if you have ever been involved in other cybercrimes like credit card theft, identity theft, stuff like that," one reporter asked him one morning. Uchewuba did not answer; he simply climbed into his car and drove off in a hurry.

"Hello?"

"Hello, Johnbosco," said Ginika. "Have you heard that the FBI arrested Uchewuba?" He had just seen a news story on CNN.

"No, oh," Johnbosco replied.

"It was on the news this evening. Christian said he was arrested for wire fraud last night."

"Oh my God!" Johnbosco broke down over the phone as he listened to Ginika.

"To be honest with you, I never expected your brother was that bad, but things started making sense when I recalled a news thread I saw on TV some time ago. It was an EFCC list that Nkiru and I took notice of. Uchewuba's name was on that list, but we did not give it much thought at the time because we were not sure it was actually your brother."

Apparently, Uchewuba had been into wire fraud in the United States for a long time; he had been shipping cars and other material things to Nigeria with proceeds of the crime. The FBI had been on his case discreetly for over two years and had initiated contact with the Nigerian authorities. To cover his tracks, Uchewuba had passed himself off as a scriptwriter and movie promoter in the United States. To nail him, the FBI needed solid evidence and witnesses to his nefarious activities, and they were happy to learn of the copyright case. The search of Uchewuba's house was to gather evidence directly linked to his wire fraud charges, but secondarily to provide supporting materials for the witness they expected Ginika could play in court.

Meanwhile, Johnbosco and other relatives of Uchewuba had started putting pressure on Ginika to stop the case in the US when it was obvious that Uchewuba was headed for jail. They also encouraged Uchewuba to make a direct plea to Ginika so they could settle things out of court, but by the time Uchewuba changed his adamant stance on his claims, it was too late. Ginika mentioned to them before the judgment that it was then too late; if only he had heeded earlier calls to backtrack, but Uchewuba had felt he had a solid case and was bent on reaping rewards from another man's work without any remorse. At one point, Uchewuba had been convinced that Ginika had no case.

A dejected Ginika had complained bitterly to Nkiru how he would lose all motivation to continue with his blogging if he lost the case. At that point he was on the verge of losing the case, or so it seemed, because of the complicated nature of providing evidence that he had authored the blogs. Like every other essay published on Facebook and other social media platforms, anyone could claim to have first authored the work, but that did not provide substantial evidence required to prove ownership. The proof of copyright required a person to prove that he or she had first put the material into a fixed and tangible form. As Barrister Shittu explained to Ginika, if he voiced an opinion or narration to someone, that voicing did not guarantee his copyright ownership. As a matter of fact, a person could write that story down and claim copyright as long as he was the first person to put the material in a "fixed and tangible form".

Winning the case meant everything to Ginika, and the possibility of losing left him emotionally exhausted. The fear of a legal loss increased when he suddenly woke up one early Saturday morning, crying. Nkiru asked him what had happened, as she had never experienced her husband crying. "I dreamed I lost the case," he sobbed. "I saw Uchewuba smiling as the judge ruled in his favour, declaring that my lawyers could not present any proof that could convince him I owned the work." It was the same Uchewuba's face he had seen in a dream that tormented him when he lost at the second round of screening for the Shell postgraduate scholarship at university. Ginika did not go out of the house that weekend and did not go to church the next day. The repeated plea from Nkiru that his depression was a good reason for him to attend church fell on deaf ears.

"At this point we need to be on our knees and ask God to intervene. There is nothing He cannot do. He knows it is your sweat and will not allow Uchewuba to silence you," she pleaded.

But after the FBI entered into the picture, things had turned around for Ginika. The FBI had advanced evidence to nail Uchewuba on wire fraud and had asked that he accept a plea bargain, but a stubborn Uchewuba would not do it. He insisted he had done nothing wrong. To further build the case against him, the FBI had contacted Ginika's lawyers for support to show that Uchewuba was into fraudulent activities. It was a win-win for Ginika's lawyers given the opportunity it provided for them to gain access to Uchewuba's computer and potentially provide evidence of his hacking activities.

"As you may know, this is not the Nigerian system even though I believe we will get there someday," Ginika said to Nkiru as they landed at the Dallas/Fort Worth International Airport. "The matter is now interwoven with a federal criminal case; it is no longer me versus Uchewuba. It is the US government versus Uchewuba. Even if I withdraw the civil case, the criminal case will go on, and there is no way Uchewuba will not taste the US jail system as a result of this case."

When Johnbosco had put pressure on Ginika to help secure a soft landing for his brother, Ginika had said, "I am very sorry. My hands are tied at this time."

With the hacking case evidence trickling into the public awareness as the wire fraud case with FBI evolved, the rest of Ginika's childhood friends started recalling Ginika mentioning that his email had been compromised. He had asked his mates to disregard any suspicious email request soliciting for any monetary support on his behalf. The Yahoo groups, which had earlier been quiet, became active again as Ginika's court case dominated the discussions, and they watched things develop while offering support as they could. Unfortunately for Johnbosco, this happened to be a very difficult time because he was caught up in the mix and had to read all sort of insults and insinuations aimed at his younger brother in the forum. Not everyone knew Uchewuba was Johnbosco's brother or that Uchewuba's brother was even a member of their Yahoo group, but those who knew moderated their contributions.

Ginika took days off from work and booked flights to the US for himself and Nkiru to attend what was going to be the last court session of the case, during which judgment would be pronounced to determine the owner of the work.

Exhausted, Ginika and Nkiru made their way to the court in the company of their friend Ogbonna, who had been with them when it all started and who had almost become a celebrity in his own right, having been the person who attended the court proceedings with the lawyers on behalf of the complainant, who was not resident in the United States. "One trip, one trouble every two years," Ginika said out loud. "But I am sure to win this time around, God willing."

Ginika was bombarded by questions from the press: "Mr Ginika, can you tell us what you are expecting today from the court? Do you think Mr Uchewuba will be going to jail? For how long do you think he should be put away? What are your plans after your right to the material is restored? Did you know he was into wire fraud before he stole your work? Is it true he is a childhood friend of yours? Is it true he is a respectable member of your society back in Nigeria? Is it true he planned to run for election back home with proceeds of his crime?" And on it went until they entered the courtroom, which was packed to the brim due to the publicity.

The judge read out the court's findings: "On the count of unauthorized and wilful stealing of a written work and passing off same without any acknowledgements, the jury finds Mr Uchewuba guilty, and the court hereby gives the full right for the material in question to Mr Ginika Ogadimma. On the offence of intentionally hacking Mr Ogadimma 's account with the intention to steal and then actually stealing materials, the jury finds Mr Uchewuba guilty. The court hereby sentences Mr Uchewuba to six months in prison with a fine of ten thousand dollars. We hope his sentence will serve as a deterrent to others. On the case of fraud and cumulative stealing of three million dollars' worth of savings from poor US families, including that of Mr Wilcox, whose unfortunate death resulted from the crime, Mr Uchewuba will spend the maximum sentence of six years behind bars."

The judge continued, "Given the reviews from the victim impact assessment, I believe this is the right thing to do because you have caused so much harm to the victims of your fraudulent activities here in the United States. Only God knows the other people who may have fallen prey to your antics in your home country, Nigeria, and I pray they find closure by these findings and possibly any further charges that may be brought against you when you are deported to Nigeria after serving your sentence here in the United States. You are a very dishonest person and have covered your criminal wire fraud tracks all along by posing as a genuine creative arts director, but your fraudulent nature had no boundaries. Stealing became your nature and was enshrined in your DNA so that any area of life you found yourself in, you did nothing else but steal, be it money or intellectual property. This serves as a warning to the youths of today—stealing does not pay. The long arm of the United States law will find and bring you to justice. It is better to channel your energy to more productive things. Mr Uchewuba had the opportunity and capacity to do that but chose the wrong actions."

Ginika could not hold back his tears of joy and sorrow as they walked out of the courtroom. He was happy to have won but sad that he'd had to go such a great length to claim what belonged to him. He was sad that it was someone close to him who had wronged him and who, unfortunately, would be going to jail. Nkiru held Ginika's hand as Ogbonna put his hand on Ginika's shoulder while the members of the press swarmed them one more time as they exited the court building.

This time, Ginika was ready to address the press. He raised his head as he looked into the different cameras. "I wish to thank the American people for all the love and support they showed as I fought for my rights even though I do not reside in this country. I thank them for believing in me and hearing my side of the story even when the high and powerful in society and the news media could have easily diverted the course of the narrative on technical grounds. What the court has done today reaffirmed the fact that hard work pays, and you can count on the system to protect you and your work from vultures and thieves who may want to reap where they did not sow. The court confirmed that we cannot hide under the proliferation of materials on the internet and steal other people's work and hide it in jurisdictions we think may not be reached by the actual owners. They confirmed that, wherever you are, once you steal, you will be caught and punished irrespective of whether you stole physical or virtual property. As you know, Facebook representatives were here in court and will duly receive the details of the judgment. As Mark Zucks said the day he attended one of the court sessions, changes will be made so that intellectual property rights are protected. There are still a lot of open issues here and there that need to be tightened as social media evolves, but this case has paved the way and will kickstart reform. I also want to thank all my classmates and Yahoo group members around the world who offered all kinds of help and suggestions that helped us prove our case in court. The case, we knew, was a no-brainer, but we also knew that the law does depend on hard facts, and those facts they helped put on the table. I also have a legion of followers back home in Nigeria where, by the way, a similar case is winding its way through the system. Hopefully it will gain traction for a positive outcome from the insights and reasoning behind this court's judgment today. I want to thank my good friend Ogbonna, who is right here with me, for standing by and holding forth the fight here in the US while we tackled the Nigerian end. He was instrumental in my discovery that my material had been stolen in the first place, and if not for him, I might have had to watch my own movie premiere just like every other person, and the fight might have been lost for being too late. And, of course, I cannot forget my lovely wife, who was there to suggest the next actions and make all the necessary contacts to drive public opinion on this case in social media. She was also in the war room of prayer and made sure God heard our cry. I thank you all from the depths of my heart." When he was finished, they made their way into their car and zoomed off.

Six months later, the book was launched with first release in the United States. It was subsequently released in Nigeria. Millions of copies sold within the first week of release. Ginika became a celebrity in the real sense and set out on a book-signing tour, taking time off from his regular banking work to talk to audiences on his experience. He received invitations to motivational speaking events both in Nigeria and abroad. Most importantly, Ginika was happy that the book preceded the movie as he had intended instead of the other way round, as Uchewuba had planned. Six months after the release of the book, the movie premiered in Dallas, the same city where the theft of the script had been revealed.

This version of the movie had been directed by another childhood friend of Ginika who had gone ahead to become one of the leading film directors in New York. Chinedu understood the script and had experienced the setting first hand, so he found it easy to follow the mind of the author as the story explored all the twists and turns that characterized the life of a typical child of a civil servant in the eighties, moving into the nineties, and subsequently into the jet age of the internet and social media.

With the movie tickets sold out, the hall was full and a smiling Ginika sat there with Nkiru enjoying the crowd and eating popcorn while nodding his head and murmuring quietly, "I saw it coming!"

"What did you see coming?" Nkiru asked.

"I saw it coming." He smiled again. "The whole episode! I knew that bastard was probably up to something when he kept pestering me for the next episode, but I never knew Uchewuba would be that desperate to hang on and hang himself."

"Wait! Wait." Nkiru paused. "Don't tell me you engineered this whole thing, honey!"

"Not exactly. I expected some kind of publicity from a copyright case, but I didn't expect that Uchewuba was into wire fraud. And I didn't expect my friend's brother would end up serving a jail term, a situation he brought on himself. I have no regrets for what has happened." Ginika smiled.

Lightning Source UK Ltd.
Milton Keynes UK
UKHW011330010920
369165UK00002B/666